Blue wolf : an Alix Thorssen m

FIC N    82

McCl
Liberty

BLUE WOLF

BLUE WOLF

AN ALIX THORSSEN MYSTERY

Lise McClendon

Walker & Company New York

First published in the United States of America in 2001 by
Walker Publishing Company, Inc.

Published simultaneously in Canada by Fitzhenry and Whiteside,
Markham, Ontario L3R 4T8

Library of Congress Cataloging-in-Publication Data

McClendon, Lise.
 Blue wolf : an Alix Thorssen mystery / Lise McClendon
 p. cm.
 ISBN 0-8027-3352-2 (hardcover)
 1. Thorssen, Alix (Fictitious character)—Fiction. I. Title.

PS3573.E19595 B55 2001
813'.54—dc21

                                                    2001023801

Series design by M. J. DiMassi

Printed in the United States of America

2   4   6   8   10   9   7   5   3   1

Author's Note

One of the first wolves reintroduced to Yellowstone National Park in late 1995 was Number 13, an older male with grizzled hair, nicknamed "Old Blue." Shy and a little slow, wildlife officials were not initially optimistic about his survival. But he rallied and lived two years with the Soda Butte Pack before dying of natural causes in February, 1997. Gray wolves continue to breed and spread. To read more about the Yellowstone wolves, check the Web sites at <www.yellowstonenatl-park.com/wolf> and <wolftracker.com>

Thanks to Diane Boyd, wolf biologist with the U.S. Fish & Wildlife Service, for her expertise. Also to Michael K. Phillips and Douglas W. Smith for their book about wolf reintroduction in Yellowstone National Park, "The Wolves of Yellowstone." Any mistakes are my own.

This book is dedicated to my Wyoming friends Chris, Mike Chuck, Emilie, Tim, Carol, Marcia, Betty, Tom, Jennifer, and the rest. The words a young girl wrote in her diary more than a hundred years ago could not be more true today: "God bless Wyoming and keep it wild."

BLUE WOLF

THE prairie's breath moved the girl's blond hair against her neck. She twitched, curled a lip, looked at the stars. Thick as cream, the same as every night. Every day was the same when you were fourteen. Time stood still. Just yesterday, and a year, her father had disappeared. It seemed like yesterday.

The sheep made low sounds as they milled on the dark hillside. She could smell their oily wool in the air, on her hands. Her mother's idea, this month among the woollies, and not a bad one. The nights had cleared her head, the days warmed her muscles.

She looked back at the dark sheep wagon, a loaf of green bread against the purple sky. Wanda's alcoholic snore, courtesy of Wild Turkey, rumbled through the wagon's cracks. It was going to be hard to wake her when it was her turn to watch the sheep. Might have to smack her with one of her raggedy Mickey Spillane paperbacks.

The girl pulled the jean jacket tight against July's chill. Her hands felt stiff, too cold to sketch. She liked to draw by starlight, listening to the scratch of the pencil against the paper. Instead she walked around the flock, picking her way down the easy slope with the long stick Wanda claimed had been around since Jesus was born.

Where were those northern lights Aunt Sig had promised? Nothing was for sure, not anymore. Not even a moon tonight. She craned her neck, paused for a shooting star. Thousand-one, thou— They never lasted long enough. All the good stuff got snatched away. The howling sound she'd been told was coyotes sounded pretty close. She should be alert. Instead she ambled on, dimly aware of the gray mass of sheep to her right. Another shooter. Then another. The sky was alive with them. One so long she got to thousand-three. If only she could draw a shooting star, she was thinking when she saw him.

The wolf had stopped thirty or forty feet off, nose twitching, eyes set on her. This was no coyote. She stared at the cold yellow light of his eyes, fascinated. He was as big as a ram, with long, gangly legs and big feet. His fur ringed his face like a lion's, both black and gray, almost blue. He seemed to smile at her, but she wasn't afraid, or smiling either. She just stared, and held her breath.

His breath came out in little puffs in the cold as he swayed on his feet. His tail was high, twitching, black-and-white hairs twinkling against the night sky. Their eyes locked, and the girl felt something strange inside her, a wild, unexplainable feeling, a pure glass thing that could easily break but if held safe and nurtured could make everything whole again. Like white-hot energy pouring into her from his animal heart, so precious and untamable that tears smeared her vision.

And when she wiped her eyes, the wolf was gone.

1

FISH & GAME TO HEAR EVIDENCE IN WOLF SHOOTING

A hearing is set for this afternoon in the Teton County Courthouse in the shooting and killing of an endangered gray wolf on a private ranch inside Grand Teton National Park.

Marc Fontaine, horse wrangler for the large Wooten Bar-T-Bar Ranch, has admitted to National Park Service employees that he shot the wolf on ranch acreage late last Thursday night. He says the wolf attacked him while he was checking the stock.

Evidence is expected from wolf biologists in Yellowstone National Park, where the gray wolf was reintroduced in 1995. There are now over one hundred gray wolves living in the greater Yellowstone ecosystem, which includes Grand Teton NP and Jackson Hole.

The wolf, according to local wolf trackers and forest rangers, was part of a small pack that formed last year, yet unnamed. The wolf is thought to be #145, a young black female who had not yet been trapped, tagged, or collared.

Controversy has been swirling since the shooting about the nature of wolves, whether they attack humans. There have been very few reported cases of healthy wolves attacking men. The carcass of wolf #145 is being tested now for rabies.

✦

OP dog," she said.
I looked up from the canvas and found Queen holding two
hand-thrown pottery mugs. "Excuse me?"
"The alpha male. The one with the biggest balls. That's what I
see in that one, that's why I painted that cold light in his eyes. See
the way he seems to look right through you? You're nothing. He
doesn't care what happens to anybody else, as long as he's top dog."

I took a mug of tea as I set the stretched canvas of the wolf
next to the others leaning against the log wall. The small cabin was
as it always was—warm, lively, and smelling of paint. The artist's
words rattled me for a moment.

I squinted at the large head of the wolf. She'd painted it almost
as a portrait, no landscape, no reference points, just Wolf with a
capital W. Personality typing with color, the royal purple in his fur,
the bluish cast to the shadows. I wasn't sure if the cold yellow of
his eyes was because he was the alpha male or just because he was
a wolf, but I was not artist or biologist. Only the art dealer. Sometimes that meant I had to think like a customer, not a critic. Most
of the time, in fact. Anyway, I liked the piece, even though staring
straight into the eyes of a huge carnivore, teeth and all, made me
feel like flattening my ears and whimpering along on my belly. "It's
a great piece. Very haunting."

"Those black-powder types, they'll like the raw power," Queen
said. "They'll think of themselves, won't they? If I ever did anything for a market, and I'm not saying I did in this case"—she
waved her mug toward the wolf canvas—"well, let's just say I know
he'll sell."

"He? You've given him a name?"

Queen paused with her mug on the way to her lips. She was
still a striking woman at sixty-something, with long gray hair and
an amazing black streak at the widow's peak over her forehead, a
streak so dramatic I often wondered if it was real. But everything
about Queen was so authentic, without pretense, from her
weather-beaten, unpainted face and her muumuus in bright
colors, even to admitting that once in a while she painted for the

market. I admired her for that, and for her self-sufficiency, living at the end of the long gravel road, using only wood for fuel and cooking in the long Rocky Mountain winters, bartering with friends for food, living without a car in a motorized world, without a need for society in a crowded, people-oriented world. She had neither television nor radio, although she'd put in a telephone a few years back. If she needed company, she often said, it came down the road for her. Here was her world, complete, unique, and satisfying.

But now she cleared her throat, a nervous crease across her brow. "No," she said. "I've given the piece a name. I call it *Imminent Domain*." She looked at me and smiled. "My father was a lawyer. But this is *imminent*, with an *i*."

I raised my eyebrows and waited for more. Did this painting have some personal connection? Queen Johns guarded her past closely. I often thought of her as a paragon springing fully formed into this place. But that didn't mean I wasn't curious.

When she didn't continue, I moved on. "I brought up some papers. Did you hear about the wolf that was shot?"

"No." Her voice was very low. "One from Yellowstone?"

"They think so. On the Bar-T-Bar."

"Aaah. Bud Wooten. That son of a bitch would do something like that. Spend his last few years in some country club prison, I suppose." She squinted. "Is he still alive?"

"Yes. Do you know him?" Another unanswered query; she only sipped tea. "They're into trail riding and horse breeding these days, not much in the way of cattle."

"Is that where you took your horse?" she asked.

"Right." Queen often surprised me with what she remembered of our conversations. "Old Valkyrie needed some taming."

"Have you ridden her?"

"No. I sold her to them. I felt bad enough about it that I haven't even visited her."

The quick-fire questions had an edge, as if she was steering the conversation. She'd done it before when I asked about her old connections. As if people she'd once known were somehow suspect from knowing her. I opened my mouth to ask her about the

Bar-T-Bar and how she knew the Wootens, but she hopped up and asked for the newspapers.

"Thank you, Alix. You know I appreciate kindling for the stove." She smiled her crafty old smile, the one that made people tell half-funny stories about her being a witch.

"Just don't push any small children in," I said, smiling.

"Only if they're plump!" She cackled and threw her long hair back. "Now, let's finish with the paintings. I'm not sure I have another one for you besides *Imminent Domain*. They want wildlife, right? That's their thing. Lions and tigers and bears. And wolves." She tapped her chin. "I might have to work up something else for your committee. How long until the auction?"

"Two weeks. But we really need to get the brochure done this week."

"Well, we better hope there's some dusty ol' thing in the back of the closet then."

The dusty old thing we found was vintage Queen, a ten-year-old oil landscape done in swirling winter colors, aspens and rocks and hills with a sky only she could produce, the kind of sky that made you feel like flying. She slapped it with a dustcloth while I bit my tongue and hurried it away to be cleaned properly at the gallery. She insisted I take a few winter apples in exchange for the sack of groceries I'd brought up, a winter ration of peanut butter and sardines and cheese. Going to Queen's cabin was like stepping back to a friendly village where you shared your wealth, and it was shared with you. I always left feeling lucky.

Jackson was quiet when I got back to town. October is a waiting month, when shop owners take vacations, when employee dormitories are hosed down and disinfected, when locals have a chance to reacquaint themselves. The air was crisp, the sky a humming blue. I made a note to wash the front plate glass as I went through the door with the canvases.

The Second Sun Gallery normally got its share of walk-in traffic, located smack on the town square with its kitschy antler arches and grassy shade. But in October the leaves were almost all gone, scattering in gutters, brown and brittle. The walk-in trade was just as lively.

The door chime echoed as I stepped into the silent spaces of the gallery. No employees this time of year either. A good time for the Auction for Wildlife put together to support the Teton Land Trust, a loose organization of hunters, ranchers, and conservationists. I'd been working on their auction for three years now, finding artists and art, cementing relationships that kept Second Sun afloat in the dicey gallery universe. Good for business, and a welcome break at a slow time of year.

I propped the two canvases up on the desk in the gallery and switched on the lights. This week I'd actually sold a piece by a local artist, Martin Ditolla, that I'd had up for two years. The excitement in his voice was almost worth the wait. On my list today was to re-hang the main gallery and ship the Ditolla.

But first to clean the landscape. On the way to the storeroom the phone rang. It was Carl Mendez. "You going to the hearing?" he asked.

"I'd have to shut down the gallery." Even as I said it I felt ridiculous. There was little business. "Don't you fly today?"

"It's hit-and-miss. There's talk of doing some wolf-tracking now, since the climbing is slowing down."

"Is the mountain covered now?"

"You can't see it from your window, can you? Come out and see it yourself. Covered in white since Saturday. Dazzling."

"So dazzling it'll probably attract more crazy climbers wanting to conquer the Grand Teat. Did you have any rescues yesterday?"

"Not a one."

"I'll try to get some nimrods to climb up without ropes. How's that?"

"Anything to fly the chopper."

Carl Mendez sounded happier than he had in a long time. He'd moved to Jackson in August after leaving the Missoula Police Department, and gotten a temporary gig as a helicopter rescue pilot for the mountain rangers. How long it would last, no one knew.

"You and that chopper. You're inseparable."

"Yeah, listen. I can't make dinner tonight."

"You're not doing night flying, are you?" The protective tone in my own voice made me cringe. It occurred to me, not for the first time, that I wasn't thrilled about Carl's obsession with helicopters. He ignored my prying.

"Let me bring you over some lunch. On my way to the hearing."

The morning was long and quiet. I cleaned, pondered frames, wrote descriptions for the brochure, rehung, repainted. Carl showed up about twelve-thirty with cream of mushroom soup in Styrofoam cups. I washed a couple of spoons, and we settled in around the gallery desk.

"Kevin's going to testify, I heard," he said.

"So that's why you're going." Kevin Stoddard was a Fish and Wildlife biologist who lived in the other side of Carl's Park Service cabin.

"I haven't talked to him about it. I've been curious, though." Carl smiled. He'd cut his hair again. Now it was air force buzz, very butch. Black hair hugged his skull, showing off his square face, black eyes, warm skin. I reached over and plucked a drop of soup from his chin.

"Have you seen any wolves out there?"

"No. Kevin told me they're around, though, making their way toward the Elk Refuge."

"I'll bet. Dinner served up, nice and neat."

"Yeah, some refuge." He looked up at the canvases. "Hey, you got a wolf."

"Do you like it?"

He stepped up to Queen's painting and cocked his head. I liked to hear his responses to paintings, since they were completely unstudied, without any veneer of cultural bias. If he said a painting reminded him of a childhood nightmare or the color of puke, I knew it would take a certain type of collector to buy it. And probably take a long time selling.

"The eyes are really good," he said. "And this color here in the ruff. Looks like moonlight shining on him." He looked over his shoulder at me. "How much is it?"

"It's part of the wildlife auction. I suppose it'll go for two, three thousand."

"Out of my league."

"Did you want to buy it? Since when do you collect art?"

He folded his arms and examined the painting some more. "Will you frame it?"

"In this green wood." I lay the piece of framing wood next to the canvas on the side table in the gallery anteroom. "You really like it, don't you?"

"If I had the money."

"You can like it without the money."

"Yeah, but then you begin to envy, then hate the person who can afford it. Then your whole attitude toward the piece gets twisted."

"I see. Better not to like it at all then."

He frowned at me. "You don't get it. Either you've got money, or you don't. If you don't, you wish you did. You wish you had the money to buy things you really love. Like this wolf. What's its name?"

I'd been around art and moneyed folk all my working life, and I still had a hard time with this attitude. A person couldn't really own a painting, in my mind. He could pay a certain amount of money to enjoy it privately, but it belonged to anyone who viewed and enjoyed it. You couldn't stop that just by owning a painting. Ask any heiress who loans out her paintings to museums. Art, like all beauty, belongs to the beholder. Once the artist sets the beauty free, it is there for the taking, for everyone. Why be bitter about the size of your wallet when right now you are enjoying the painting as much as you ever will? Why does buying a painting affect your enjoyment of it? Viewing a painting of a wolf is the same as seeing a real wolf: a priceless memory that no one can buy, borrow, or steal.

"The name? *Imminent Domain*."

"Weird name. That's a legal term, isn't it?"

"That's spelled differently. *Eminent*, with an *e*. This is imminent, like threatening. And domain, like where you live. I guess it means their territory is threatened."

"I like it. Just wish I could afford it. Oh, well." He looked suddenly at his watch. "So have you got next week figured out? Pencil me in for some hikes?"

I glanced at him, then back at the wolf. "I always take the week off to paint. It's pretty intense. I told you."

"All painting all day makes Alix a dull girl."

"It's not work. It's fun, it's very rewarding. It clears out the cobwebs. I get really excited. And I don't get many chances to do it nonstop for a week. Besides, I've got all the last-minute auction stuff to do too."

"So no hikes then?"

I looked at him, his jaw tightening. "I told you that weeks ago, Carl."

I'd been trying to work out his reaction ever since. Did he want some other kind of girl, the kind who is eager and athletic and peppy? The kind who drops everything to do whatever he wants? Did he want me to change to please him, to be someone else? Was this some kind of Latin power test? I felt a hardening of my heart, and hated it.

"I'm late. Gotta go."

"Let me know how it goes, will you?"

He was half out the door. "I'll try to call tomorrow."

I watched him walk briskly down the boardwalk, his khaki climbing pants and hiking boots a blur. He was fit and tanned and full of enthusiasm, enough to qualify any man for hunkdom. He did seem happier out of law enforcement, but how long would that last? The last two months had been interesting, having Carl around almost all the time, getting to know him on a day-in, day-out basis. And him getting used to the strange convoluted life that is my life in business in Jackson Hole. He'd caught the end of the crazy season, then watched, amazed, as things turned deadly quiet, only climbing bums and recreational vehicles touring around.

Leaning my face against the cool glass of the window, I felt the doom again. I'd been feeling it off and on for a week, but attributed it to boredom and the lack of business. Now it sat heavily in my stomach and felt a tug from Carl Mendez. This one wasn't going to make it: that was the message. He wanted somebody I wasn't. I didn't want to change, I wanted to be me, self-sufficient, independent. Like Queen, a woman who could be solitary and happy. How did Carl—or any man— fit into that?

Standing straight, I tried to shake it off. I doomed everything from the start; that was the way of the Viking world. Doom and gloom, maybe a happy moment here and there to divert you from the fact that all ends in fiery hell and that's that.

Well, fuck that, I told myself. It didn't have to happen like that. I went into the bathroom and grinned at myself.

"I'm happy." I put my shoulders back and admired my profile. "He likes my breasts. He said so. How many guys would do that?"

All guys like tits, moron. I smacked my lips and smiled into the mirror.

"Don't be such a gloomer."

I gave my pale cheeks a little pinch and tugged at a piece of chapped lower lip. Get to work, I told my scruffy dishwater hair.

I shut the bathroom door, gravitating back to my old railroad desk. In the pencil drawer I fingered the old photograph, pulling it out into the light of the gallery windows. My former partner Paolo Segundo stood with his back to the camera, tending a steaming pot on the stove, laughing back at me over his shoulder. He wore a white undershirt, the kind he called a wife-beater, with his shoulders bare. He had a small black mustache and gleaming teeth.

The photo was old, ten years at least, from the New York days. I ran across it last summer in a box of letters too painful to read again. But the photograph drew me like a magnet, that beautiful man cooking for me, gleaming with sweat in a third-floor walk-up one New York summer. I was happy then. I tried not to think about the rest of it—the other women, the betrayals, the falling-out, the mistakes I'd made, the losing him forever. No, just this moment, as if time could stop, could be put in a glass jar like a lightning bug and admired and held close to the heart. I closed my eyes and put the photo to my forehead.

Just one moment. Sometimes it was all you ever got. I didn't want to think that, but when I looked at Paolo from long past, I felt it down in my toes.

✦

"Alix! Turn some music on, it's a goddamned tomb in here!"

The voice boomed back to the storeroom, where I'd spent the afternoon framing, crating, and making busy. The biggest excitement was the discussion with Lillian, who owned the jewelry store next door, about what we were going to do about the troublesome woodpecker who had taken to waking me each morning with his attempts to dig insects out of the wood siding of my building.

Morris Kale stood in the middle of the gallery, hands in his pockets. He gave a shout of greeting as I emerged.

"I can get Frankie to lend you some rap if he'll take his headphones off. Frankie!" He waved his hands in front of his stepson's face, but the teenager shot him a look.

"Hi, Frankie." I waved at the boy. He didn't respond. To Morris I said, "Is he still doing any artwork?"

"He's taking it in school. Audrey was just saying that those sessions he had with you this summer really helped."

"Well, he's a good kid."

In truth Frankie was a pain in the ass, moody, smart-mouthed, and lazy: the kind of teenager everyone who thought twice about having kids had nightmares about. Our sessions at my studio this summer, all four of them, were a concession to my friendship with Morris.

"Come to look at the new paintings? I picked them up from Queen this morning. They're ready for the printer."

I propped them on the desk in the gallery. Morris made nods and oohs; he liked them. I was pleased, as I was whenever an artist I liked and admired was approved by others. Like children, I imagined.

Morris leaned close to *Imminent Domain*. "This wolf. Wow." I felt a buzz happening about the wolf painting. "The energy, the intelligence she puts in there. Amazing. You go to the hearing?"

"No," I said.

"You should have heard them, the hunters, going on about the wolf tearing the beating heart from its prey. About the inhumanity of allowing a wolf to take down an elk because you could hear the elk's cries of pain. Somehow humanity was never something I associated with wolves. Intelligence, yes, but they aren't human, you can't think that way. You'd think some of those hunters had never blasted apart a furry animal."

As president of the Teton Land Trust, Morris Kale had to make peace with all sides—environmentalists, hunters, ranchers, animal-righters, even hikers and bird-watchers. It was a slippery tightrope never successfully crossed, but always interesting. Today he seemed to be wearing his environmental hat.

"And you, Morrie, you blast our furry friends?"

"Gave it up years ago." He gave me a friendly wink. He was tall with a yachtsman's look to him, not a hunter's. He still had a good head of hair, prematurely gray. His oversize chin dominated his face. "Already got the ego full up on diesel."

"So that's where that belching smoke is coming from."

He laughed roundly—he was getting a little round about the middle since his retirement to Jackson Hole. Only forty-two when he offloaded his daddy's lucrative New Jersey dry-cleaning chain, he'd spent six or seven years trying to spend his millions. His wife was giving him some help in that department, but I wondered if it was enough to keep the man busy.

Now Frankie, there was a project.

The boy was tugging on a weaving on the far wall. I clenched my jaw, blinked hard. By this time Morris had seen what he was doing and gave another ear-shattering bellow at the boy.

"That kid." He shook his head, smiling. "He's a sweetheart." But his eyes told a different story, a sadder one.

"How's Audrey?" I asked. Frankie's mother seemed a safer subject.

"Been on a decorating frenzy, feathering the nest for winter. Curtains and rugs and sofas, you oughta come out and see what she's done."

"We have a meeting at your place soon, don't we?"

"She'll give you the grand tour, I'm sure."

"Can't wait." I turned away, hoping Morris didn't see the lie on my face. "So, what else happened at the hearing?"

"They had one of the wolf guys from Yellowstone come down and talk about who this goddamn wolf was, as if it had some address and social security number. Trouble is, they never tagged this one. That made him a little embarrassed."

"What did Marc Fontaine have to say?"

"You know him? Seemed straightforward enough. He said it was dark, he heard the horses getting restless. Thought it might be a bear. Then out of nowhere the wolf just charged him. The biologist says it's not common behavior, in fact, hardly ever happens."

"Unless the wolf has rabies."

"And they don't know that yet."

"I don't see why they had the hearing before they even knew."

"Some wolf people, an offshoot of that group protesting over the buffalo hunts up in Montana. They started calling the Fish and Wildlife office, haranguing them."

"Was it Candace—All One All Wild?"

"I hope not. Whoever they are, they've made some threats to Marc Fontaine too."

When things got this twisted this early, they tended to spin into the irrational zone. Who wanted more violence? If you shot a grizzly bear in self-defense, nobody blamed you. If you shot a grizzly bear and thought it was a black bear, an easy thing to do, you got a "stupid" ticket. If you knew it was a grizzly bear and it wasn't attacking you, you were in deep shit. Which it was in Marc's—and the wolf's—case, we might never know.

Morris was staring blankly at Frankie, who bobbed his head to unheard rhythms. A chill went over me, a bad vibe. Where it came from, what it meant, I didn't know.

"I feel sorry for Marc. It's a no-win situation," Morris said softly.

"I hope everybody calms down after the ruling."

Morris straightened. "I better run the paintings over."

"Let me wrap them, Morrie." The phone on the desk rang. A soft voice. "Queen? That you?"

"Hello, Alix. Can you hear me?"

"Yes, barely. Can you hold on a second?" I set the receiver on the desk as Morris Kale picked up the paintings.

"I'll be careful. Frankie can hold them on his lap, it's only a few blocks. Come on, Frankie. I'll talk to you tomorrow, Alix."

"Okay, Morrie. See ya, Frankie."

"Tell Queen thank you. Gorgeous as usual."

The two exited, Frankie tripping over his voluminous pants on the way down the steps.

I picked up the phone. "Sorry, I had a customer in here. Queen?" Dial tone. "Damn."

I looked up her number quickly and dialed. It rang a long time. I hung up, dialed again, and let it ring. At last she answered.

"Alix?"

"Sorry. We got cut off."

She cleared her throat. There was a long pause. Finally I said, "I got the paintings cleaned up. They look great." Another pause. "Thanks again for the apples. I ate one on the way down, very tasty."

Still nothing. I walked to the door of the gallery, locked it, turned the sign to Closed. I got a sudden panicky feeling.

"Is everything all right? Are you sick?"

"I'm fine." She sighed. "I don't know why I called. Thank you for the groceries. I hope—good-bye."

"Wait! You told me thanks already. Was there something else?"

"No, you're busy. I—"

"I'm not busy. That was just Morris Kale picking up your paintings to take to the printer for the brochure. He says thanks, by the way. And I have loads of time." I pulled out the desk chair loudly. "There. I'm sitting down, I'm comfortable. Can I do something for you?"

"Is he gone?"

"Nobody here but us chickens."

She paused for a long time. "It's a favor, and I'm not used to asking for favors. I don't like it. So let's call it a bargain."

"Okay, what are we bargaining?"

"I have two paintings for you. You can do whatever you want with them. Sell them, auction them, burn them, I don't care."

"Two paintings. I see. And my part of the bargain?"

Another pause. Then the words tumbled out of her. "Twenty-five years ago next month there was a hunting accident in Jackson

Hole. A boy was killed. I want to find out what happened, who investigated it, how it was undertaken, everything you can find." She paused as I mulled this. "That's all. Just information."

"Information."

"The who, what, why, where, all that. It was in the newspapers. But you might have to do some digging. Not much."

I dug my fingers into my forehead. This was hardly what I expected. What did a woman who thrived on solitude, an occasional jar of peanut butter, and a steady supply of oil paints really need? A stack of paperbacks, a winter coat? A dog from the shelter maybe. But information on a twenty-five-year-old accident?

"This boy," I said. "Someone close to you?"

"If you don't want to do it, if you're too busy, just say so. I'm imposing. I know it. I thought the paintings might be enough."

"I'm not too busy. It's just surprising, Queen. You never mentioned a boy or an accident."

"It's not that important. If you don't want the paintings, I can find someone who does. I just thought you and I were on—oh, some wavelength. I have these feelings about people."

"I feel that too, Queen. I always enjoy our visits. And I do want the paintings." Coming out of my fog, I did a quick calculation, and it cleared $2,500 easily, even not knowing the size or quality of the pieces. With two months until the Christmas rush, very welcome greenbacks, and easy sales here or to Santa Fe or Telluride dealer friends.

"I just need a little more information. What, um—what was the boy's name?"

I held my breath, hoping it wasn't a relative of someone I knew.

"Derrie—Derek Wylie."

I wrote it down, registering both the relief and the nervousness in her voice. My own relief: the name was unfamiliar. I asked her to spell both the names. She did so, carefully.

"And he lived here? Anything else? A date of the accident?"

"November nineteenth. Twenty-five years ago."

I scribbled down the date. A long time ago. "Shouldn't be too hard to find."

"So you'll do it."

"Sure, Queen. I can scrape up something. If there was something in particular you were looking for, I'd know what direction to take."

"Everything you can find. Can you make copies of reports?"

"Newspaper stories?"

"Or police reports."

"All I can do is try. I don't know what sort of walls get thrown up after twenty-five years." I thought for a second. "You're sure you don't want to do it yourself? I could drive you into town, it wouldn't be a problem."

"I never come down the hill." Her voice was harsh, clipped. Then she softened. "Besides, dear, you wouldn't get your paintings then."

She was seducing me with those paintings. It made me wonder what I might find out about Derek Wylie. Was it some gruesome thing I'd have nightmares about? The saccharine in her voice was odd, but nothing twenty-five years old could be that terrible, could it? Besides, the paintings would be worth it.

"I should be able to get this together in a few days. Is that soon enough?"

"Oh, yes. I have one piece ready for you now. I didn't show it to you today. I quite like it. And the other is half finished."

"Great." I dug into my forehead again. Why was I surprised? Queen has always been eccentric, never traveling into town, living alone off the land, in contact with only a few neighbors. Her life was a mystery to me. Why would I know about her connection with this hunting accident?

I took a breath. I was flattered by her offer, I realized. Only an art dealer would want what she had to barter, and she'd chosen me.

"I'll give you a call as soon as I get something."

I hung up the phone. On the square a devil gust of wind picked up a clutter of brown leaves and dirt, twisted them into a tower, and sucked them down the street, where they disappeared behind a white Caddy pulling an Airstream trailer. They came out the other side in an angry, disorganized twist, assaulted a golden retriever tied in front of the drugstore, then disappeared around the corner.

Where were they going, those leaves?

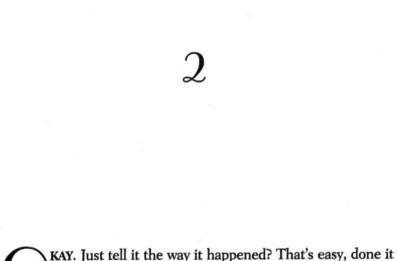

2

OKAY. Just tell it the way it happened? That's easy, done it seven or eight times already. Aaaah. It was after midnight. There're just three of us out there this time of year, none of the summer help. Hal—my punk brother—and old Farley and me had played some cards in the cabin. Me and Hal got the cabin. Farley, he likes the old bunkhouse, especially now that it's empty. Colder than a witch's tit out there, but he don't care, he's used to it. Just ask him about the winter of 'fifty-three, he'll tell you about cold.

"Been damn cold at night since mid-August, you notice that? Frost on the twenty-fifth. So, I hear the horses. It's not common that you hear them at night. They settle down pretty well.

"The southeast pasture, only thirty acres, it's not much for the horses. There's eighteen of them now. We lease more in the summer. I was a little worried, what with them being so close to the aspens. That thick forest along the south fence, all heavy woods in there. Good cover for bear, cougar, wolf. I didn't really think anything'd bring down a full-grown horse, but they could sure do some damage, cut an animal up good. So every night I'd walk around the perimeter at dusk, making some noise. Sorta like leaving a scent just in case.

" 'Course I had my gun. That's the point, Danny boy. I walked the line earlier that night, doing my usual thing, touching fence-posts, even taking a little whiz out there. Nothing like the smell of piss to scare off the prowlers. But I never saw nothing, just the shadows out in those woods.

"So I hear them, after midnight. Farley had fallen asleep in his chair, snoring so loud I almost missed it. The snorting and whinnying and all. I grab the shotgun and head out the door, not even taking my coat. Had to run across fifteen acres to find them, running in circles, nostrils flaring. I tried to tag the bay, she's the easiest, but even she wouldn't settle. Alix's old horse, that bitch nag, she rears up like some demon movie horse.

"There's mayhem for a few minutes, horses rearing and bumping into each other and screeching and biting. I figure it's a bear. They stink like a son of a gun, and horses can smell them for some distance. I head around the herd for the back fence, keeping the gun at the ready. I don't see a thing. I stop and listen, but I don't hear nothing but the damn horses.

"I'm just about to fire up into the sky, scare off whatever it is. I don't feel like going no closer to the forest. I can't hear nothing, but something's out there. I know it. The horses know it. I tip the gun barrels up, and that's when the wolf comes outa nowhere, from my right. I don't see it—it's a dark night, and there's no moon. It's almost on me, then I swing the gun around and let 'er go. I could feel its breath all wild and angry. I felt the teeth on my arm almost the same time as I pulled the trigger, so that's how come I got no bite. Yeah, lucky, if that beast is rabid. It's gotta be rabid, doncha think? I never hearda no wolf attacking like that, except maybe in old stories, Jack London and all. But none of these wolf guys think they do that, unless I was crowding in on their kill or something. Well, I tell them, it happened to me, you trying to tell me it didn't?"

Danny Bartholomew hit the stop button on his recorder and picked up his empty coffee cup. "Got any more?"

"Help yourself." I wrapped my hands around my third cup of the morning. "That's quite a story."

Danny came back with more coffee and sat down again at the gallery desk. "Yeah, I got an exclusive. The AP says they'll pick it up."

"Marc sounds shook."

"He should be. He could go to jail for it. That nimrod up in Montana did, and he said he thought it was a dog harassing sheep."

"He did happen to skin it for a souvenir. Legal to shoot dogs, isn't it?"

"As long as their owners don't complain."

I sighed. "Things had been going so well with the wolves and the ranchers."

"I wouldn't say that. There have been more wolves killed by the Fish and Wildlife folks than they tell you. That whole pack by Dubois was shot."

Last night's low-tech meal churned in my stomach with my morning coffee—Spaghetti-O's and bad TV movies, with a dollop of microwave popcorn. Nary a peep from Mendez.

"Is that the end of the interview?"

He squinted cagily. "There's a little more."

"Something juicy? I'm getting wolf fever."

"Not sure I can use it. Sort of like incriminating yourself."

"Marc knew there was a wolf out there?"

The reporter shook his head. "Not saying. Wouldn't be prudent." He smiled. "Now what did you really ask me over here for this morning? I know it wasn't to share your fabulous coffee."

"Oh, it was. But you're right. There's something else." Danny B and I go far enough back that we know each other's curiosity streak and when it needs scratching. He'd scratched mine just now, so I obliged him by offering up my own slender tidbits.

"I need to find out about an old hunting accident. It happened twenty-five years ago."

"Why?"

"Somebody asked me, it's an info swap. You and I know about those, Danny."

"Twenty-five years ago, that's old news. It won't be on computer. The *News* computerized about ten years ago." He frowned. "That means digging in the Devil's Own Clip File."

"Not fun?"

"Tedious and boring and time-consuming, and to top it off you have to deal with Maymie Tubbs."

"Who?"

Danny grimaced. "I can't believe I let that slip. Don't repeat it." He leaned close. "That's what we started calling Russ. Mr. Mason."

"Your editor?"

"Bad, isn't it? Sharon started it. And we can't seem to stop."

"I saw him in Bermuda shorts walking his dog the other day. Maymie Tubbs. Yeah, I like it."

"It's so bad. It really is." Danny laughed, his elfin body shaking in caffeine-jagged hysterics. When he wiped his eyes, he gave a gasp and slapped a hand on the desk. "I thought of something."

"No Maymie Tubbs?"

"That's one source. The other is Dutch Abbott."

"Who's that?"

"Steel trap of Hole history. He wrote a column for the paper for years on fishing and hunting. His grandparents started the Jackson Mercantile on the square way back."

"The one that's now the Gap?"

"All the old stuff is gone."

"This used to be a whorehouse. We could have reenactments. Like the Civil War."

"So, you're not getting any these days?" Danny smirked. "What happened to Heli-Man?"

I kicked him under the desk.

He was laughing again as he slipped his tape recorder into his bag. "I'll have Dutch give you a call. He's past eighty, but sharp as a tack. Can still hear, even though he taught gun safety for years." He turned at the door, serious. "Word is, the wolf story is going to be on national news tonight."

"I'll try to catch it. Give my regards to Maymie."

✦

When Dutch Abbott called a couple hours later, I didn't hesitate to shut down the deserted gallery and hightail it out of town. It was a Tuesday, the air held the nostalgia of warm fires and deep forest secrets, and the sky was clear enough to write on. I pointed the Saab Sister, my '67 beast-on-wheels, west across the Snake River's gravel beds, through the rolling ranchette suburbs, and finally down a narrow rutted lane to a small log cabin. A wisp of smoke rose from the chimney; a rusted blue pickup listed in a pothole, its gun rack empty. I held tight to the steering wheel as the car's wheels jumped through the last ruts, then parked next to the pickup.

The cabin had the same feel as Queen's, solitary, cozy, the last bastion of the West's true personality. The man—or woman —alone, needing nothing but a bushel of apples, a cord of wood, and a friendly horse. Or in this case, a pickup truck. I brought some of Queen's apples and bribery material.

Before I reached the top of the porch's four steps, the door opened. From his stooped shoulders the old man peered at me, his white eyebrows low.

"You the nosy one Danny told me about?"

"That's me. Alix Thorssen."

He gave me another look over. "Thought you'd be a man."

"Are you disappointed?"

"What's in that bag?"

"Apples. And three Hershey bars."

"Chocolate? Who you been talking to? Get your behind in this door. Pronto, girl." He shooed me past him into the tiny cabin and slammed the door shut. "I got some tea brewing. You take whiskey in yours?"

"I'm trying to go straight."

"Hmmph." Dutch hobbled over to the motherly woodstove, where a kettle stood steaming. He looked into a teapot on the table and added more water from the kettle. Drops of water on the cast iron hissed and danced. "I only got one kind of tea. No choices."

"That's okay." I set the paper bag on the table. "Danny tells me you've lived here all your life."

"And then some. You gonna get out that chocolate or not?"

In a few minutes we were ensconced in sprung but comfy armchairs, tea at the ready, chocolate broken up on a plate, warm and fortified. The log cabin was a museum of old fur hides: coyote, beaver, fox, bobcat, cougar, bear. Heads of deer and elk, wide, flat moose antlers over a doorway, old photographs of proud men with guns and dead animals.

"You like hunting?" Dutch asked, watching me eye his cabin decor.

"I don't have any strong feelings about it. I don't hunt myself."

"That's your answer then." He cocked his head. He hadn't shaved in a couple days, and white stubble sat on his chin like grubby snow. "What do you do then?"

"I'm an art dealer. I have a gallery down in Jackson."

"Sell art?" He wrinkled his nose. "That any fun?"

"It has its moments. It's pretty slow right now."

"Of course, it's hunting season."

I nodded. That was obviously the reason. "Your place reminds me of Terry Vargas's. You know him?"

"Vargas." He scratched his chin. "Up on the pass?"

"The Flying V. You might have known his father, Pierce."

"Percy Vargas? Sure, I knew him. Used to take some of his dudes hunting up by Two Oceans. Hell of a guy. Dead ten years now, ain't he?"

I nodded, never having known the elder Vargas. The younger was Morris Kale's cochair on the Wildlife Auction, and a well-known piece of work. "His son has the ranch now."

"I remember the snot-nosed brat. He improved any?"

"He wipes his nose now."

Dutch let out an explosive laugh. "So what you want to know, Miss Alix Thorssen? Or you just come up to wreck my arteries with chocolate?"

I set my cup down on a pine table. "It's about a hunting accident that happened twenty-five years ago. I was hoping you might remember something about it."

He took a bite of chocolate and worked it around his tongue. "I might. What are the particulars?"

"All I know is the name of the boy who died. Derek Wylie."

Dutch laid his hands on his knees and stared at me with dark blue eyes. He didn't say anything for so long I got worried. But at last he cleared his throat.

"Sad thing. Very sad. It has been twenty-five years, hasn't it? Seems like just last year."

He wrestled himself to his feet, took his cup with gnarled fingers, and poured more tea from the pot. "You want more?"

"No, thanks."

He shuffled to a high cupboard, strained for the bottle of Wild Turkey, and gave himself a healthy splash. On the way back to his green plaid wing chair with singed corners, he glared up and said, "Better than a damn flu shot."

"Just have to drive back into town, or I'd join you." And I would have. Tea and Turkey by the fire in a snug cabin on a cool fall day—what more could a gal ask for?

"All right. So what makes you want to dredge up all this tragedy from long past?" Dutch asked after blowing and sipping on his toddy for a few minutes.

"Somebody asked me, that's all. Somebody who can't let it rest."

"Hmmph. Damn well oughta." He squinted. "Who?"

"Somebody who knew the boy." A calculated guess.

He waved his bony hand. "I wrote it all up in a column, trying to get these fool kids to take a hunter safety course."

"What happened?"

"Three teenagers—friends, I guess. All went out hunting for deer one day, only two came back. Gun went off, that's what they said."

I stared at my tea. "That's all?"

"Oh, there was probably more to it. But the parents kept it under wraps, didn't even let the boys' names out to the paper. Said it would prejudice people, and they had their consciences and all."

"But Derek Wylie's name was out."

"Couldn't very well keep that outa the papers. And no more

harm could come to him. I think the parents was probably right. It was an accident, a terrible one, but like the man says, they do happen."

"You don't know who the other boys were then?"

"Never wanted to know." He looked across the room at a bookshelf. "I got that column somewhere. In those albums."

He waved me over to the bookshelf, and I pulled out a dusty oversize photo album crammed with yellowed newsprint. Maybe if I could borrow the old man's column, photocopy it, and get it to Queen, I could call it done. This field trip was fun, but I couldn't really afford to leave the gallery dark every day in pursuit of her whims. The ancient Viking soldiers in my head began to chant: Work, work, work. Bad enough I was taking next week off.

"That the seventies? In the middle there, the ones with the picture of the handsome guy on the top."

"Ah. You mean the ladykiller." I grinned at him. He popped a big hunk of Hershey bar in his mouth.

I pawed through September columns, then October. Then December and finally, out of order, came the November batch. At the end of the month was a column titled, "Tragedy Could Have Been Avoided." I read the headline aloud.

"That it?"

"Uh-huh. And it coulda been. Senseless. Hunting should be peaceful and a mental game, bringing you back in touch with nature, those roots you lose by sitting all cozy under the roof every night, watching television, working on your damn computer. Shouldn't cause you to lose the only thing that can't be brought back."

I slipped the brittle newsprint out of the album and smoothed it on the table. "Okay if I borrow this?" I scanned down the double column width quickly, looking for details, names, places, and had a quick impression that my search wasn't over.

"Sure, just bring it back whole. Don't have any more copies. Sit down, girl."

I realized I was impolitely itching to go now that I had the goods in hand. I laid the clipping down by my backpack and sat down to finish my tea.

"You don't remember anything else about the incident, do you? Someone who investigated it, maybe?"

"Only person I talked to was the boy's mother. She was mostly incoherent, so I couldn't use her in the story much. Women get that way, when it's their boy."

"No police or deputy or Fish and Wildlife man?"

"Oh, there was a deputy, by the name of—oh, hell. Can't remember."

"It's been twenty-five years, Dutch. I don't expect you to remember everything."

Still he frowned, irritated. "Might be in the column."

I retrieved the clipping. Running my finger down the faded type, I ran into "Teton County deputy Farley Platt." I repeated it aloud.

"That's him. Farley Platt. A bronc buster doing a little deputizing on the side."

"He still around here?" I thought of the Farley on Danny's tape. It wasn't a common name.

"Hell if I know. I ain't exactly a social butterfly these days."

As if to contradict, the old black telephone sitting next to the plaid chair rang in an ear-shattering trill. Dutch Abbott picked it up solemnly.

"Who's this? Markie? Yeah, I called you. I heard about what you did, and I wanted to thank you for it. 'Course I mean the wolf. Damn fine piece of gunplay."

I stood up to give a semblance of privacy to the conversation. I knew he was talking to Marc Fontaine, new Jackson celeb. It turned my stomach a bit to hear the glee in Dutch's voice at the death of the wolf. In my mind I could see her, a sleek black streak against the blue-white snow, lunging, sniffing, running, her breath hot in the cold air, her essence red, steaming, sinking into the last bit of fall pasture near the aspens.

I looked up at the skins on the walls. They had all died this way. It was the way men lived, by killing animals, either to eat or to eliminate animals that ate what men wanted. It had been going on for thousands of years, and would go on for thousands more, no matter how many televisions or computers or sports cars the world filled up with. It was part of who we are.

The fox skin was red-orange and fluffy under its ashy dust. I ran my hand down the still-elegant tail. Dutch had launched into another compliment.

"There's no two ways about it, so quit beating yourself up. That wolf was out to kill you. It was kill or be killed. That's the law of the jungle, boy. I taught you that myself. You gotta think like a wolf if you want an elk. Didn't I tell you that? You always was a good shot. I'm proud of you, boy."

It went on like that. My only consolation was that Marc seemed to need some convincing. There was hope for him yet. He was young, he hadn't seen all the game disappear like Dutch had, he hadn't needed to blame wolves for those losses likely as not due to range cattle in elk pastures. Times were different now. I couldn't wait to read how Danny put his own spin on the incident, assuming Maymie Tubbs would let him.

Dutch hung up, his face flushed with excitement. He shook his head and said, "Damn," under his breath, smiling. "You hear about that?"

I nodded.

"First man in sixty years to kill a wolf in Jackson Hole. Shoot, that's something."

"He could be in a lot of trouble."

Dutch waved a hand. "Those Fish and Wildlife boys are hunters. They know where their bread is buttered."

I gathered up my backpack, tucking the clipping inside carefully. "Those Fish and Wildlife boys brought back the wolf." I shouldered the pack. "Thanks for the tea, and the column, Mr. Abbott."

"Oh, call me Dutch. Everybody does."

"Great talking to you, Dutch. I'll bring the column back in a couple days."

"Bring more chocolate, and you're always welcome."

Outside the sun had almost sunk behind the Tetons, the days getting winter-short. High up the smell of snow hung in the pine trees. A squirrel was scolding somebody. I looked back inside as I got into my car and saw Dutch with his head back in the chair, eyes shut. In his hand was a piece of chocolate. He looked just about as happy as anyone I'd ever seen.

Things didn't go as well at the county sheriff's office. A very nice woman with nicotine-stained fingers and a hairdo from hell told me that personal records of deputies and closed cases were not public domain, and thus were out of my reach. I was wishing I had another magic Hershey bar when I was rescued.

Kevin Stoddard wore a gray federal uniform that looked starched and uncomfortable. Biologists must rarely wear their regulation duds. His hiking boots were caked with mud, and he had gotten a new haircut since I'd met him out at Carl's cabin. He nodded seriously toward me, then requested a transcript of yesterday's hearing from the clerk. When she rose reluctantly to locate it, I turned to Kevin.

"Things calming down?"

He put both hands on the edge of the Formica counter. "Not really. You hear about yesterday?"

"I heard you testified."

He clenched his jaw. "I have a bad feeling about the ranchers. They're not going to take the government's word that we can handle it."

"Have there been threats?"

"Sightings. Coming out of the woodwork. Got six calls today that folks had seen a wolf on their property."

"Are you taking them seriously?"

"What choice do we have? There's a system, and by God—" He pursed his lips.

"Where are these wolves supposedly?"

The clerk came by with an armful of paper and slapped it down in front of Kevin. A waft of cigarette odor followed. "That's half of it," she grunted and shuffled off.

"Three of the sightings were in the valley here. One north of the park, up by Flagg Ranch. And two were up the Gros Ventre. That one we definitely have to look into. Two sightings in forest land not far apart."

"Near cattle?"

"That's the funny part. There's no cattle—or sheep—around there. So who's calling in these sightings, and why? Near some old hermit's place. A woman."

I straightened. "Do you remember the name? Was it Queen Johns?"

"Could be. I think that was it."

The other half of the transcript arrived in loving arms. The clerk produced a form for Kevin to sign and returned to her desk. I watched Kevin size up his prize and wondered if Queen had called in the sighting. That didn't sound like her. She would like having a wolf in the neighborhood.

"Say, Kevin." He stopped trying to figure out how to lift the transcript. I moved a little closer. "Is it possible to get copies of old case files from here? Something very old, like twenty-five years?"

"A crime?"

I shook my head. "Hunting accident investigated by the sheriff."

"I don't see why not. You just have to fill out one of those Freedom of Information forms at the counter. Anything that old isn't privileged."

I spun around and saw the forms on the counter, next to requests for birth and death records. Walking over, I held one high and said loudly, "You mean these forms, Kevin?"

The Fish and Wildlife biologist looked confused, then saw the annoyed look on the clerk's face. He smiled and slapped the pile of paper. "Right. Freedom of Information. It's a wonderful thing."

It ended up costing a few bills to get the clerk to agree to a late tomorrow delivery. Her name was Gail Poppler. I didn't mind the money, since poor Gail was going to have to sift through microfilm. I had had a few bad experiences with runaway microfilm and learned to stay away from it. I made a mental note to bring Gail a carton of Marlboros—whatever it took to make her happy.

Back at the gallery, I turned on the lights and planned to conduct business for a couple hours in the late afternoon. But instead I called Danny at the *News* office and found out Farley's name was indeed Farley Platt. So I locked the doors again and headed north in the Saab Sister. The evening sky turned purple as I watched, the Grand a majestic white cone with its cohorts Teewinot and Moran chumming up on both sides. A wispy boa of violet cloud twisted between them—a sight worth shutting down the gallery for. I opened my window and smelled the cold wind laced with sage. Ahead a small herd of umber-and-buff antelope browsed near the sawbuck fence. I wondered if they'd heard the wolves, if they remembered wolves somewhere in their genes.

The Bar-T-Bar was a small, meticulous ranch, one of several small ranches left private when the national park was formed. It was the sort of place Americans dream about when they think of going cowboy: golden pastures, mountain backdrops, gleaming horses, weathered barns, log ranch houses, the smell of latigo and the clunky sound of bootheels on boardwalk.

When I stepped out of the car at the cabin and bunkhouse where Marc Fontaine and his crew quartered, the first thing I heard was the long, lonely, throaty howl. I stopped in the gravel drive. The cry echoed off the mountain granite and faded. It was the sound of grief, of mourning, and it pierced right through me. I shivered and pulled my coat closer. Where had I heard that before? For a moment I was paralyzed, remembering old pain, old grief, old wounds.

The howl was gone. The ranch air lay silent again. But somewhere, close by, lived a wolf.

3

THE cabin was empty. In the corral across the drive three horses pranced in the dirt. The light was going, too dark for me to go trekking around in barns and pastures looking for Marc. I turned left off the porch and walked around the back to the pasture where I'd last seen my horse Valkyrie. The grass was gnawed down and dry. Not a horse in sight. But I put my fingers into my mouth for a loud whistle that used to get her galloping my way.

Nothing. I put a hiking boot on the bottom rail of the split rail fence and shivered. The wolf's howl had had a strange effect on me. I felt electrified, jumpy. Looking up at the wide sky, I felt like a speck on a giant green ball.

"That how you get dinner? Or is it boyfriends?"

I spun at the gravelly voice. A skinny, bowlegged cowboy with a drooping gray mustache and a beat-up black hat stood grinning at me.

"Give you a scare, did I?" The cowboy took off his hat and scratched his nearly hairless head. He wasn't any taller than me but perhaps had sat a little taller in the saddle in his younger days. His clothes were stiff with dirt. "I could say I'm sorry, but that'd be lying."

"Well, we can't have that."

He grinned some more. "Farley Platt." He reached out a gnarled hand. I felt his calluses and let go. "And you would be—besides trespassing?"

"Alix Thorssen. I tried the cabin, but no one was home. I sold my horse to Marc this summer. I guess she's out in a far pasture."

"Could be. What's she look like?"

"Dark, almost black. Tall and pretty wild, no markings."

He scratched his head again and put his hat back on. "She's over here in the corral. Hal's been running her through her paces."

Farley led me across the yard. I hadn't even recognized Valkyrie. There she was in the corral, saddled, with a young cowboy on her back. I couldn't believe my eyes.

"He's riding her."

" 'Course he is. No horse can't be broke."

Broke. That's what we do to horses. I felt a little sad watching her turn to Hal's commands, left, then right, forward and back. She looked happy, though; she wasn't fighting it. All those years I'd had her, she had only let me hang on bareback, usually flat on my belly. She was a picture horse, a wild free thing, Black Beauty, symbol of raw power and freedom. She would bite and paw the ground, ever defiant. I realized now I preferred her that way.

"Is she okay?"

Farley gave me a side glance. "Oh, don't worry, girlie. She's getting fat on our grain, and I hear tell she's got herself a big stallion friend."

"I want her to be happy."

"Well, I heard her tell a good sheep joke the other day. Had the whole stable in stitches."

I gave Farley a grin, then watched Hal work her. He dismounted after a few minutes and walked over to us, leading her. Farley gave quick introductions while I rubbed the old mare's nose and cooed in her ears. I guess she remembered me, because she tried to bite my shoulder.

"Hey, you."

"She's got a temper on her. I usually give her a treat after exercise. That's why she's grouchy," Hal said. He looked a lot like

Marc, lean and short with blond hair and weathered skin. "We're taking good care of her. Marc told me you wanted that."

"I hated to sell her." Valkyrie let me pet her nose again. "But I just couldn't afford it any more."

"Come out and ride her sometime," Hal said before leading her, tail switching, back to the barn.

"Farley," I said as she and Hal disappeared, "There's another reason I came out here." He scratched and nodded. "To talk to you. I was talking to Dutch Abbott, and he mentioned your name."

"What's that old coot up to?"

"Eating chocolate and drinking whiskey and taking it easy. Looks like the life of Riley to me."

"I'll be goddamned. That cuss could talk your ear off." He squinted suspiciously. "Why you talking about me?"

"An old case when you were a sheriff's deputy. Long time ago, twenty-five years. A hunting accident where a boy named Derek Wylie was shot."

I saw the recognition in his eyes, even in the dusky light. He rubbed his cheek. "What you want to go mucking around in that for? That's done and gone."

"I know. But somebody wants to find out what happened, and she's asked me to look into it for her."

"Somebody? Do I get to know who?"

I couldn't see why he shouldn't know. "Queen Johns."

He jerked his head up and stared at my mouth like I might revise my words. Finally he shook his head. "You better come into the cabin then. Getting damn nippy."

Farley lit a fire in the woodstove, rummaged in cupboards for cups, and poured us each half a beer before I made him sit down at the scrubbed pine table and get down to it. He sighed, as if I'd caught him in a lie. His gnarled fingers wrapped around the chipped mug, and he squinted out the dark panes of window glass, then back at me.

"Guess it doesn't surprise me," he said, "though after all these years, I'd almost forgot myself."

"What doesn't surprise you?"

"Somebody asking around about it. I never felt good about the whole thing back then. It all got swept under the carpet. And it wasn't my dirt, so what the hell, ya know?"

I twisted my mug of warm ale and pushed it away. Uneasiness about this job reared its ugly head again. Something was going to make me wish I'd stayed in the gallery, safe and bored. Something always did.

"Just start at the beginning, Farley, if you would."

"Thing is, there ain't that much to tell. Three boys went out deer-hunting together, along south of Highway 22. There weren't many houses out there then, fewer anyways. The deer would come down toward the river bottoms, looking for forage. I guess they went out early that day—it was fall, colder than now."

"Mid-November," I said.

"Right. So first thing any of us hear about it is about eight o'clock that night when somebody from a house along there called in. Said there had been an accident with a gun. We wanted to bring an ambulance, you know, but they said it was too late for that."

"You went out there yourself?"

"Right, me and Shorty—Lester Smith."

"Is he still with the sheriff's department?"

"Shorty bought the ranch years back. Keeled over on the job, just like he always said he would. He was right rotund, nobody was much surprised."

Sympathetic yet eager looks from this side.

"So me and Shorty find these two boys, all hangdog they was, and we followed 'em on foot, with flashlights and Shorty's old shepherd on a leash. Took close to an hour to find the body. It was their friend, that Derek Wylie. Never forget that." He shook his head.

"He was dead then."

"Long dead by the looks of it. Coroner said later it probably happened eight to ten hours before we found him."

"So long?"

"That was curious. I asked them boys what took 'em so long, and they said they was scared and didn't know what to do. They knew he was dead and weren't sure which of them shot him, or even if it was them at all. Maybe it was some other hunter, they says."

I raised my eyebrows. "What did the coroner have to say about that?"

"Coroner says he was dead. Never had a chance to compare casings. Never knew who killed the poor kid."

"So what happened then, in the woods?"

"Me and Shorty wrapped the kid up in our coats and carried him back to the truck. We couldn't leave him out there all night, and we sure as hell weren't going to stay out there on the lookout for bear. Had to throw that coat away."

"Was there an investigation?"

"That night there was a big hoohaw down at the sheriff's. The kid's mother and father were there, of course, they had to identify the body and all. Nasty scene. And the folks of the other kids, the two that probably shot him, well, they put up a big front, whisked those kids away and had lawyers do all the talking." Farley scratched his scalp. Either he had lice or a nervous habit. "That kinda behavior puts a different cast on things in my book."

"Like they got something to hide?"

"Why not let the boys make their statements and go home and let the chips fall if you done nothing malicious? Hell, hunting accidents are a dime a dozen, at least they used to be. Some rube shoots his buddy thinking he's an elk even though he's wearing a pea green jacket and a watch cap. He moved, says the hunter. He was in the woods."

"Do you think that's what happened?"

Farley shrugged.

"What happened after the lawyers showed up?"

"Everything about them two boys got stonewalled then. I think the sheriff just took our statements of what we saw, what they said out there on the scene, and just threw up his hands. He'd never seen something like those lawyers. And the sheriff then was Chester Gass, and he'd been around for a long time."

"Sounds like those two boys were from rich families."

"Oh, yeah, that's right. The kind used to getting their way, all the time."

"Did you know them?"

"Nah. Shorty did, sort of. But their names, no, I don't remember 'em."

"Did you know Derek Wylie?"

Farley swallowed hard. "He hung around town a lot, getting into trouble. We had a couple run-ins with him, but he wasn't a bad kid. His father lived in town, but he was on the road a lot, sold something, cars or cash registers or something."

"His parents were divorced?"

"That's right."

"But his mother lived here. You said she came down to the station, that both his parents were there."

He cocked his head. "Uh-huh."

"Do they still live around here?"

"The father took a flyer after the boy got shot. And the mother, well, you know about her."

I stared into his eyes, a ripe awakening washing over me.

Farley's wrinkled old hide softened. "Queen," he whispered.

I looked at the toes of my hiking boots on the dusty plank floor for a minute, listening to Farley chug his beer. Outside the sound of a truck pulling up, doors slamming, and boots on the porch signaled company. I felt slapped—and stupid. Why else would Queen have been so interested? I got up and fed a log into the woodstove, then turned back to Farley.

"Why wouldn't she tell me that?"

The old man had only time to shrug before the two brothers came into the cabin, accompanied by a blast of chilly air. Marc Fontaine was a good deal older than his brother, with a receding blond hairline, hat line across his forehead, and a few scars for character. He was too rugged to be called handsome but had a great smile that he turned on me. In a matter of a few minutes I was ordered to join them for chow over in the kitchen of the main house. We pulled on our coats and tromped across the gravel into a large ranch kitchen where a huge pot of beef stew awaited us. Helping ourselves to spoons, bowls, crackers, and large glasses of milk, we sat at the long table and ate.

The talk, what there was of it, related to horses. Valkyrie was given a thorough equine analysis and deemed salvageable. Wolves were never mentioned, though I was dying to ask Marc about them. But he looked tired, with dark circles under his eyes, and snapped at Hal if he spoke at all, and in the end I let it pass. Instead I asked Hal about his artwork and asked him to bring by some for me to look at. As we were clearing our dishes, the cook stepped out of the kitchen with a worried look on his rangy face. He blurted out that we better hustle back.

We huddled around the small color television, spattered with grease, set on a shelf over the large industrial sinks. Tom Brokaw was ending a spiel. On the screen came a young woman's voice and views of the Tetons, Jackson, and finally the sign over the Bar-T-Bar ranch entrance. The reporter was summarizing the incidents of the last week. I snuck a peek at Marc. He squinted impassively at the screen.

> According to Fish and Wildlife Service spokesmen, the gray wolf has shown great adaptability and fertility in the years since a handful of wolves were reintroduced. Officials had hoped the wolf wouldn't stray too far, too fast, but incidents between wolves and livestock have increased.
>
> Another issue brought to the forefront by the latest wolf kill is that of private ranches inside national parks. Grand Teton National Park, one of our youngest parks tucked next to our oldest, Yellowstone, poses special problems. Numerous small ranches like the Bar-T-Bar continue to operate alongside special wildlife conditions. In his Denver home, where he spends his winters, Bar-T-Bar ranch owner Jerome "Bud" Wooten told us of his struggles to keep ranching his grandfather's spread in the shadow of the Tetons.

The camera cut to a shot of Bud Wooten, seventyish, balding, and barrel-chested, wearing a denim shirt and Levi's and silver belt buckle, by a large fireplace next to what looked to my practiced eye like a Charlie Russell oil. His face was large and weathered, the prototypical cowboy, yet I knew he was more accurately a millionaire oilman.

My grandfather, Curly Wooten, came out to Wyoming with a string of mules around the turn of the century, thinking wrongly that there might be some gold. Instead he found a golden opportunity, you might say, and traded the mules for some of the most beautiful rangeland in America. When the park came in, we were promised we could stay, and we've been trying. It's not easy, or cheap, to raise livestock with grizzlies and wolves around, with killer winters and thin hay crops. You have to love the land, and we do. We'll be here, the Wootens, as long as we can, and the land will be there even longer. With or without wolves.

No mention of Marc, no support expressed—the bastard. The reporter wrapped up the story, obviously finished before yesterday's hearing. We all started to move away. The shot of Bud Wooten, his study in Denver with its guns and elk heads and art and branding irons, stuck in my mind. What he'd said was nothing special, but I felt the difference between his version of the cowboy, false and fat, and the real thing standing here, lean and hard and left carrying the bag.

As I said good night, the wolves were howling again, this time back and forth across the valley, a wolfen telegraph.

"Farley," I said, tugging his sleeve at my car. We watched the brothers continue on into the cabin. "Did you know Queen Johns back then?"

He stuck his hands into pockets of his wool jacket. "Went to school with her. She was a wild thing. Not far different from Derek. Getting into trouble, and the like."

"But she left and came back?"

"Went to college somewhere. Came back when Derek was a baby, that's when I saw her again."

I looked at his craggy face, half hidden by the shadow of his battered hat. "Was she a friend?"

"You might say that." He turned to me, then away, then back again. I waited. He would tell me whatever it was if he wanted. I couldn't force him.

A wolf howled. Farley said, "People called her crazy, you

know. Said she was out of her mind. But she loved that boy. I know she did, 'cause I saw them together, from when she first moved back. I saw her all the time with Derek and—" He rubbed his hand over his mouth and chin.

"You were close?"

"I haven't seen her in all these years, since Derek died."

"When did she get divorced?"

"Soon after she came back. He divorced her, that Dominick Wylie. Said she wasn't fit to be a mother, that she had crazy fits and wasn't safe around the boy. It warn't true, none of it."

"Derek lived with his father then?"

"For all the good it did him." He turned up his collar. It was getting cold. "He wouldn't let Queen see that boy but one day a month. It was cruel. She cried and cried about it. Then one day she just quit crying and started painting. That was when she moved up into the hills in that cabin, away from everybody."

"Away from you too?"

He shook his head. "She still let me come see her once in a while. But she changed. Maybe she was a little crazy. Something was gone from her, something that—don't know how to describe it. Maybe Derek dying did it for good. I know it turned her hair white."

An owl hooted in the trees. The night was dark. "Farley. You said you thought the dirt got swept under the rug. What dirt?"

He pursed his dry lips and hunched further down in his coat. "Whatever really happened to Derek Wylie out there. But after twenty-five years, we may never know."

Farley veered off toward the dark bunkhouse, an ancient log building slung low against the pastureland. I watched his hunched shoulders disappear into the shadows. Did he love her? Did he blame himself for Queen's divorce—with reason? So much time had passed, and still his feelings for her, and her dead boy, were keen. I wondered if twenty-five years from now I'd still be pining for Paolo, and what good that would do me. A romantic idea, but bad for living.

The cabin's door opened, and Marc stepped out into the glow of the porchlight. He set his hat hard on his head with one hand. In the other was a rifle. I paused, jangling my keys.

"Feels like winter," Marc said, squinting into a cold breeze off the mountains.

"It's coming."

He peered my way. "You hear about the mess with the wolf?"

"Hard to miss. That where you're headed now?"

"I moved the horses from that pasture. I never figured a wolf could take one down." He exhaled a cloud of air. "Until the other night, that is."

"That's what you think was going on?"

"What else? There's no foals out there. And the wolves'd been hanging 'round. Like tonight, we'd been hearing them closer, and more often."

"Well, it'll turn out all right. You were defending yourself. Like Dutch said."

"You know Dutch?"

"Just met him today. I was up there when you called."

"Dutch doesn't know the politics of wildlife and ranching, not any more."

"I bet you never thought horse wrangling involved politics."

"Horse wrangling's a lot easier than people wrangling." He gave a very small smile. The events of the last few days weighed heavily on him. He squinted into the shadows of the mountains. "I like the land. I believe like the Indians we can't own it, but we get our little time to take care of it. But in a way it owns us—it makes its demands on us, and either we cowboy up or we're gone. I guess the other night was the land's way of checking me out."

"Well, hell, Marc, you cowboyed up."

"I suppose I did." He didn't sound too thrilled about it.

"You didn't have a choice."

He frowned. "I'd like to believe that. In that split second, I believed it, but—" He shook his head.

"Nobody who hasn't been right there—having to decide to kill or not—can make those judgments. Christ, the wolf was attacking you." He pinched his lips together. "Right?"

He scraped the gravel with his boot toe. "When I was a kid, I had a dog. Charger, a big purdy golden lab. Sweetest dog in the world. One day one of my buddies came over and brought his little sister, she must have been three or four. She loved Charger, she was always petting him and talking to him. We got bored with that and went outside. Then the little sister is bawling, and she has this big tooth mark across her face, right below her eye. Her mother comes for her, she's bawling and hollering. Everybody thinks Charger has bit her. Charger just sits there, his tongue rolling, sweet as ever, wondering what the fuss is about.

"But my father comes in from calving, and he sees what's going on. He takes Charger out behind the barn and puts a bullet through his head. He couldn't stand the bawling."

A shooting star lit up the midnight blue over the Tetons. Frost gathered on the blades of grass. I clutched my coat tighter across my chest. "Your father never looked for the truth?"

"Sometimes, you just gotta stop the bawling," Marc said. "Next time you see me, I'll be making change at Kmart."

"Mr. Wooten won't fire you."

He looked at me, his blue eyes cold and dark, and raised one eyebrow. "Good to see you, Alix."

He strode slowly across the drive and climbed over the corral's fence. I got into the car and watched his shadow cross the light powdery earth of the corral. Bad enough he second-guessed his decision to kill the wolf, bad enough he's testifying and getting written up, bad enough he might get fined or arrested. But he might have to give up horses and the only life he's ever known.

At the tall log gate of the ranch, under the swinging iron Bar-T-Bar sign, I stopped the car to let a car pass. The headlights came slowly, from town. It was cold in the car, and I wanted to go home. What was Carl doing tonight? I felt twitchy from the wolf's sad cry and some memory it touched, and Marc's depressing story. Was it too late to call Carl? I looked at my watch as the truck came into the beams of the Saab Sister's headlights.

A man standing in the pickup bed caught my eye, his face in a shadow—a ski mask? He held a white bucket, and in that split second before I blasted the horn, he yelled, "Killer!" and threw the bucket of blood over the car.

4

WITH the gun blast I quit honking the car horn and flattened myself to the seat, pressing my face straight into a ratty hole and snagging my lip on the edge of an exposed spring. I whimpered, held a hand to my mouth, and waited for the blood-slingers to return. I listened for the truck. Nothing. The owl and wolves had scattered into the dark forest.

Footsteps. I rolled onto the floor, a nasty place in a very old car, cold, oily, and reminiscent of every french fry that ever escaped. I moved my hand to include my nose.

The door was flung open with an oath. "Alix? You all right?"

I opened my eyes and removed my hand, hoisting myself up to the seat. The windshield was a dark, slimy mess. Marc stood in the open doorway, rifle in hand.

"Was that you? The shot?"

"Warning shot, that's all. Scared 'em off."

I slithered out of the Saab, which had died and lurched forward when I hit the deck. On the ground around the car was the dark stain of the liquid. I bent toward it and smelled the rich, dank smell of blood.

"Is it real?"

Marc nodded. "Third night of it. Sheriff tells me somebody's been stealing blood from a slaughterhouse down by Big Piney." He sighed. "Seems like somebody's pissed off at somebody else all the time."

At close to midnight I got home, cold, tired, and wet. The doors of the Saab were frozen shut so tight it took a kick with both feet to escape. Marc had insisted on a complete car wash in the cold, pitch-dark night. The cowboy could be gallant, you had to give him that. Now I stumbled down the alley, unlocked the back door with stiff fingers, and spent a long minute struggling with the deadbolt on the inside.

I stripped and took a hot shower, staying in until I felt more or less normal again. With a glass of wine I slipped into my pajama sweats and thick wool socks, then hopped into bed. I didn't even look at the answering machine. I'd had enough for one night.

Ensconced against the pillows, I sipped and tried to unwind. The conversation with Farley echoed, as the excitement of the bucket of blood receded. Why had Queen never said she was related to Derek? Why the secrecy? Did she think it didn't matter? I ran over Farley's story of finding the boy's body in the woods. Who was with Derek that day? That was who I needed to talk to. Could it be that no one had ever gotten the straight story out of them?

And what would the official report say? Would it be different from Farley's version of the events? Had he forgotten something, some name, some detail, some important fact that the report would clarify?

The knot on my nose began to tingle. I knew what that meant, that I was curious, or shall we say, nosy. This was a bad sign. I had to finish the auction brochure, figure out the placement, talk to Terry Vargas about procedure. Plus I wanted to hole up and paint next week, even though Carl had other plans. Lots of details, and I, girl once mocked as a snapping turtle with a brain and a bra, could not stop thinking about a forest clearing where a young boy's life had gone out like an underfed flame.

I sunk lower under the comforter. My apartment over the gallery had its pluses. Number one was location, near "the office." A big second was the quiet night, at least from neighbors. None of the other stores along this side of the town square had apartments overhead; I was alone. I could play music as loud as I wanted (with the windows closed); I could entertain anyone I wanted. It was private, just the way I liked it.

I closed my eyes, still holding the last of the wine in the glass. In the quiet the sound of the wolf's howl out at the Bar-T-Bar played again in my head. A wave of pity or sorrow that washed over me seemed at first connected to the late hour or the wine. That mournful, lonely sound. It was endless, going on and on, like the bawling in Marc's story, a cry for help, a wail from somewhere deep in the soul. Somewhere forgotten, somewhere far away and too close by. A place so primal, so close to the being, that like the face of God it was best not looked at. Yet, this sound. This terrible sound.

My eyes flew open. I sat up, sloshed my wine onto the comforter.

The wolf. The searing howl.

I bent over double, a sudden pain in my gut. I had heard that howl years ago. It came back like a freight train through the prairie night: the hillside, the sheep, crazy Wanda, the summer twilight that seemed to last and last until its final moist purple droplets were sucked into the void. The smell of the grass, the oily woollies, the whiskey. And the wolf: blue-haired, yellow-eyed, full-throated. With a single swooping cry it carved a hole in my heart, then patched it up again with the kind of searing tenderness and raw courage that only a fourteen-year-old whose world has collapsed can understand.

Another sound now, a gulping moan. I opened my eyes, recognized my voice. The wine was soaking through the covers. My face wet with tears, I jumped out of bed, stripped off the sheets and comforter, and left them in an angry heap by the window. The wineglass took a bounce and rolled under the bed.

I laid my forehead against the cold glass of the window, gulping air. Out on the square the twinkle lights on the antler arches seemed cold and sterile, death gates. I hugged my stomach, both willing the pain to go and hoping never to forget that moment again, that eye-lock with wildness. Blue Wolf. That blue wolf held a secret, I remembered thinking back then. He is wild and free and could lead me to the secret of surviving. Something pure and simple and golden, like a magic wand. Had I found it, and forgotten that too?

After twenty years, I should know the secret.

But in the morning all I felt was hung over, from half a glass of wine plus adventures. No blinding revelations had come to me in the night. So I made coffee, tried and failed with my hair, and went to work. I took a break from the auction brochure to call Terry Vargas about our afternoon meeting. His assistant, or whatever you wanted to call her at twenty-three and gorgeous, confirmed they were expecting me and Morris Kale at two. I hung up, strangely offended by her efficiency. Did one woman have to have it all? The hangover appeared to include a heavy aftertaste of the peeves.

I was nibbling my nails when Maggie Barlow burst in, singing at the top of her lungs. She had her boyfriend's daughter by the hand. Together they finished up "Hey There Little Red Riding Hood" with a sexy growl.

"You two sure are looking good," I said, grinning at the little girl. Her name was Lily, and she had dark brown hair pulled into spiky topknots.

Lily put her hands on her hips. "And you're everything that a big bad wolf would want. Grrrrrr." She bared her teeth, all a five-year-old might be expected to have.

"Why aren't you in school today, young lady?" I asked her.

"She goes in the afternoons, kindergarten."

I found crayons and scrap paper for Lily, then poured Maggie coffee. "You look like you might need it."

She had dark circles under her eyes, making her brown eyes sink deeper into her pale face. Her heavy sweater, although perfect for brisk fall days, was buttoned wrong.

"James's ex is out of town," Maggie whispered. "She made me play beauty shop this morning, seven A.M. He's got some big meeting about his screenplay. He was all excited about it last week, but now I'm not so sure."

"Didn't you say you'd read it?"

"Yeah, it's great, at least I think so. It's James, he's—" A cloud formed on her pretty face, turning her mouth into a frown. "One day he thinks it'll sell for millions, then he's lost all hope and he barely makes it out of bed."

"Must be a hard business."

Maggie watched Lily drawing. "I love that kid, but if all I am is an unpaid baby-sitter, what sort of a relationship is that? I don't want to be that kind of a creep. And yet, what the hell am I doing?"

"Maggeeee!" Lily yelled from the back.

"What, sweet pea?"

"I have to peeeeeee!"

When they came out of the bathroom, I gave Lily a cookie from my secret stash. She dribbled crumbs happily.

"I have to go check out a claim," Maggie said. "Did you hear somebody put a rock through the window of the All One All Wild office? Things are getting nasty. I've never seen folks so galvanized on an issue."

"Aren't they in the same building with the Land Trust?"

"Right next door. Do you know the director, Candace?"

"She's on our auction committee." Candace, at first blush, seemed to be a hard-nosed, unlikable sort, with an agenda she wore on her sleeve. Morris Kale had invited her to be on the committee, and I'd heard him bemoaning that decision. I wondered suddenly what sort of a pickup Candace might drive. And if she had a penchant for blood.

"You don't look like you want to know her," Maggie said, looking at me curiously.

"Somebody has been delivering buckets of cattle blood to the Bar-T-Bar."

"Ick." Maggie grimaced. "You think it's All Wild?"

"It was somebody who thinks Marc Fontaine is a killer."

"It may not have happened exactly the way he says."

"You think he's lying?"

Lily wiped her hands on her corduroy skirt, making greasy stains. Maggie took her hand. "Come on, sweet pea, time to go." She looked at me. "Wouldn't you—to cover your ass?"

"His ass?" Lily piped up.

"Don't repeat that, missy." Maggie rolled her eyes, grabbed the girl's hand, and waved good-bye.

As I swept up Lily's crumbs, I thought about Marc and his story about his dog, and Bud Wooten on television. For a moment I mourned the end of the cowboy days. Very few men lived like Marc Fontaine any more. The West had once been full of cows and cowboys, but it had changed a long time ago. Gentlemen ranchers like Bud Wooten didn't even live on the land any more, and their employees were expendable. My mourning for Valkyrie's wildness felt the same way: an inevitable but sad passing of something good and pure.

Carl called. I kept sweeping, cradling the phone under my chin.

"Where the hell have you been?" he blurted.

"What the hell do you mean?"

"Didn't you get my messages?"

"Oh. I was out all day, most of the evening too, out at the ranch where I sold Valkyrie."

"I waited for you for two hours at Merry Piglets, and you never showed up. I left you a message, we were going to meet at seven, but you never called or showed up or anything. I think that is very rude."

I swallowed, digging my fingertips into my forehead. I seemed to be doing that a lot lately. "Assuming that I would just arrive where you command is very misguided." There was a long silence, broken only by heavy breathing. "Did you have a nice dinner?"

More heavy breathing, then finally, a "Yes."

"Mine was leftover beef stew, not particularly good. Then I got sloshed with a bucket of blood."

He didn't respond. In the background I could hear someone talking.

"Where are you?"

"Huh? In the Fish and Wildlife office. Kevin let me use the phone. I may take them to track the wolves this afternoon." Another pause. "Listen, can we have dinner tonight?"

"I've got a meeting at Kale's for the auction. It starts at seven."

"I won't be back till at least six if we go looking for lobo."

"We really don't have to eat together every night like we did." It was a relief to have a little space again.

"Whatever," he muttered. Voices again, now raised, shouting. "What's going on out there?"

"A group of people arguing with the chief. They're getting pretty heated."

"Maybe you better use your police training and defuse 'em."

"Right, okay, we'll talk later."

He hung up. A frisson of resentment bloomed. Was that jealous tirade just an act? A fit of pique because he had to eat alone? He obviously wasn't interested in our conversation. The question was, was he interested in me? Or more to the point, was I interested in him? Carl Mendez was an attractive, complicated, sexy man who'd moved here because of me—or had he? Jackson Hole had lured many pilgrims with its natural wonders, incredible beauty, and the sense of being one of the chosen few who manage to live in paradise. He'd found a way to combine his love of the outdoors and his work. Why did I think it was me at all?

The drive out to Terry Vargas's ranch on Togwotee Pass was one I usually relished, but not today. Not only had the sunshine disappeared behind dark clouds, my mood had also darkened. I'd tried not to think much about a future for me and Carl, but now it seemed I couldn't get anything else into my mind.

The questions bombarded me as the Saab climbed the hill that led to the Flying V Ranch. I had to put the car into second and was soon joined by a big black pickup truck kicking up dust behind me. Morris Kale waved and parked next to me at the fence next to the ranch house. We walked up to the door together.

He knocked loudly on the wide, sawn-plank door weathered by the elements. "That wolf painting, wow. I can't quit thinking about it."

"Yeah," I said, still distracted. "Blue wolf, to a T." I realized what I'd said and tried to smile as if he had the faintest idea what I was talking about.

The door opened, revealing the rangy figure of Terry Vargas, in jeans, flannel shirt, and immaculate beard so dark he had a glint of the devil on him. He greeted us warmly, ushering us into his buffalo-plaid living room with majestic mountain views and veritable zoo of stuffed heads. Their glass eyes watched as we were served tea and finger cookies by the assistant, Georgia. She was all business today in skin-tight black slacks and a low-cut ribbed sweater. The glass eyes weren't the only ones ogling her chest.

"I've asked Georgia to take some notes, so I don't forget what we talked about." Vargas smiled at the woman, who took her cue demurely, pulling a notebook from thin air and opening a fancy fat pen. He sat back in a brown leather armchair and brushed invisible dust from the tips of his snakeskin boots.

"Before the meeting tonight," Vargas said, "I want us all clear on the auction procedure. Now, I've hired Jake Laughlin to auctioneer. He's done a few charity auctions, and you know him, he's got quite a voice on him."

Morris sat forward on the plaid sofa. "Laughlin? The artist? I thought we were getting a professional auctioneer."

"He has two pieces in the auction, Terry," I pointed out. Plus Jacob Laughlin was one of my least favorite people in the Jackson art scene. He was always bugging me to hang elk-bugling scenes in the gallery, and I was always refusing. Last time I hadn't been too nice about it.

Vargas shrugged. "He's cheap. If you want somebody else for his two paintings, I can do it myself. I don't think people need a real quick style, like we're auctioning cattle."

I eyed Morris to see if he was going to protest further. He had his head cocked and eyebrows furrowed. "How cheap is cheap?"

"Free. And he's donating one of his paintings outright."

Good old Jake. I took back all my negative thoughts. Morris gave me a questioning look, and I nodded.

"What else?"

"Next, we've got a problem with Queen Johns."

My turn to sit forward. "What problem?"

Vargas paused to tent his fingers, then to dig his thumbs around his chin hairs.

"This auction is for the Teton Land Trust. We all agree with that, I hope. We believe the land is sacred and should be preserved as is, in open spaces for ranches—"

"And wildlife. And hikers and skiers," Morris added.

Terry frowned at him. "Right. Well, Ms. Johns doesn't see it that way. She's holding people off her land with a shotgun. I was up there myself this morning and saw it."

Georgia sat up, eyes wide. "She threatened to kill me. I wasn't even on her property."

"Hold it," I said. "What is this about? Why were you up there?"

"Wolves. There's been reports of wolves near her cabin. The Wildlife Service went up there to check out the reports, and she held them off with her shotgun."

"She owns a shotgun?"

"A big one," Georgia said.

"They're all big, dear," Terry told her. "But she did threaten us. And the agents. I imagine she'll be arrested this afternoon."

"Arrested?" I should go right now. "Listen, Terry. You can't cut her out of the auction. She needs that money, and she's donating her share just like everybody else."

Morris, Terry, and Georgia took a moment to frown at me. Finally Terry said, "What's it to you? You don't exhibit her, do you?"

"She's my friend, Terry. And she doesn't have many."

"I wonder why," Georgia snipped.

"Look, she's eccentric, we all know that. But she is a great artist—Morris was just saying so—and her paintings will bring a lot of money to the Land Trust. Isn't that what this all about?"

"I don't think she'll help the Land Trust if she's in jail during the auction. Not good publicity in my book. In fact, it will seem that we support ecoterrorism. Bad enough we have those All Wild nuts on the committee."

"Candace Gundy isn't bad," Morris said. "Just passionate."

"For the wrong thing. It looks bad, and you know it. Don't be such a wimp, Morris. We are a conservation group. We are conservatives and conservationists. We don't need to be associated with a bunch of whackos disrupting the work of federal agents or legitimate ranching interests."

"Queen is not an ecoterrorist!" I said. "No one thinks of her that way."

"They just think she's crazy," Georgia said.

I refused to look at the girl, she was making me so angry with her little outcries. "You're making generalizations about the Land Trust, Terry. I know for a fact some of them aren't conservative politically."

"Oh, you mean the movie stars. Sure, they can afford to be liberals because they aren't making their living off the land. They're a bunch of hobbyists. Running around playing cowboy, finding endangered species in foxholes, or fancy bats in their barns."

The venom in his voice was stabbing. Morris stared at the floor. This summer he had found a strange strain of bats living in an old barn on his ranch, and it had been written up in the paper.

"I didn't mean you, Morrie. You've got your own weird ways, but at least you're giving it a try, aren't you." But we all knew what Vargas really felt. He cleared his throat. "Let's move on, can we? If you aren't ready to make a decision on Queen Johns, we'll have to bring it to the full committee tonight. It'll probably take hours. I thought we could just get it out of the way, but if you're so all-fired worried about the old biddy—"

"Really, Terry," I cautioned.

"She's an old biddy if I ever saw one. I call a spade a spade. She's a nut, she's off her rocker living up there alone. If she was my mother, I'd sure as hell throw her—"

"Let's move on, Terry," Morris said sternly. "What other auction procedures are we working on here?"

Vargas reddened. He was really put out by Queen Johns. It was amazing the things that set people off. He smoothed his hands down his jeans.

"The food's all set, right?" I asked.

"Yes," Georgia said. "The caterers have everything planned out, with the buffet line starting with fresh fruit and vegetables." She went on to describe all the food and table settings. I was too angry at Terry Vargas to think about whether the napkins should be flat or rolled with little raffia ties. After a few minutes of Georgia's listings, I excused myself.

"I've got a lot of work to do," I said. "I'll see you tonight."

"Don't go away mad, Alix," Terry said, standing and smiling. But it would take more than his superficial charm to cool my jets. "We can work something out on this Queen Johns issue. I'm sure you'll see why it—"

"—why it has to be your way? I doubt it."

He stood silently, staring at me.

"I will never see why you feel the need to punish Queen Johns like this. And make no mistake, that's what you're doing. It's your organization, she doesn't belong. She's only an artist, not a rancher. She doesn't have a conservation easement or a herd of cattle. She's only a crazy old woman. You can do whatever you want to her and she isn't going to sue you, is she? She's got no one, Terry. No one."

"Alix," Georgia said, standing next to Vargas. "I think you're overreacting. Terry isn't trying to be vindictive. He's just concerned about bad publicity. And she is a dangerous woman, I could see that for myself."

"Thank you for the warning, Georgia. I've known her for seven years, and I've never felt anything but welcome at her cabin. And as for vindictive, well, I'm surprised at you, Georgia. Three syllables."

Stupid Stupid Stupid.

On the drive down the hill, the words pounded in my head. I wish I had been talking about Georgia, but she was too calm and reasonable for that. No, it was me who was stupid, flying off the handle at Terry Vargas and Georgia when I had to work with them for another week on this stupid stupid stupid auction. It was too late, and would be too unprofessional, to quit now.

I smacked the steering wheel with my palm. At the bottom of the hill I hit the highway with a vengeance, but at Kelly I made a turn toward Queen's. What the hell was going on up there?

I had plenty of time to wonder as I wound my way up the Gros Ventre. The clot of pickups and cars parked along the dirt road was my first clue I wasn't too late. Queen never had visitors, but someone had put the word out about the wolf sighting. Or maybe about Queen herself, with her shotgun. I threw the Saab Sister into the ditch and ran up the road toward the cabin.

A green U.S. Wildlife Service pickup sat by her door. I knocked and called her name, then reached for the knob.

"Queen? You here?"

The cabin was empty, the afternoon sun streaming in the west window. On the table sat a mug. I felt it; it was cold. Had she been standing off these guys all day?

Out the window was her woodpile, an ax stuck into a log, a log-splitter awl next to it. The clearing was full of wood chips but nothing else. I peered into the trees, wondering which way they were. Then I heard the shot. As I ran out the back door, I thought I had been hearing way too many guns. Something had to stop, and I only hoped it was the bullets.

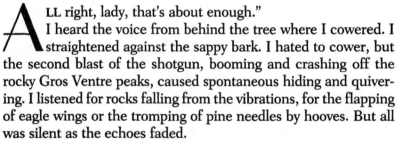

5

"ALL right, lady, that's about enough."
I heard the voice from behind the tree where I cowered. I straightened against the sappy bark. I hated to cower, but the second blast of the shotgun, booming and crashing off the rocky Gros Ventre peaks, caused spontaneous hiding and quivering. I listened for rocks falling from the vibrations, for the flapping of eagle wings or the tromping of pine needles by hooves. But all was silent as the echoes faded.

"Put the gun down now," the male voice said. I stepped out from behind the tree to peer through the trunks to another clearing, darkening with shadows in the afternoon sun. On one end, in the shadows, stood a group of officials, neighbors, and hangers-on. On the other stood Queen Johns in a fuchsia muumuu, holding a big gun. I crept closer, trying to get a look at her without causing bodily injury.

"Then get outa here," she said, her voice strong. "You got no right to set those traps, or use those dart guns. I never complained about a wolf. If I did, I'd be the first to tell you."

I reached the last ring of trees and paused in the lee of a pine trunk. The clearing was marshy with reeds and snake grass on the opposite side, and mounds of blue-green grass and moss. The grass had gone brown on top from the summer sun, but was still green where the spring—uphill somewhere—kept it moist, the sort of magical place where you expect to find a doe and fawn bedded down, or maybe a unicorn. The slanting sun from the west shone on Queen like a spotlight, illuminating dust motes and pollen, and the tangled branches in her long white hair.

She raised the gun at the men on the other side. "I said git. And I mean it."

A ranger in a gray Forest Service uniform stepped forward. "This is public land, ma'am. Forest Service property. You don't have rights on this land."

"I'm a member of the public, aren't I?" she demanded, squinting at the man. He grimaced, his weathered face trying for a look of conciliation.

"Yes, you are. But we have a greater good to think about. We are trustees for the entire public."

"Don't do me any favors then. You never did. You let Mason Brothers come in five years ago and log, right up the road from me. That was you, wasn't it?"

The ranger shrank back.

"Did you ask me about that? And then the runoff came, and the creek behind my place was full of mud from that clear-cut. All the fish were gone. Tell me whose good was that for? Ask that wildlife ranger how that helped his fish."

Another uniform stepped forward. "These decisions aren't easy ones, ma'am. We balance all the good and the bad that can come out of it and try to do what's best. This time we need to set these traps so that we can collar this wolf, if there is a wolf. That's all. We don't want to hurt him, or even move him. We just need to know which wolf he is."

"So if he gets caught feeding on your precious beef, you'll know which one to slaughter. That's what you mean."

"Sometimes that happens, yes. Wolves learn, they're smart animals. If cattle are easy prey, they come back. And that means trouble."

"Well, there isn't any trouble out here. No cattle. So git on back to the flatlands."

The forest ranger said, "These forests have grazing permits, ma'am. There are cattle here."

"There sure as hell don't need to be."

Queen slipped a hand in her pocket of her muumuu. She broke the stock of the shotgun, dislodged the spent shells, reloaded. When she put it back together, with its satisfying metal clunk, the rangers looked at each other. A rancher from down the road raised his rifle to hip level. Uneasiness spun through them like the plague.

I stepped into the sunshine, plastered a beatific smile on my face. Finally Queen blinked and turned my way.

"Hi, Queen," I said. I took another small step toward her.

"Keep back, miss," the wildlife agent said. "We don't want any trouble here."

"A bit late for that, isn't it?" I smiled again at Queen.

"Alix," she said, puzzled. "What are you doing here?"

"I have some news for you. A report." I turned to the quivering mass. "But if you're busy, we can do it some other time."

Queen squared her shoulders and glared at the men. "They want the wolf. But they can't have him. He belongs in the wild, not with them. They want to kill him."

"Mrs. Johns, please!" A small bespectacled man wearing a navy flannel shirt stepped forward. "We don't want to kill the wolf. It's a scientific thing."

"Science schmience. Bugger off, Leroy."

"She's crazy, Leroy. Don't even start with her. Loonie." The mutterings of the crowd consoled Leroy, and his flannel shirt wilted again behind the rangers. Leroy Leonard, the high school biology teacher—I wondered how he knew Queen. I'd never heard her talk that way to anyone.

"Maybe we could talk about it inside, Queen," I offered. "It's getting cold out here."

She kept her gaze on the men. "Talk is done, isn't it, boys?" Her smile froze them. Their eyes were glued on the gun barrels.

"Well, I want to talk, Queen," I said. "Let's just leave them out here with their little-boy games. The wolf isn't anywhere around here now. Those blasts of the shotgun were brilliant. You scared off the wolf."

Her dark eyebrows gathered in thought. "I suppose he's miles away."

"On the other side of the pass, I bet. Halfway to Dubois." I turned to the wildlife agent. "You're setting traps?"

"Just two. They're humane, they don't hurt the animal."

"If they catch it."

"That's right. We might not even catch the wolf. Maybe the reports were all wrong, maybe it was a coyote."

The rancher with the gun spoke loudly. "Wasn't no coyote. It was black with gray grizzles. And it was big. A wolf, no doubt."

The agent sighed. "We're just doing our jobs here, ma'am."

I dared another step toward Queen and lowered my voice to a conspiratorial whisper. "That wolf is too smart. They'll never catch him." The shotgun sagged in her arms and she looked suddenly very tired. "Come on, Queen. I'll make you some tea."

The men stood like statues in the blue-green autumn shadows as I took Queen's arm. She had powerful shoulders from years of chopping wood; her muscles rippled as she shifted the shotgun to her other hand. She stopped halfway through the trees and looked over her shoulder. The men had their heads together, talking.

"I'm watching you!" she yelled. The men's white faces peered toward us through the dim light. "I won't forget."

She spun back and began crashing through the kinnikinik on the forest floor. I kept up behind her, glad to see the cabin. It sat dark now in the twilight. She pulled open the back door, propped up the shotgun, and went immediately to the woodstove.

"No wood." She headed back toward the door. I caught her arm.

"Let me," I said. "I've still got my jacket on."

Queen sneered. "Think I'm an old lady, do you? I've been chopping wood every day of your life."

I stepped aside. She seemed so different than the day I picked up the paintings. That day she'd been full of quips, talking about the alpha wolf like a *Ms.* magazine ball-breaker. Today she was embattled, even bitter. Defensive and angry.

With a few quick drops of the awl, the wood was split. I opened the door as she hustled in, arms full. I filled the teakettle and set it on the stove as she lit the wood inside. She stood staring at the flames, arms crossed.

"Have you been out there all day?"

A toss of her hair over her shoulder was the only answer. The water boiled quickly, and Queen silently laid out tea bags and cups. She seemed calmer, unwinding little by little. As we stirred the tea bags, the men tromped silently out of the trees and across the edge of the cabin's clearing. Queen watched them, anger flaring across her face.

"Get offa my property," she said quietly. Then she turned to me. "They've got no right to be here, chasing away the birds and the little animals. Wolf, they say? What about the trout in the streams, the jack rabbits, the squirrels? They don't know all the beings that depend on this forest."

I turned away from the window, sat down on the edge of one of her frayed wicker chairs, and stirred my tea. Queen continued watching until the clearing was quiet. The trucks started up, and drove away. Finally she sat down. It was very quiet, only the snap and crackle of the fire accompanying the high, waffling sounds of the nighthawk outside.

"Have you seen him?" I asked. "The wolf."

Queen cocked her head, a coy girlish look transforming her face. "Maybe I have. Maybe I haven't."

I set down my teacup. "I'm not one of them, Queen. I'm your friend."

"Beware people who call themselves friend."

I sat back in the uncomfortable chair and picked a piece of green paint from the old wicker. "Was I wrong, Queen? Aren't we friends?"

Her head jerked up. For a moment I expected her to throw me out. Then she softened, blinking gray eyes that showed every year of her age.

I went on. "I talked to some people about the accident. The one where Derek Wylie was killed."

She straightened, regaining composure. "And? What did you find out?"

I paused, then said it. "I found out he was your son."

She stood up and turned toward the window again.

"I wish you'd told me that," I said.

"I don't see why it makes a difference. I didn't have anything to do with the accident."

"But if you could direct me to people who were there, who knew Derek."

"I thought you were going to find police reports, newspaper articles. That's all I asked. I don't want you to look around at Derek. He was a good boy, he—"

Her voice broke. She hung her head. When she spoke again, I had to strain to hear her.

"I didn't do right by Derek. I was young, and I thought the world owed me. Derek's father was a son of a bitch—like most men. No, worse. We shouldn't have gotten married, it was a mistake from the beginning. But then there was Derek.

"Such a pretty boy, everyone said so. And sweet and kind, not the sort that he ended up tearing around town with. He was living with his father then. They used to fight a lot, I heard. Dominick was hard to please, hard to live with. I didn't see Derek much after he was twelve. Dominick thought it was better I didn't. After all that happened before, I suppose he was right."

"You were divorced when Derek was a baby?"

She turned to me: "Who told you that?"

"An old friend of yours."

She squinted at me menacingly, then turned again toward the window. All she could see, I guessed, was her own reflection: an old, sad woman trying—and failing—to forget.

"You do have friends, Queen."

"That time is gone. I have no one."

An eerie echoing of my words to Terry Vargas.

"I'm your friend, Queen. But maybe it would be better to leave Derek's death in the past," I suggested gently. "It can't do any good now to dredge all this up."

She sighed. Her voice had lost all its power and sounded

fragile. "I don't want to remember. But every night for the last month I see him in my dreams, running through the forest. He is confused, he is alone, and I can't help him. But I have to help him. He needs me, he's cold and afraid. I have to find out what happened to him, even if it is to say good-bye."

It was a curious speech, almost as if she didn't believe he was dead. I thought of Farley's tale of the two coats, the sling that bore Derek's body back. He was gone. Yet he lived, inside his mother's head.

I sat trying to figure out a way out of this, a way to salve her sorrows and not reopen the wounds. The boy had been gone for twenty-five years. He was dead. Life goes on, even in grief. I knew that as well as anyone. The sun comes up, breakfast has to be eaten, dishes washed, night falls again. Queen had made a life for herself up here—alone, yes, but a productive life full of beauty and close to nature. It could even be said, an enviable life.

She was looking at me. "I saw him," she whispered.

I blinked. "Derek?"

"The wolf. I saw him right outside here. I bury my garbage, but he dug it up. He stood right there and looked at me."

I stared, following her hand pointing outside.

"I started leaving him things. I know I shouldn't, that they get used to it. But he was so beautiful, a wild thing so big and full of life. He made me feel alive just to see him. And glad."

She turned, her eyes watering. "I was glad to be alive. I haven't felt that in so long. After Derek died, my heart turned to stone. Maybe it had been going that way for a while. I worked hard, I built this cabin with these two hands. I chopped wood, I grew my garden, I caught fish. Every day was a struggle, not only in the material world but in here." She laid a hand over her heart. "Every day the stone hardened inside me, until I couldn't feel anymore."

She stood in front of the window again. "Then he came. He's an old wolf, like me. That was him in the painting."

I returned her smile. "I wondered."

"When he turned his yellow eyes on me, I wasn't afraid. The first couple times I was just curious—when would he come back, what did he do while he was gone. But one day it changed. I was outside painting, it was nearly dark but almost balmy, an Indian summer evening, the kind you want to bottle up and sprinkle on your sheets all winter.

"I looked up at the sky. The stars were twinkly and pale. Then I felt this—this presence. I stood very still, but I remember my dress was blowing in a gentle wind. It was orange and must have stood out like a highway flagman. But I just stood there, listening. I couldn't hear anything, but still I felt the wolf was nearby.

"I had a brush in my hand. I stood right there, by the easel. The rest of the paints and the palette were on the wood table there. Then I saw him, just fifteen feet away, like he was magic. You know, the oil paints smell very strong, and the wolf was sniffing the air. So I held the brush out for him. He took a step toward me, but he wouldn't come any closer. So I put the brush down on the grass and backed away from it. Slowly he came forward, stopping to smell the wind, to look into the forest. Finally he put his big black nose right up to the brush. He took a lick of it, and his tongue had a big blue patch on it. I started to laugh. I tried not to, I didn't want him to run away. But I couldn't help it.

"He looked up at me, and you know what he did? He smiled."

"The wolf smiled?"

A grin split her face. "He smiled. And my heart felt so—so strange."

"Your heart was glad," I said.

"And it still is. So you see why they can't trap that wolf. He is my—" She bit her lip. Her gray eyes squinted at me, then at her lap. How lonely she must be, up here by herself, no relatives, few friends, stubborn, willful, independent. How vulnerable to the whims of men like Terry Vargas.

My wolf. Is that what she was going to say? One couldn't own a wild wolf. But that smiling wolf had entered her heart that had been closed for years.

"I call him Blue," she said.

"What?"

"Because of his tongue. Old Blue."

I felt a cold shiver down my back. The howl from the Bar-T-Bar. The gaze from a wolf twenty years ago. Two wolves, years apart. That stabbing pain in my stomach from last night was back. I bent over.

"What's the matter?" Queen stepped closer.

I tried to straighten, to be rational. "Nothing. A little stomach-ache."

"No, it's something, I can tell. You're pale."

I looked up at her. I tried to talk normally, but my breath only came in spurts. "Just that I saw a wolf once. Years ago, when I was a kid. And it had the same sort of effect on me."

Queen sat down. "How did it feel?"

I swallowed, tried to think how to describe it. A tornado inside my chest, a two-by-four upside the head. "Like a thunderbolt. Stabbing right through my heart."

She nodded solemnly. "What did you do?"

"I told my Aunt Sig and my Uncle Myron, and they didn't believe me. They said it was a coyote."

"That's what I thought at first. I'd never seen a wolf. But he was so much bigger than the coyotes I've seen. And different." She shook her head. "For a while I couldn't believe my eyes. I thought I should call somebody. But after that time, with the blue tongue, I'd gone too far, he lived inside me."

She thumped her chest. "Inside here."

My own chest felt full to bursting. I stood up. "Can I use your bathroom?"

In the cramped, spotless space I splashed water on my face and peered into the mirror. I looked like hell. What was happening? My body felt sore, like whiplash had struck my spine, my neck, my brain. Why was this wolf memory having this effect on me?

I pushed back my damp hair. My father's hunting jacket felt heavy and warm. I stripped it off, splashed more water on my arms and neck.

"Get a grip," I whispered into the glass. The bare bulb over the sink glared down on my gray cheeks. I took a deep breath and tried to expel the weirdness. I closed my eyes, seeing again the hillside in northern Montana, the grass, the sheep, the stars. And the wolf. That night, that singular night. How is it possible to remember one night so long ago, so vividly?

I shook my head. This was nuts. I straightened my shoulders, patted my face dry, grabbed my jacket. Back to reality, girl-child.

Queen was peering at me curiously. I gave her my brave, together face. "I have a meeting tonight. I better go. You'll be all right?" I glanced out the window. Would the wolf show tonight? Probably not.

She crossed her arms across the fuchsia muumuu. I saw she was wearing jeans underneath, and big work boots. "I should be asking you—are you all right?"

"I'm fine. You won't do anything, will you? About the traps."

"Oh." She raised her still-black brows. "Them."

I slipped into my jacket and headed for the door. Her cryptic ways were back, and for some reason that reassured me. "I'll talk to you tomorrow."

"You'll keep working, then?"

I turned back, hand on the doorknob.

She said, "Looking for Derek, for what happened to him. It's important."

Memories of the wolf lived inside me. Derek lived inside Queen. You don't really *lose* a child when he or she dies. The part of you that is the mother or father remains, clinging to that empty space that was filled by your child. This is grief. With time that space moves further back in the mind, but it is never gone. Time hadn't worked its soothing magic on Queen. In spite of the passing years, the space in her heart for Derek was still too close.

There weren't going to be answers, not real ones. Not after twenty-five years, I knew that. But *something*, some end to the turmoil. Until the painful probing was done, the boy—and the mother—would never rest.

"If you want, Queen. Yes, I'll keep looking."

She smiled, a bittersweet smile that betrayed both the restlessness of her soul—and the heartbreak. It stabbed my own heart all the way into town.

6

THREE minutes in my apartment, and I had Aunt Sig on the line. On the drive home I barely saw the razor-edged peaks looming in the twilight. Almost hit an antelope on the flats. Was passed by three pickups and a Lexus—not unusual, as the little sister Saab's rubber bands are wearing out. But I didn't care this time, I didn't flash my headlights or anything. I was thinking about Aunt Sig.

Sigrid, my mother's younger sister, by ten years.

They had as much in common as bananas and grapefruits. They were both fair and blue-eyed, but Sigrid was taller and stronger, from a lifetime of ranchwork, a straightforward woman of the old mold. I hadn't seen her in five years, but in an instant we were chatting. I filled her in on my life. She expressed sympathy once again for Paolo.

"Time marches on, Aunt Sig."

"Yes. Yes, it does." There was sadness here, and I remembered that her grandson, my cousin Robbie's son, had died two years before, only a baby. I had never even seen him. I asked about Robbie and his sisters. All were well, producing more children than I thought possible in such a short time.

"Remember the wolf, Sig? The one I saw?"

"Wolf?"

"When I stayed with you that summer. You thought it was a coyote, but I insisted it was a wolf."

"Oh, yes, vaguely. You showed us a picture you drew of it. Didn't look much like a wolf to me. Wolves are much bigger."

"In my notebook. That's right. I'll have to dig that out. Did you ever have any other wolf sightings up there?"

"I've heard of a few over the years, lone wolves coming down from Canada. It's always been a problem, but not much of one. The coyotes are worse."

I was now itching to hang up and once again had to force myself to be polite. "Whatever happened to Wanda? That woman who shepherded for you that summer."

"Wanda? Oh, Wanda Leachman. I don't know—wait." Muffled talking. "Myron says she cleaned herself up and went to college. She's in Missoula, working for the university now."

"That's hard to believe."

"She was nothing but trouble. We lost a number of lambs that summer, and I know it was because Wanda was off boozing."

"Booze? Wanda?"

"Don't play innocent with me, young lady," Sig laughed. "I never could tell your mother about the bad influence of that woman on you. You learned more curse words that summer."

"What the hell are you talking about?"

We laughed about my summer adventures, and finally I had to plead the upcoming committee meeting and ring off. I made a mental note to keep in touch with my aunts and uncles; they were much more fun than parents.

Seven o'clock. I could be a little late. I opened the trunk that served as an end table by the sofa and began rifling through the detritus of my life—art notebooks, clippings of shows, brochures and catalogs, high school scrapbooks. Most of it was junk, but as a collector I have an irresistible urge to save everything.

It was at the bottom, a ratty black-and-white notebook with

lined pages unsuitable for drawing but used nonetheless. I settled onto the sofa, stopping to read such gems as: "Wanda taught me how to pee standing up last night. She has to pee a lot. It's not very easy, especially with tight jeans. She makes it look easy, but I have a feeling cleanliness is not her strong suit. She uses old catalogs for toilet paper."

There was no illustration, thank goodness. But three-quarters of the way through I found the rudimentary pencil drawing labeled "Blue Wolf. Seen July 22." He had a big head and sticklike legs splayed outward, with paddle-size feet and a bushy tail. His head was down, ears forward, eyes big and ringed with black. I looked for a smile, but the mouth was just a squiggly line.

The drawing was crude and childish, with proportions off, but that was it, the image of the wolf I'd seen that night. None of the feeling was left in this portrait. How could I draw that moment, that thunderstruck feeling? I sighed and set the notebook on the sofa.

More later, but now, in the adult world, I had another meeting to wrangle.

Morris Kale's ranch was the sort of place hard-luck itinerant salesmen dream about when they think of the word *millionaire*. Brightly painted, gaudy, impeccably appointed with white fences and brick chimneys, three stories rose from the vast lawn, with thick shakes on the roof, gabled windows, stables and barns in matching red siding, a big ol' flagpole flying the colors of money.

Cozy was not a word that came to mind at the Kale's, despite eight fireplaces all burning tonight. Since they moved in, Audrey Kale had had the full-time job of redecorating the enormous place, and tonight the new walnut paneling in the great room shone like a duke's hunt club. The man-size granite fireplace with antique wood mantel held six logs in various stages from coal to spark. I seated myself to one side of it as the meeting began, to enjoy the distraction of its crackle and warmth in the cavernous room.

Terry Vargas quickly wrested the meeting away from Morris,

and was in the process of alternately boring us and pissing us off. The combination at least kept us awake. Candace Gundy from All One All Wild wore her standard uniform—hiking pants and boots with a ratty brown sweatshirt that matched her butch haircut. She was small-boned and could be pretty when she wasn't sneering. An artist, a banker, three businessmen and one woman, real estate people, museum director, doctor, three lawyers: we doodled and drank coffee and discussed and voted until it was certain that Terry would get his way or pout. He was really getting on my nerves as we broke at nine for a ten-minute respite.

I headed for the food laid out on the long bar at one end of the room. Audrey Kale, lurking this evening in the background as the perfect hostess, stood behind the bar, freshening up trays and ice. Her nervousness overshadowed any real enjoyment. Several years older than Morris, tanned, coiffed with blond highlights, dangling gold from ears and fingers, she played the part well, but it was a part. Her gray blouse was starched and pressed to perfection, her eyes full of something close to resignation.

"These wontons are incredible, Audrey," I said as I heaped a couple onto my plate. "Did you make them yourself?"

"Oh, no," she said, eyes darting as if she would die of embarrassment if anyone thought she even approached a stove. "Are they good? I haven't tried them."

"Delicious."

She eyed the food, up and down the bar, as if she wanted to try it all. Then she straightened, sighed, and smiled sadly. I recognized the face: she was on a diet.

"Morris tells me you've been doing some redecorating," I said.

With a flurry of relief Audrey led me into the bedroom wing, where she'd redone a guest room in a southwestern Indian motif, a soothing peach-and-blue scheme. Nothing innovative, but pleasant. That was Audrey. I nodded and cooed, glad to be away from the meeting for a moment. I always enjoyed poking around the bedrooms of strangers.

"This is Frankie's room," she said, gesturing to a closed door. Inside the familiar thump of rock music came through. "We can't go in there. He let me repaint it last summer, but he's pretty private. Teenagers, you know. He does have one of the paintings he did for you this summer up on the wall."

After reading my notebook, I wasn't sure I wanted to remember what fourteen was like. Full of angst and hormones and muddleheadedness. Even pain. Better to grow up and forget it. But not that one night—I didn't want to forget that. If I could just put my finger on what happened that night I saw the wolf.

Audrey was down the hall, opening another door. "This was my daughter's room. But she's married now, so I thought I'd just do it all over."

The darkened room brightened as she flicked a switch illuminating bedside lamps. The dark walls were padded and covered with navy blue fabric that invited touching—some sort of cushy velvet. It wrapped the room in midnight, perfect for an insomniac. I spotted a small oil painting over the sitting area and stepped across thick carpet to look at it.

"I found that in the attic. It must have been Morrie's, but I've never seen it hung up," Audrey said. "I liked the colors in here, light but not so bright they would be out of place."

The piece was abstract, swirls of white and blue with spots of sunny yellow and fuchsia that did complement the room's color scheme. An element of flight hidden in the swirls, an anxiety to run, to flee. "Very nice. Who's the painter?"

"I don't know." Audrey peered closely at the canvas. "It says here, 'Q, 75.' "

Q? Could it be Queen? She'd been painting for years, long before I met her.

"Alix."

Morris stood in the doorway. He frowned at Audrey, then paused as he took in the oil painting. Anger flared in his eyes, then something else—sorrow? Then he turned to me. "Terry is making a vote on Queen. You better come back."

A clatter of voices echoed down the hall as I scurried behind Morris. In the great room I stood by the bar as Morris glowered from behind the sofa, arms crossed. Candace ran a hand through her chopped brown hair, ruffling it more. She whispered to the chairman of the Wildlife Museum board, a lawyer who specialized in environmental issues. Several other clots of people talked, elements of shock and confusion on their faces. Terry Vargas stood at the end of the room with his hands on his hips.

"All right, quiet down now. Everybody's here." He glared at me with an insincere smile. "We're going to have to take a vote on this now. There's only a week until the auction, and we can't let it go."

"Wait a minute, Vargas." Candace stood up. "Why are you ramming this down our throats? This isn't necessary. If we don't want to take a damn vote on it, we don't have to."

"Since when are you one to turn your back on controversy, Candace?" asked a woman in charge of finances.

"That is not the point, Pam. The point is, we don't know what is going on. We don't have the facts."

"We sure as hell do," Terry said. "Sit down, Candace. We're not going to duke it out."

"Why not?" she demanded. Nervous wiggling around the room. "Care to take it outside?"

Vargas laughed, then choked himself off at her serious stance. "Let's just vote and go home. This isn't worth getting into a rankle about. She's just one artist. We've got plenty."

I opened my mouth to speak up for Queen, but Candace cut me off. "Who here wants to condemn a woman, throw her out of the auction just because one chauvinist pig can't take the heat? Who here wants to be on the kangaroo court of Terrence Vargas, safari hunter, pillager of the wild, and all-around jerkface?" She turned to the chastened group. "Well, speak up! Who wants to join this farce? Stand up and be counted!"

"Candace," Morris said softly. "I think we can resolve this without insults."

"You have a lot more faith in the process than I do," Candace said. She flopped onto her chair, her face red with anger.

"That's not saying much," Vargas sniped.

"Let's wrap this up," Morris said. "Maybe we better vote on having a vote."

"Can I say something?" I said, stepping forward. "Queen Johns is an artist, a very good artist. You all know that from shows she's had, in my gallery and others, and from other auctions. But also she is a woman living on the edge. She has no backup plan. She makes her living, what there is of it, from painting. That is a frightening thing—"

"I'll say," piped up the artist.

"What I'm trying to say is that although you may not think what she did was right, don't jeopardize her livelihood by a quick, unthinking vote. She needs the income, she really does. And she deserves it."

In the pause that followed, a murmuring rose up that ended with someone saying, "Forget the vote," and another muttering assent.

"Does anyone want to vote? Raise your hand," I said. There was no movement from the crowd.

"Wait just a second," Terry bellowed. "This is my meeting, I call the votes."

"Actually, Terry," Morris said softly, "it was my meeting."

"Too late. It's done." I smiled up at his hot black eyes. "Anything else on the agenda?"

Vargas's jaw clenched and reclenched. He shuffled angrily through notes on the table in front of him and adjourned the meeting.

I hit the fancy powder room on the way out, as much to avoid Terry as to use the facilities. When I stepped into the yard everyone had scattered into the night—everyone but Terry and Morris. Their voices carried from the circle drive where Vargas had parked his pickup. I slowed, hoping it would break up before I had to walk by them to my heap.

"You never back me up. This is just like you, Morris, just like your sorry ass."

"Terry, you know that's not true. You were out of line back there. You have to calm down."

My footsteps crunched on the gravel as I tried in vain to step softly. The men turned to me, and I froze. "See ya later, guys."

Terry moved toward me menacingly. "And what was that calling the vote?! I'm taking her paintings out of the auction. I don't give a rat's ass what you or any of these other pissants think about it. She's out!"

I looked at Morris and back at red-faced Terry. "You can't do that," I said. "Just because she . . . she what? She threatened you with a shotgun? Is that what this is about?"

"She is mentally deranged. She is a lunatic. I am the chairman of this auction, and I will do whatever I have to do to keep her out of it. She's bad for the auction and bad for the Land Trust."

My shock at his high-handedness changed to rage. "What kind of publicity is that going to give us, Terry? 'High-rolling Ranchers Give Destitute Old Lady the Heave-ho.' That'll play really well in the papers."

Vargas brought his chin in an inch. "They don't have to find out about it."

"What if they do?"

"You mean you'd tell them, is that what you're implying? You'd sabotage the auction? That's actionable, Miss Thorssen."

"Oh, you're a lawyer, are you?"

He pointed an indignant finger at my chest. "I can sic a lawyer on you so fast you won't know what happened to your wallet. We don't need you on this committee. You're here strictly out of courtesy of the Land Trust. And if you think we'll be needing your services next year, think again. This is my organization, not yours."

With that he spun on his heel, jumped into his pickup, and screeched away, shooting gravel against our legs. Morris and I watched him spin the rear tires around the corner and the tail-lights fade into the night.

"Christ," I whispered.

"You shouldn't egg him on, Alix. He gets heated up, and he can't stop. He won't back down, he's not made that way."

"You're always making excuses for him, Morris." I peered into Kale's face. Why did he do that? I wanted to ask but bit my tongue.

Morris frowned toward the end of his long drive. The white fence glowed in the starlight. To the north the tips of the Tetons, shining with snow, looked eerie and small. Around us the thick night bore down, heavy with the evening's tensions.

"Good night, Alix." He moved toward his hulking ranch manse, the glow in its multipaned windows warm but lonely. I watched him walk, hunched over, slow-paced. Then he turned back as if to say something. But he only gave a small wave and went into the house.

I stopped the Saab Sister at the top of the hill, a mesa where the village of Jackson lay glittering below in the trees. Through the open window I smelled the cold air and shook myself. If I was a wolf, how would I feel? I closed my eyes and searched for answers. The memory of the sheepherding night was dulled now through the evening's jarring tensions. I opened my eyes and sighed.

"If I was a wolf, I would be hungry," I said aloud. If I was me, I'd be hungry too.

Jackson was quiet, with trailing wisps of wood smoke filling the sky. I stopped at the light at the corner of the square as two women ran across the street in front of my car. Following their trajectory I spotted the bonfire. Flames—smoke—yes, it *was* a bonfire in the middle of the town square. The light changed, and I eased out, looking at the fire. A group of people were clustered around it, with a good contingent of our local cops talking to them. A thumping of drums rose as I turned the Saab down the alley. I parked and walked back around the block and across to the square to see what was happening.

A man in a fur headdress was beating a large round drum, Indian-style. He wielded large hide-covered drumsticks. He wore only a bone chestplate and leather pants, the rapid action of his brown, muscular arms apparently keeping him warm. That and the bonfire. It rose six feet into the night, the yellow flames licking dangerously close to the surrounding trees. A policeman was arguing loudly with two women who were protecting the flames with their bodies. The rest of the people, some twenty or thirty, stood mesmerized by the drummer. I stared at the headdress that hung down his back. He bent down to beat the drum, and I saw the tail of the animal swing around from behind his back. It was a wolf hide.

Suddenly a man appeared from behind the bonfire and began to chant. It made no sense to me, just sounds, consonants, wailing to a beat. The crowd turned as one, their eyes glued to the singer now. Two policeman standing nearby talked to themselves, heads together. Bonfires were no doubt against the law in the park. But nobody was doing much about it. Yet.

A white flash strobed through the darkness. The papers were here. I looked around for Danny but saw only a photographer, a tall cowboy in a King Ropes hat. I skirted the edge of the crowd toward him. But he moved, kneeling to take shots of the drummer and singer from ground level.

I was closer to the policeman now. He said to one of the women, "You have to have a permit, ma'am. This is not a picnic."

"I call it a picnic. With music," one woman said. I knew that voice. Candace Gundy, with her spiky brown hair lit up with fireglow. As someone at the meeting had said, she was everywhere there was controversy.

"Then we got sound ordinances too, ma'am. It's after ten o'clock—"

"The hell it is. It's nine-forty-five."

The policeman checked his watch and sighed.

I stepped into Candace's line of sight and waved. "Hey, what's all this?"

But just then the singer changed from his baritone chanting to a yip-yip-yooooheee! Now he was the wolf. Candace and her friend joined in the chorus, and soon the whole crowd was howling like wolves. I smiled at the policeman.

"Looks like fun," I offered. He shut his eyes and pinched his nose bridge. The drums were going strong, a crescendo of rhythm and howl until the singer dropped his voice, slumped his shoulders, hung his head. The drums stopped. The crowd stopped too, except for Candace, who couldn't help a last yip. Then she stepped up next to the chanter.

"Thank you, Clyde." She turned to the drummer. "Ronnie. You are magnificent." The hunky drummer, his long black braids swinging over his bare shoulders, grinned, eliciting more yelps from the females in the crowd. "Now, quiet please. Clyde will lead us in a prayer for the wolf."

Clyde stepped forward. He was a short, dark man, with black hair falling to his shoulders from a high, round forehead. He wore a red-and-yellow blanket coat with gray feathers fluttering off the shoulders. He pushed his hair back, then held his hands heaven-ward.

"Brother Wolf," he began, his resonant voice booming over the crackling bonfire. "Bless this night, your night, with your wild voice. Sing out into the darkness, tell us of your hunt, speak to our hearts of the danger, the beauty, the smell and sounds of the earth we love. Bring your tawny breath close to our ears so we may hear your sorrows, your cry for help, your lonely walk on this planet. We are one, Brother Wolf, we walk beside you."

From behind us the red lights of a fire truck began to flash hypnotically, washing the crowd in a bloody glare. Clyde, with eyes shut tightly, continued the prayer. But the rest of the crowd watched the firemen jump off the truck and quickly screw the big firehose into a hydrant. I took a step back, toward my building. Watching a drum-and-song rally was one thing, a cold shower was another.

"When the snow falls, we see your track, Brother Wolf," Clyde intoned. "We walk in your footsteps, we learn from you, we take strength in your strength, we turn our noses to the wind and find solace in the warmth and abundance of the earth."

The screech of the wrench turning on the hydrant squealed over Clyde's voice. He paused as the crowd began to scatter. I took off for the street. At the boardwalk I turned to see the firemen pointing the hose at the bonfire, and the water shooting from the nozzle. Into the stream ran Candace Gundy.

"Stop!" she hollered as the force of the water picked her up and tossed her several feet. Her cry was drowned with water. She fell at Clyde's feet. The Indian singer frowned at the firemen, then at Candace, then nodded to the drummer. Ronnie picked up his drum. They stepped neatly over Candace and disappeared into the night.

From her puddle, Candace balled her fists and shouted curses. The photographer knelt behind her and fired off several shots until she turned, a muddy mess, shivering and wet, and gave him the finger. The flash blinded her.

Ah, Candace, anything for the cause.

7

I arrived early at the county clerk's office the next morning, a carton of Marlboros under my arm. The door was locked, and I leaned against the institutional white walls, thinking it would be a relief to turn my mind from the obsessive wolf-contemplation of yesterday. There had to be something less contentious than the art auction or wolves. And I was determined to find it, even if it meant digging up old secrets.

In bed the night before, trying to sleep, I had wondered what Queen was up to. I had no doubt she would do something to those traps, hide them, steal them, at the very least make them inoperable. She wouldn't allow the wolf with the blue tongue to be captured and collared. I saw her point. The radio collar would only make it easier for the Fish and Wildlife people to track down and kill the wolf. It wouldn't mean fewer sheep or cattle would be killed necessarily, only that the right wolf was punished. I fell asleep with the image of Blue Wolf loping across the grassy hills, his bicycling gait comical and endearing. Only man could hate an animal for being so like himself.

The clerk, Gail, spotted me as she walked toward the door

with her keys. She frowned at her watch and unlocked the door. She was ten minutes late for work. With a great show of slow-moving bureaucracy she took her time putting her coat and purse away, turning on lights, dusting off the counter, rearranging her bra straps, and patting down her towering hairdo. My punishment for showing up so early.

"Now." She pursed her lips. "What is it I can do for you?"

"We talked about an old hunting acccident report. A couple days back." I fingered the carton of cigarettes, trying, and failing, to be nonchalant.

Gail adjusted her glasses, found a spot, cleaned them on a handkerchief. "That's right. You were in some kind of big rush."

"Right. I got hung up last night. Got here right after you closed up," I lied.

"Uh-huh." She gave me a squint through her still sticky lenses. "Well, I found it. For what it's worth." She turned back to her desk, plucked a paper from her in-box. "It's not much. I warn you."

I reached for the paper. She kept her fingers on it until I slid over the Marlboros. I snatched up the page and scanned it quickly before reading. Most of the sheet was full of fuzzy typewriting; that was good. But names had been blacked out in heavy ink. My hopes sank.

"They used to do that," Gail said, pointing at the blackouts. "For kids, and also for anybody they liked. So it didn't come out in the papers someday."

"So much for freedom of information."

Gail sniffed. "No such thing, not in a small town, sweetie." She looked me over, held out the Marlboros for inspection. "I read that, you know," she said.

I tried for disinterest. "You know these folks?"

"Oh, sure. The sheriff, and Farley Platt too. He's an old friend of my cousin's."

"I talked to Farley. Well, thanks. I really appreciate your looking this up." I knocked the counter with my knuckles.

"I missed my trip to the nursing home yesterday. I take them cookies and sweets once a month." Gail scratched into her beehive hair. "Only one who'll miss me is old Sheriff Gass."

I stopped halfway to the door and turned. "He must be getting on. What is he—?"

"Ninety-one. Has his sharp days though. If you get there before his nap." Gail gave me a wink. "Which starts about nine A.M. "

In the hallway I checked my watch. It was only eight-twenty. I had time for another stop in the county offices, to my old buddy the coroner. Up the stairs to second, I found the office open. A young redheaded secretary sat typing, listening to dictation on headphones. She nodded at me, kept typing on a computer, then took off her headset.

"Can I help you?"

"Is Peg—Miss Elliott in?"

"Not yet." Her eyes moved to the clock on the wall, registered a small annoyance. "Can I do something?"

I explained about the autopsy report, its age and importance. "It may have been sealed by the court. As far as I know, it never came out in the inquest."

The secretary frowned. She was thirtyish and efficient, just the sort of person Peg would hire. "I'll have to do some research and get back to you. What was the date again?"

The old man sat in a wheelchair parked in a sunroom filled with straggling geraniums. The nursing home was reasonably cheerful. For a nursing home. Several other wheelchair-bound residents sat quietly in other corners of the sunroom. The old sheriff wore thick glasses and held a book in his lap but stared not at it but out the steamy, smudged glass at the outline of the mountains in the distance. He looked up when I spoke his name.

"Nobody's called me Chester since I left home." He strained forward. "Do I know you?"

His withered frame tucked into the blue blanket was still lively, although he looked much too small to have ever been an authority figure. His bald head was spotted with freckles above the milky eyes. He laid a bony hand on his book, a Tom Clancy adventure.

"No, sir. May I sit down?"

"Help yourself. Got no other company coming. You one of those students looking for an old person to write up?"

I introduced myself. It took only a few sentences to sum up my search for Derek Wylie's details. "His mother has never felt really good about the answers she got back then. And now it's twenty-five years past. I guess she feels like it's time to know."

"Twenty-five years. Yup. I retired right after that."

"You remember it then—the accident?"

"There's plenty lost in this funny old noggin o' mine." He began to chuckle, then cough. He pulled a big handkerchief out of his shirt pocket and spit into it. "Now," he said finally, "where was we?"

"Derek Wylie, the hunting accident. Specifically, Mr. Gass, I'd like to speak to the boys who were hunting with him. Do you remember their names?"

"Names? You want names? You're asking for the moon. I got ninety years worth of names rattling around up here, and you expect to just pluck one out?"

I slumped, chastened. "Well, can you tell me what happened when they brought the body back to"—I checked the photocopy of the microfilm record I'd gotten from Gail—"to the morgue?"

He scratched his ear with long, yellow nails. "That was when the lawyers came in, loaded for bear. I remember that. That son of a bitch who thought he walked on water."

"A lawyer? Do you remember his name? Or what he looked like?" Or *anything*.

"Never was good with names. He was in politics though, I remember that. Both him and his daddy. Governors or senators or some such."

"Was he your age?"

"Oh, no. His daddy was my age. This one, the son, he'd already been something, assistant governor or something. Thought he'd been sainted by the pope."

I scribbled on the back of the copy—"thinks he's a saint, lawyer, lieut. gov? daddy in politics too, arrogant." Now here were some clues. An arrogant lawyer. I hoped there weren't too many fathers and sons in Wyoming politics.

"What did he do?"

"Started telling me what to do. Like he was sheriff. I can tell you, that didn't sit too well. But he started pulling out injunctions and restraining orders and the sort o' thing we didn't get any too often. It went on for hours, and I never even got my hands on those two boys. Never did interview 'em and find out what happened. I figured they was dirty, the way the lawyers and the parents was acting. It weren't no simple accident, not with the caliber of those lawyers shooting off their mouths." He ran a tongue over dry lips. "Can you get me a drink of water, miss?"

I returned a minute later with a glass of water to find Sheriff Gass with eyes shut. It must be nap time, I thought. I stood with the water in my hand, wondering what to do. Then a resident in another wheelchair coughed loudly. Mr. Gass started.

"Here's the water." I handed him the glass and sat down again. He sipped loudly, then gripped the glass in both hands in his lap, dripping water all over the Clancy novel. The navy was used to wet conditions.

"Thank you. I seem to need an awful lot of water at my age. Now what were we talking about?"

"The Derek Wylie accident. You told me about this lawyer who—"

"Aaack." Mr. Gass waved one hand. "He was nothing compared to that Vargas son of a bitch."

I squinted. "Did you say Vargas?"

"Father of one of the kids. Nastiest bunch I ever run into. Most folks are pretty pleasant, especially when their kid might be in trouble. Most folks don't want to piss off the sheriff. But not them Vargases." He shook his head in disgust.

The mountains were crystal clear in the morning sun, so bright it hurt the eye. I stared too long, then caught myself. "The Vargases from the Flying V? Pierce Vargas?"

"Never met a more disagreeable man in my entire life." He squinted at me now. "You know him?"

"He's been dead for a while."

He looked at the mountains, then at the old woman in the

other corner. "That's going around. It's enough to make you take up religion."

"So it was Terry Vargas?" Was there another son?

"Never laid eyes on him."

I wrote T.V.? on the paper and sat, thinking. Mr. Gass didn't seem to mind the pauses in conversation, just scratched a fingernail idly against the page of his book, staring.

"Was there anyone else involved that might still be around, another deputy or the county attorney?"

The sheriff worked his mouth, thinking, then shook his head. "Can't remember no more."

I stood up. "Thanks for all your help."

"Leonard," he blurted. He slapped his book. "County attorney. Worthless as tits on a rooster."

"Leonard. Was that his first name?"

"Last name."

I scribbled again. "You have been so much help, Mr. Gass. Is there anything I can bring you from town?"

"You coming back?"

"Sure. What would you like?"

He smacked his lips. "A fifth of bourbon would go down nice."

"I'll see what I can do. You'd share, of course."

He grinned broadly, showing me his odd collection of teeth. "Drinks all around. A regular party."

A trip to the nearest convenience store netted Mr. Gass a big bar of chocolate, which the nurse at the home said would be better for his health than bourbon. He would be disappointed but I didn't want to be the instigator of a nursing home bacchanal. The codger was napping by the time I got back so I scribbled him a quick thank-you to go with the chocolate and left again.

Back at the Second Sun I got together all the information I'd found for Queen. One article and one police report. I made photocopies and spread them across my desk to read carefully. Dutch Abbott's column was a lament on the uselessness of hunting accidents, and a plea for hunter's education and safety classes. He was really a drone about it. Very few facts about the case itself, except a quote from the mother of the victim, unnamed here: "Why did it have to happen?"

Queen was still asking that question.

Case: Derek Wylie
Date: November 19, 1975
Duty Officer: Lester Smith

Call received at approximately 8 P.M. Officers Smith and Platt proceeded to the Malone residence on Fish Creek Road. Met——— and ——— who led officers through the woods for approximately one hour. At approximately 10 P.M. body of Derek Wylie was located in a clearing some seven miles south/southwest of the Malone place. Identification in wallet included driver's license and school ID card. Examination by Deputy Platt of the body indicated he had been shot through the back of the head with a single bullet. The body was cold and stiff. Emergency medical care was ruled out. Deputy Smith examined by flashlight the surrounding area and found two shell casings. Platt and Smith carried remains of Mr. Wylie back to the service vehicle where he was laid in the backseat and removed to the hospital morgue.

Witnesses ——— and ——— explained at first interview that Mr. Wylie had been shot, maybe by one of them, by accident while hunting for deer. Neither could say who fired the shot. Neither saw the deceased fall but discovered him together some minutes later. The victim was already dead, they said. Witnesses drove their own vehicle back to the courthouse. Deputy Platt reported they did not speak to him there but drove immediately away.

Next morning, Nov. 20, witnesses refused, through attorneys, to be further interviewed. Their guns were not available for inspection. Attorneys said the young men were feeling bad about their friend the night before and threw the weapons into Jackson Lake.

December 3. Coroner's inquest ruled death accidental. No witnesses called.

Signed.....Deputy Lester Smith

No witnesses called. Another case of efficient lawyering, or negligent jurisprudence? Maybe both, I thought as I folded up the two photocopies, put them in an envelope, and addressed it to Queen. I wrote a quick note, telling her I'd call soon, that I was still working on it. I didn't mention Terry Vargas. I wasn't sure Sheriff Gass was referring to him, or a brother, even a cousin. The old man's reliability was another factor—but he did seem positive. The orneriest customers, like traumatic experiences, were the hardest to forget.

I slipped the letter in a box on the corner as I walked through the chilled autumn air to the *Jackson Hole News* office three blocks away. One of the joys of living in the center of town was not having to drive everywhere, although increasingly the grocery store was farther and farther into the suburbs, the hardware store now specialized in "This Is Your Brain in Jackson Hole" T-shirts, and the bookstore sold leather coats for $600. I could still get a double shot of espresso at the Shades Café, and for that I was eternally grateful.

When I arrived at the newspaper office, refreshed by the cold air and thoroughly caffeinated, I found the newsroom empty. Yesterday was their deadline day. The twice-weekly had been published this morning, and everyone was taking the morning off. I plugged the machine in the lobby and got a copy, glancing at Danny Bartholomew's byline on the wolf saga. There was Marc's interview, worked in piecemeal with the facts about the Yellowstone wolves and the concerns of local ranchers. To my disappointment, it was balanced, fair, and objective. It wouldn't start any riots, or help either side. That Danny, a model reporter. No mention of the secrets he wouldn't let me listen to on the tape, the ones that might incriminate Marc. I had an idea that Marc had seen the wolves before, or at the very least heard them howling as I had, and had gone hunting wolf that night, ready to take out an adversary. That he regretted what happened, I didn't doubt.

The door opened behind me with a gust of cold air. I held on to my paper as the man bustled around me and the counter that separated the rabble from the reporters, and continued back into an office without a word. Danny's editor, Russ Mason. He disappeared into his office in the back of the open newsroom and shut the door.

I spread the paper on the counter. On the lower left was a photograph of Candace Gundy slopping in the mud and wet, next to a shot of Clyde the Singer giving his wolf prayer. Clyde looked better. After scanning the front page and finding a second-section blurb on the Auction for Wildlife, I got bored and wandered through the desks to Mason's office door and knocked.

"Enter."

"Mr. Mason? I'm looking for some help in finding some back issues of the paper. Is there someone who can help me?"

He frowned, an impressive sight on an expressive face. "Isn't there someone at the desk?"

"Afraid not."

"Come back later. Somebody who knows how to do a computer search can look it up for you."

I looked out the window. I didn't want to come back later. "I don't want a computer search, just the paper from a certain week. It's old. I can do the work myself. If you point me in the right direction."

Mason rattled the paper. "Do I know you?"

I introduced myself. "Danny Bartholomew is a friend of mine."

"Oh, right, last winter, the Wort Hotel."

I smiled. And waited.

"That was good copy," he admitted. He eyed me, then pushed himself up and past me out the door. I followed him to the north end of the building, where a stairway led to the basement. It was musty and cold down here, and I had no great hopes for finding newspapers in any sort of shape. But he opened a door, flipped on a light, and ushered me into a warm, comfortable space that smelled strongly of newsprint.

"This is the official archives, so be careful with the copies. No cutting, tearing, or otherwise defacing the papers. You will be fined $50 if a paper is defaced. If you need a copy, you can bring it upstairs for a Xerox. Otherwise make notes on your own paper. Here"—he pointed to wood shelves labeled with dates—"is 1995 to the present. There, '90 to '95, over there '85 to '90. Before '85 is on microfilm, or we've lost it. The owner before 1985 was a negligent and greedy son of a bitch. Fortunately he's no longer with us."

His footsteps echoed heavily up the stairs as I eyed the microfilm reader. I couldn't get away from the beast. I had volunteered so bravely to do the work myself. No Gail to slip ciggies to.

I ran my finger down the little white boxes, looking for November 1975. The files only went back to April 1972. Must be when the paper started. Or the negligent son of a bitch had lost all the early copies.

I pulled down a box labeled October/November 1975 and threaded it on the reader. The newspaper was a weekly back then, it appeared, instead of today's biweekly schedule. The paper's masthead hadn't changed much. In '75 it was a little funkier, more western. Today it had a clean, modern look. Lots of pictures, lots of ads, that hadn't changed.

What was I looking for? I doubted the official report of the hunting accident as told to the newspaper would have anything new in it. I found it in the November 22 issue, bottom of the front page, a very short article. "Local Boy Dead in Hunting Accident." Just the bare facts, attributed to Sheriff Chester Gass. He didn't mention a Vargas. A headache was growing with each realization that sooner or later I was going to have to talk to Terry Vargas about this. It was a moment I wasn't relishing, not after last night.

I scanned the rest of the front page. Ski season was set to open at Thanksgiving, snow conditions willing. The Chamber of Commerce had high hopes for vacation bookings. Jack Dennis had just remodeled on the town square. All thrilling news.

A quick scan of the rest of the issue was equally revealing of the rather shallow interests of the resort community. Tourists, tourists, tourists. But how could I complain? They were my bread and butter too.

I turned the beast's knobs to go back a week. It almost got away from me, but I wrestled it to a stop, squinting at the fuzzy screen. Muttered curses about microfilm. Too far back, end of October. I scrolled forward slowly to the next front page.

November 1. Condominiums open at Teton Village. Fire season declared over. A lone wolf trapped near the Idaho border in the Hobacks was brought to Jackson for viewing in a specially made pen.

Wolves in Wyoming back then? The story was brief, with a fuzzy photograph. I scrolled ahead to the next issue, and found a follow-up article. Environmentalists were protesting the scheduled death of the wolf by threatening to release it if the order wasn't changed. A rally in the town square, similar to Candace Gundy's of last night, included Indians, animal righters, environmentalists. The photo showed a motley crew of fascinating costumes, including what looked like a pair of black-powder mountain men in the background.

Land use issues were just beginning back in '75, with zoning, development, and growth big controversies at the county commissioners' meetings. Ranch news, school news, ski news. I scrolled on. I wondered what happened to the wolf. Had it been freed by the ecoterrorists? Had it gotten its death sentence? Nothing in the next issue at all. Lots of stuff about a fall arts festival, music, art, concerts. A big development okayed over the outcries of anti-growth protesters.

Then, on the next front page, the report on the wolf. "Wolf Shot by Midnight Intruders." Somebody had gotten itchy and decided to make sure the wolf didn't get released. More outrage by animal's-righters, more protests by Sierra Club, World Wildlife Fund, Defenders of Wildlife.

So Marc Fontaine hadn't shot the first wolf in sixty years. There had been this wanderer, possibly down from Canada like my own. The wolf: feared by ranchers, hated by hunters, revered by those who had never seen one. Strange the sort of emotions wolves brought out in people, pure hatred of an evil creature so foul he should be wiped off the face of the earth. Or pure joy in the essential untamability of the beast, its solitary yet social nature, its so-human emotions. That smile on Queen's wolf, how it had changed her, made her feel again. And my own single moment of unexplainable wonder.

I focused on the reader's badly lit screen and trudged through articles, from concerns about wood smoke pollution to local bond issues. Snowmobiling accidents, a memorial service for a local girl who committed suicide, Park Service concerns about winter climbing accidents. Amazing how very little changed. Our tiny marks on the geography of a place were erased quickly and filled in with new people, new marks. Only the geography stayed the same.

Two hours passed, and I hadn't found anything relating to the hunting accident but the single two-inch, one-column mention. As if Derek Wylie didn't matter, his death just a blip, a tiny ripple on the smooth surface of life. Queen had a right to be angry. Her boy was gone, and too quickly forgotten.

I rolled up October/November and got down December/January. In mid-December there was finally a mention of him again. A memorial service had been held at the high school, organized by a group of students. At least he'd had friends. His father, Dominick Wylie, was mentioned as a "successful farm implement salesman." Queen's whereabouts and occupation were not mentioned. A grandmother was listed, Adelaide Johns of Jackson.

Derek was a dedicated student, the article said, who kept people laughing with his antics. A member of Spanish Club, 4-H, and manager of the freshman football team.

Staring at the screen, I felt a wash of sorrow pass over me. This was all there was of Derek Wylie, all of his short life that remained. What would he have been? We would never know. His mother's memory, his only legacy.

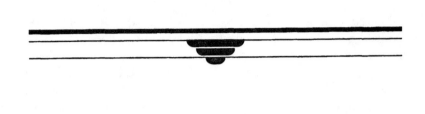

8

SINCE graduating from Bozeman Senior High, it's been my policy not to reenter high schools. When it must be done, well, it must be done, but expect an adolescent wave of peer pressure, fashion anxiety, and hair envy. Not to mention sweat sock smells and duplicator toxicity. So I waited until nearly four o'clock the next day to make my appearance at the doorway of the classroom of Leroy Leonard.

The evening before had been quiet, and this morning I was all business, even a few customers in the gallery. But I was jumpy, and ready for a chat with Leroy.

The biology teacher had achieved a small renown in environmental circles for his projects with students, testing air pollution in town, counting frogs in Yellowstone Park, and lately, casting wolf tracks in plaster of paris. What exactly he was doing up at Queen's I didn't know, but I assumed it related to his wolf-track study. I peered inside the door's window and saw a long line of round plaster casts of tracks lining the bookshelves under the windows. I didn't see Mr. Leonard, but I opened the door and stuck my head in.

"Mr. Leonard? Leroy?" My other, subversive school visitation policy, calling teachers by their first names. "Anybody here?"

A crash in a corner closet preceded the appearance of the biology teacher. He was carrying a dusty book, and looked a bit dusty himself.

"Leroy Leonard?" I stepped into the room and introduced myself. "I was up at Queen Johns's the other day."

He straightened his glasses and took a last blow on the book. His brown hair going to gray was unkempt and his glasses smeared, but he wasn't an unattractive man, in a cuddly way, wearing another flannel shirt.

"Ah, yes, the day we almost got killed." He frowned. "I suppose I should thank you for saving my life."

I didn't take this seriously, and from the tone, I doubted he meant it that way. "She was pretty hot under the collar."

He barked a sarcastic laugh. "That she was." He took the book to his desk and began to sit, stopped as if remembering me. "Something I can do for you?"

I leaned against a student desk, folding my arms. "Queen knew you. I was surprised at that."

He sat down, obviously anxious to get on with his dusty book. "I know plenty of local people. I've lived here thirty years."

"Right. But Queen doesn't. Not anymore." I peered at him. Thirty years would make him at least 50, if he moved here to teach after college. He looked younger, and fitter. "Did you know her son, Derek?"

His hands fingering the book stilled. He blinked. "Yes, why?"

"I bet it's been a while since anybody asked you about Derek."

He looked away, out the window, and didn't answer. Someone else had mentioned Derek to him recently—when he was up at Queen's?

"Was he your student?"

"Who?"

"Derek Wylie."

He nodded, his face sullen. "It was terrible what happened to him."

I let the pause lengthen then asked, "Did you know any of his friends?"

"What's all this about? Why are you asking all these questions?"

"There are a lot of holes in the reports about his death. Just trying to fill them."

"What for? Are you writing an article?"

"Maybe. Was Terry Vargas one of his friends?"

Leroy Leonard jumped from his chair and went to the window. "I don't appreciate this kind of interrogation. I'm busy. Please leave now."

"You talked to Terry up at Queen's cabin, didn't you? Did he tell you that he still hated Queen, that he had it in for her?"

Leonard spun to face me, his face red and eyes bulging. "What the hell are you talking about? He never said anything about hating her. He thinks she's crazy, we all do. She came after us with a shotgun, for chrissakes. Scared the piss out of us." He lowered his voice. "She's just like Derek, passionate, impulsive, and dangerous. She's got to be stopped before she kills someone."

"Why was Derek dangerous? What did he do?"

Leonard shook his head. "I didn't mean that—he, well, he was a sweet kid, he really was. He just didn't think things through. Got in all kinds of trouble around town, stealing beer, joyriding, that sort of thing."

"What was he passionate about? Hunting?"

"No, no. I never understood that. The accident and all. Why he went hunting. He didn't really like to hunt. He told me once he felt so bad for the deer, like his own heart was being ripped out."

This was the first time somebody had told me what Derek was like. "And Terry, was he like that too?"

"Terry?" Leonard gave a sharp laugh. "He was just like he is now."

"Gun nut? Hothead? How would you describe him?" I said. Leonard paled and covered his mouth with one hand. "Terry was there that day, wasn't he? On the hunting trip where Derek was killed."

"I never said that. I don't know that." Leonard began to shake. He clasped his hands together to stop them. "Please leave now. I have work to do. I must ask you to leave."

I stepped up to the wolf tracks frozen in white plaster. They were as big as a human fist, with claws like a dog's. "Nice castings. Did you find tracks up at Queen's?"

Leonard nodded. "Now please leave. I'm sorry, I can't talk anymore."

"You have relatives in this town, Mr. Leonard?"

He squinted. "Are you threatening me?"

"No, I'm sorry." I tried to give a disarming smile. "I just ran across the name of an attorney named Leonard. Teton county attorney?"

"Uncle George, he was—" He clenched his jaw tightly and looked out the window, pale as plaster.

I turned at the door, gave him my best toothy smile. "Don't worry, Leroy. This is just between you and me."

Through the twilight on the drive back into Jackson from the high school I thought about Terry Vargas. I had no doubt now that he had been hunting with Derek that fateful day. But what did that prove? It could still have been an accident. And if the knowledge inflamed Queen to actually use that shotgun, there would be trouble. I wrung my hands over the steering wheel and tried to figure out a way to tell her gently. I had no confidence that I was up to the job.

Carl was sitting on the gallery's front steps. He stood up and smiled, stretching as if he'd been there a long time. Annoyed by the gesture, I unlocked the front door and let him in. Readying for a hello kiss, I felt a letdown when he launched instead into the saga of the woodpecker.

"I saw him. It's a flicker, the kind with the orange under their wings." He gave a big smile. "But don't worry, I scared him off."

"He's been around for weeks. I've hollered at him a few times myself." I didn't want to burst Carl's bubble, but I'd identified the species some time back. "I doubt one more shout will discourage him."

"He's wreaking havoc on your cedar siding. There's holes everywhere."

"Do you think I can file a claim on my insurance? Act of Bird?"

Carl was looking around the gallery. "Hey, where's the wolf painting?"

"Gone to the printer's for the brochure. Did you go flying today?"

"Yesterday. It was incredible, Alix." His face was animated in childish delight as he told me of swooping over the Tetons, checking on climbers, and then tracking wolves north of the Elk Refuge. "But only tracks, no wolves in sight."

"Have you ever seen them? From up there?"

"Not yet. Kevin's seen them up in Yellowstone but never close up. Except for that dead one, and I saw it too, not much left. They've got a pool going out there, who sees the first wolf in Teton Park." He flopped into the chair. "Go get a bite to eat with me, and I'll tell you the latest in the wolf shooting." He grinned.

"Tell me now, is it good?"

"You've got to break bread with a man before he releases his secrets."

I fixed him with my steely glare, then pounced, tickling his ribs. "Tell."

He groaned and laughed, pushing my hands away. "Promise to eat?"

"I love to eat. And love to eat with you." He waited. "I promise," I said.

"The rabies report came back. It was negative."

Marc wasn't going to like hearing that. "What does that mean?"

"Probably that there'll be more investigation. That wolf, if you can believe your friend the horse wrangler, didn't act like a regular wolf. That's what Kevin says."

"You sure put a lot of stock in Kevin's opinions," I said.

"Hey, he's a smart guy. He's studied wolves, but not as much as the Yellowstone team, of course."

"I thought his specialty was elk."

"That and the wily wolverine. He's seen a couple of those, but they're pretty scarce too."

"Why did they have him testify at that hearing anyway?"

"To explain why the wolves were coming out of Yellowstone, and particularly into Grand Teton Park."

"If only Grand Teton were a regular national park, instead of having all those pockets of private land inside it. That sure mucks up the wildlife planning."

Carl shrugged. "I guess the Rockefellers couldn't talk everybody into selling. Can you imagine actually owning a hunk of real estate like that? It blows my mind."

"How about blowing your mind on a beer or two, just for old times' sake? Seems I made a promise to a gentleman."

Carl bent an elbow toward me. When he smiled wide and his eyes crinkled, I felt I would give away everything for a life with this man. Unfortunately, or maybe fortunately, he didn't smile like that often.

"M'lady." He ran his tongue over his lips, even made a small bow. "For auld lang syne."

Dinner was a pleasant but careful affair at the Snake River Brewpub, where Carl told many stories of his flying adventures and his new friends out at the national park. He had a good chance of getting his contract renewed for a second three-month period at least, he said, and part-time work in maintenance when there was no flying to be done. I tried to concentrate on his smiles, on his charming face, but found my mind wandering back to Queen and Derek and Terry Vargas. When Carl brought up next week again, and wanting to go hiking, I set down my glass of beer.

"What?" he said, seeing my expression. "You live in this fantastic place, and you never go out in it. Alix, look around you. There is this incredible natural wonderland."

I looked around the restaurant for a distraction. But it was nearly empty, off-season quiet. I looked back at Carl in his fleece vest, plaid shirt, tanned concerned face.

"I've lived here a long time, Carl. I've gone hiking. Next week—well, I've told you how many times? This is my week to just be me, to do exactly what I want to do. It's bad enough that the auction hits on Wednesday."

"So you've done the hiking thing."

"Look, Carl." I leaned in close so I wouldn't raise my voice. "You don't need me to go hiking. You've got other friends. You keep telling me about them. Or you can go by yourself. Why is it so important that I bend to your will?"

His eyes widened. "That's how you see it—me trying to force you to go hiking?"

"After the third or fourth time I tell you no, yeah, it begins to sound like it means something more to you than hiking."

Carl reddened and kicked his chair back, pulled out his wallet, and threw a twenty-dollar bill on the table. I put on my jacket and followed his angry stomping out the door to the famous wooden boardwalks. Hands deep in his pockets, Carl glanced back and walked to the corner. He waited to cross the street with me, then escorted me silently back to the gallery entrance. I was feeling ridiculous by then, wondering why we were having this disagreement, why we were both so stubborn.

"I don't think we should see each other for a while," Carl blurted out. He was looking across the street at the town square.

I didn't so much mind conflict, but I hated good-byes. I swallowed hard.

"I—I understand," I said.

"Just for a while. We, um, it must be too much togetherness. Or something," he said.

"Okay."

"You agree?" He looked eager but hurt, anxious.

"I don't know. Yes. I mean, I've been busy, and then next week is my painting week anyway, so after that maybe."

He nodded at his boots. Then he leaned over, kissed me chastely on the cheek, and was gone.

Walking up the steps to my apartment, I felt strangely numb. I didn't need him, I thought, or I'd feel worse. I didn't want to need anyone, isn't that what I'd said? I hadn't asked him to move here, hadn't promised rose gardens or any damn thing. So why wasn't I the one who called it off?

I unlocked my door and turned on all the lights in the place, which took about thirty seconds. A chill north window was rattling the window glass facing the mountains, knocking as if to remind me that winter was coming. Cold and loneliness—just around the corner, hello! I listened to it for a minute, then took an emotional checkup. How was I doing? I was fine, just fine. What he'd proposed was reasonable, and we were both grownups. Okay.

However, it seemed an opportune time to clean the bathroom. That accomplished, the dirty dishes of a week beckoned. After an hour's cleaning I fell onto my bed and stared at the ceiling. The painting week was supposed to start Sunday. If I could get the brochure for the auction delivered tomorrow, plus wrap up inquiries on Derek Wylie, I'd be home free. But how to deal with the Terry Vargas information? I couldn't just tell Queen. A gnawing in my gut told me I didn't entirely trust her to be rational, not after the wolf trap incident. Just laying out the information was too dangerous.

What then? She wanted to know what I'd found out, that was what I was getting two expensive paintings in return for. If I talked to Vargas myself, what would that accomplish? Could I talk him into confessing his role in the accident to Queen? That seemed unlikely. I doubted I could talk him into taking a leak. What had he done about Queen's paintings? I hadn't thought about that all day.

Back in the kitchen I called Morris Kale. I looked at my watch: eleven o'clock, late. The phone rang six, seven, eight times, then was at last picked up by a breathless Audrey.

"Frankie? Is that you? Where are you?" she demanded, worried and angry.

"It's not Frankie, Audrey, it's Alix Thorssen. Is something wrong?"

"Oh. No, he was just supposed to call . . ." Her voice trailed off in desperation.

"Can I help? I could look around here."

"No, please. This is a family matter." She took a loud breath. "What can I do for you?"

"Um, is Morris there?"

"No, he—oh, here he is."

"Alix, what's up?" He sounded calm and together, a direct contrast to his wife. Maybe it wasn't as bad as all that. Frankie seemed like a typical teenager, no more taciturn, withdrawn, or alienated than most.

"Sorry to call so late. I was wondering if Terry did anything about Queen's paintings today."

"Not good news, I'm afraid. He did take them out of the auction. Took them to his house actually, and I couldn't talk him out of it."

"That son of a bitch. Aren't you cochair, Morrie?"

"I am. But you know Terry."

"Hmmm." I wondered suddenly if this hatred for Queen was rooted in the past. "Morris, has Terry ever told you about a hunting accident, from years back?"

"Um, no. What about it?"

"He was a friend of Queen's son, did you know that?"

"Queen has a son?"

"Had. He was killed in a hunting accident in high school."

Silence.

"It was a long time ago," I said, regretting my big mouth. "Don't say anything about it, please, Morrie."

Audrey was saying something to him. "I have to free up the line."

"Right, okay. But Morrie, please don't—" Then the line went dead.

I hung up the phone and paced the small kitchen a few times, thinking. What would Terry do if he found out I knew about Derek? Would that be a way of flushing him out—if Morris told him? Could spilling the beans to Morris have been a brilliant mistake? Or a tragic error? If he was just along on the hunting trip, he wouldn't, or shouldn't, react. But if he was guilty of something, as Sheriff Gass seemed to think, then what would he do?

I could hear his hateful voice from last night, threatening me with legal action. Was that perhaps a way to get to him? Re-

straining order on his taking Queen's paintings out of the auction?
That didn't sound particularly legalistic. There was no bodily
threat, no potential for violence. Was there? Maybe not with the
paintings, maybe yes with the long-buried secret of the hunting
accident. I dialed Queen's number quickly and let it ring and ring.

"Shit." I picked up my keys, grabbed my coat, and headed to
the car.

9

THE moon rose languorously over the Wind River Mountains, the high, remote peaks that formed the eastern side of the rendezvous spot favored by mountain men back in the beaver heydays. The road in the foothills along the Gros Ventre River that flowed west into the Hole twisted and turned, taking me farther into the foothills covered with sagebrush and pines. Once the reflection of the near-full moon blinded me in a flat bend in the river, and I slowed, trying to slow my heartbeat as well. The smell of a dry, cold wind laced with fish smells and the indescribable wild blew in the crack in the window.

Queen's cabin was dark. The tires of the Saab Sister crunched the gravel loudly as I pulled up and shut her off. I paused at the door, hand ready to knock, and listened to the night—a lonesome cawing, a scurrying of small feet, the wind high in the long needle pines. Where is the wolf tonight? Is he smiling, hunting, sniffing, feasting? Where is he? I felt a small ache: I wanted to see him. I wanted to feel that thunderbolt through my heart again. It had been too long.

Pounding the door seemed an intrusion. I knocked delicately, then realized the futility of that. The knob turned under my hand. I stuck in my head, called her name.

"Are you here?"

A gust of wind tore the knob from my hand, opening the door wide. Moonlight through the east window illuminated an empty armchair. I felt around for a light switch and shut the door as an overhead bulb came on. Its weak light showed the room I'd seen yesterday, unchanged but for a bouquet of flowers on the table in the kitchen.

"Queen?"

The cabin was quiet. Her bedroom lay in a back corner, near the bathroom. The door was open, the bed empty.

Where could she be? She had no car. It was late, close to midnight. I went back to my car and took a flashlight from the glove compartment. Picking my way across the yard, the moonlight helped. But once in the forest the trees blocked all light, their dense, piny presence like the inside of a ripe mausoleum. The floor of the forest was spongy with plants and fallen needles. I bumped into trees, tripped over roots. Then I came to the clearing.

Taking each step slowly, stopping and sweeping the area ahead with the small beam of flashlight, I made my way carefully around the clearing, circling it, making ever smaller circles. On the third go-round I tripped over a chain and stopped, regaining my balance on the soft marshy ground.

I looked at my feet. The chain that lay across my toes strung out for five or six feet to my right. To my left I could see a large, sharp hook, like a grappling hook, attached to the end of the chain. I followed the chain right, carefully. There was the trap.

There was no mistaking it. The trap looked enough like an old-fashioned metal-jawed model that it caused a shiver up my back. I bent down to look at the teeth. They were padded with rubber, but steel gleamed in the starlight underneath the padding. Small metal pegs were placed along the edge of the teeth, presumably to hold the wolf's leg. It didn't look very comfortable, but the wildlife biologists wouldn't do it if it hurt the beasts. They were in the wild-LIFE business, after all.

A large chunk of wood sat in the middle of the jaws. The trap had been sprung with a piece of firewood. If a wolf had sprung the trap, it would drag the trap off; nothing held it to the ground. That must be when the chain and hook come into play. They would get tangled in the forest and slow the wolf's escape.

At the crack of a twig my head snapped up. I switched off the flashlight and stared into the trees, listening. Was it from the west? I cocked my head. Only the wind in the high branches, the creaking of the bending trees, old men straightening their ancient backs. A lull in the wind, silence.

"Queen?! That you?"

My voice faded quickly into the pines. I turned, checked the clearing and trees behind me, turned the flashlight back on, caught the red-eyed glare of a small rodent before it scurried into the tall grass.

"Queen? It's Alix. By the trap."

Close, flapping wings right overhead—I ducked. The bird, big enough to be an owl, rose and disappeared into the dark. "All right, that's enough," I muttered.

As I picked my way back through the trees, an eerie vertigo seeped out of the blackness. The spot of yellow from the flashlight made it worse. I stopped against the trunk of a tree, holding on to get my balance back, switching off the light. I listened to my ragged breathing and the swish of pine needles rubbing.

Where was the wolf? I wanted him to come. I leaned my cheek against the prickly bark and tried to summon Blue Wolf. Nights were so very long, life was so long and confusing and full of dark forests where you didn't know where to turn. All you needed was a guide, a wild spirit that knew the territory. Why not a wolf? Maybe that night in the Little Belt Mountains was a vision quest, and the wolf was my spirit being. And I didn't even know it until now. That made me pretty dense. But better late than never in the spiritual department, like Sheriff Gass said.

I closed my eyes and smelled the forest smells: rich, deep, and ancient. They swirled and settled, tingling my nose. Cold seeped down my collar and I shivered. *The woods were dark and deep . . . miles to go . . .*

The blast came from far off, sound ricocheting off the granite cliffs. I was startled out of my trance, scratching my face on the pine bark. The second shot came, its pinging sound repeating three, four times. I started to run back to the cabin, ran into a tree and slowed myself down, turned on the flashlight, and bumped through.

I burst into the back door, searching frantically for the shotgun I'd seen Queen put there. Brooms, mops, no guns. I tore through to her bedroom, pushed aside muumuus to look in the back of the closet. The shotgun was gone.

Outside again, I called her name frantically, then jumped into the Saab. As I backed out, I wondered: Had she heard about Terry Vargas? Did someone—Leroy?—tell her, warn him? Had Terry shot her? Or she him? The questions popped out of my ears, mouth, fingers, as I careened down the mountain, barely keeping the old girl on the road, barely keeping my head from bursting from lack of information.

At the highway I turned right; I couldn't help myself. I followed the dark highway through Moran Junction and up Togwotee Pass to the turnoff to the Flying V. Too far, I thought. Too far to hear a shot. It must have been someone else, somewhere else.

The Vargas house was dark and quiet. The Saab balked where the drive widened for parking, as if it knew it shouldn't be there. I took a deep breath, turned around, and drove home. Crazy, that's what it was. Maybe what I heard wasn't a shot at all, maybe it was . . . a rock slide? But I knew, I couldn't fool myself. A gunshot, a ricochet, an echo, I knew. But somebody else, a stranger.

Nothing to do with me.

The phone woke me from a heavy sleep that had come late, preceded by pillow-punching and deep sighs. I had a bad feeling that all my plans to drop out of life for a week would be dashed. Nothing was wrapped up, nothing finalized. Queen was missing, armed and presumed dangerous. Terry Vargas wanted to bite my ass. The auction brochure hadn't been distributed. And from the answering machine somebody was calling my name.

I stumbled into the living room and tried to place the voice through the fog of sleep.

"Alix, pick up, it's important. . . . Alix, come on. ALIX!! It's Danny, come on."

"Danny," I said, snatching up the phone, awake at last. "What is it?"

"Christ, you are there. Whadya do, go on a bender last night?"

I rubbed my forehead. "I wish. What time is it?" I looked at the kitchen clock. Eleven already. "What's up?"

"It's Audrey Kale. She's been shot."

"Shot—Audrey?"

"She's alive, according to the hospital spokesman. Shot through the shoulder, just missed her heart. She lost a lot of blood before they could get the ambulance out to their place."

"Where did it happen?"

"At home."

I thought about Frankie, how he was missing, how scared Audrey sounded. "Who did it?"

"I don't know, but—well, they think it was Morris."

I pinched the bridge of my nose, trying to make my brain function better. "It can't have been Morris. That's ridiculous."

"The word is, he confessed."

"What? Where are you?"

"At the hospital. There's cops everywhere, county guys. Morris is waiting for her to get out of surgery, but they're watching him."

"I'm coming down. Don't leave."

My hair was still wet from a quick shower as I made my way to the surgical waiting room inside St. John's Hospital. Danny was right; everywhere were sheriff's deputies in brown uniforms, eyes on alert. One stood against the wall right outside the waiting room. I paused, looked at the deputy, and glanced inside. Morris Kale sat with his head in his hands, staring at the floor.

I found Danny around the corner in a sunny sitting area facing the Elk Refuge. The noonday sun brightened the utilitarian green seating.

"Have you talked to him?" I asked, perching next to Danny.

He shook his head. "His lawyer's got everyone stonewalled. Won't let him talk to anyone."

"Even me?"

"I imagine. It's Sonny Garrett. He almost tore my head off."

"I don't know him."

"Consider yourself fortunate. Cantankerous old s.o.b. of the old school. The kind that are used to running this state as their personal playground."

"How is Audrey?"

Danny shrugged. "She should be out of surgery by now."

I stood up, restless, hearing gunshots ricocheting off rock in my head. "Come get a cup of coffee with me."

We fiddled over coffee for fifteen minutes in the hospital cafeteria, then made our way back to the surgical waiting room. It was empty, the deputy gone. We wandered down toward surgery.

"What's going on with Marc now?" I asked as we waited. "I see you didn't use anything I didn't hear on the tape."

Danny only smiled enigmatically. "Another hearing. You heard about the rabies test?"

"Uh-huh. Does that mean Marc could be charged with something?"

"Depends on how far Fish and Wildlife wants to force the issue."

"And how crazy the animal-righters are?"

Danny frowned. "Do you know Candace Gundy from All One All Wild?"

"She's a pistol."

"She staged that protest in the town square. Now she says she's threatening to have another demonstration this week, something that will make national headlines."

"Like what?"

"Might be something at the Auction for Wildlife. I thought I should warn Morris. But maybe you could tell his cochair."

"Terry Vargas. Sure, my bosom buddy." I ran my hand through my damp hair. "What would she do? Did she say?"

"No, but—"

Danny stopped, straightening as a tall young woman strode toward us and the surgical suite doors. She paused and nodded to Danny.

"Eleanor. I guess you heard."

"And I guess you beat me to it. Again." She turned on her heel and started back the way she'd come. "Doesn't mean I won't write better copy." She walked quickly back down the hallway and around the corner. I raised my eyebrows to Danny in question.

"Eleanor Green. She writes for the *Guide*. She's young, doesn't know the scene. But she could be good."

"Sounds like you've got a rival." I turned to Danny. "Listen. I was reading up for that digging I've been doing. On the hunting accident. Did you know a wolf was captured and brought here in pens? Back in the seventies?"

"When was this?"

"Seventy-five. Somebody trapped this wolf near Bondurant. They showed him off for a while, then some animal-righters got pissed off and said they were going to release it. But before that happened somebody shot it."

"Here in Jackson?"

"Wolves weren't listed yet. Fish and Game people were going to dispose of it anyway."

"So there were wolves around back then. Interesting."

"Marc wasn't the first in sixty years to kill a wolf here."

Danny scribbled a note to himself on his pad. He'd probably be down wrestling the microfiche beast soon himself. We waited for a few more minutes until Morris and an older man burst through the swinging doors, and Danny was on them.

"Mr. Kale, how is your wife? Is she conscious?"

Morris paused, looked at Danny, then me, mute.

The white-haired lawyer held a stiff arm out. "No questions. Come, Morris."

"Has Mr. Kale been charged, Mr. Garrett? Why do the sheriff's deputies follow him everywhere?"

Eleanor Green reappeared, blocking the hallway, or trying. A deputy trailed behind the lawyer and client.

"Did you shoot your wife, Mr. Kale?" Eleanor asked briskly.

Morris Kale stopped again and stared, pale and wide-eyed, at the young female reporter.

"No comment," barked Garrett. "Deputy, can we get rid of these pests, please?"

The deputy rounded them and tried to sweep Danny and Eleanor and me aside with one arm. But Eleanor stepped deftly around him and kept walking with Morris and Garrett.

"Why did you shoot her, Mr. Kale?" she asked. "Did you have an argument?"

Sonny Garrett glared at her. "Step aside, miss."

Morris stopped again. He stared at her, then turned to Danny and me with a blank look. "It was an accident," he said quietly. "I didn't mean it. The gun went off."

"Let's go." Garrett took Morris Kale's arm and hustled him past Eleanor Green and the deputy, out the front door of the hospital, nearly dragging him into a waiting car. We pushed through the glass doors of the hospital and watched as Eleanor ran after them, shouting questions at the closed window as the car drove away from the curb. A county sheriff's vehicle followed behind.

Eleanor straightened, then scribbled on her pad furiously. The sun was bright, but a cold wind blew her brown hair across her face as she wrote.

"She's a pushy one," I said admiringly.

Danny slapped his notebook against his thigh. "I think she watches too much television."

Back inside, the hospital public relations woman told us Audrey Kale was in critical condition but out of surgery. Her condition was expected to improve, but she would probably be unstable for a few days. She wouldn't give any particulars about her medical condition, where the bullet had gone, or what damage had been done. That was up to the doctors, who were unavailable.

Danny and I ended up eating pancakes at Jedidiah's. I told him about my struggles with Carl, and he told me about what his boys were up to, about his wife's new job and the changes it would make at home. It was good to talk about normal stuff for a while, to chew on sourdough and syrup. But the Kale troubles hung over our heads like a cloud, and as we finished, I told him about the phone call last night.

"Audrey sounded frantic. Like Frankie'd been missing for a while, or at least had missed his curfew by a good length of time." I sipped the last of my coffee. "But I got the feeling Morris wasn't as worried."

"Like he knew what Frankie was up to? How old is the kid?"

"Fourteen, fifteen, something like that."

"Not old enough to drive, then. Do you suppose he took one of their cars?" Danny frowned. "Hey, where was Frankie this morning?"

"Maybe he's still missing."

"I'll find out," Danny promised. "Somehow." He looked at me curiously. "Are you worried about him?"

I shrugged. "I don't know. I was thinking about Queen. I went out to her cabin last night, and she wasn't home. I can't figure out where she went. She never goes anywhere."

Danny fished a hand inside his coat and pulled out a tiny cellular phone. "Call her."

"Wow. This is small. Just your size."

"Real funny." He smiled.

I dialed Queen's number. It rang for a long time, until I hit End and handed it back.

"Maybe she went on a trip, to visit a relative."

With her shotgun. Right.

Danny and I parted outside Jedidiah's, and I walked through the chilly wind back to the gallery, letting myself in through the front. I had had the place open so little this week, I should see if Saturday brought out a few customers. Sometimes it was the best day, other times the worst. I flipped the Open sign, turned on the lights, and scooped up yesterday's mail from the floor by the slot.

On top of the pile was an envelope without postage, with only my name and "CONFIDENTIAL" typed on the front. I felt it, held it up to the window light, and determined it was probably just paper before opening it. Inside was a single sheet of paper, a photocopy with sticky note attached. The handwritten note said: "For your eyes only. Miss Elliot says call her." I pulled it off and read.

POST MORTEM: Derek Dominick Wylie.
CASE #1334-A75

In an upper corner was hand-scribbled "Purge Immediately." I glanced down it, then sat at the desk and read it carefully. I didn't understand all the terminology, but I got the gist. As I stared at the "Findings" typed at the bottom, a group of six tourists opened the door, their laughter and talking filling the empty spaces of the gallery. I stood up at the desk to greet them, smiling and nodding, even with my finger on the autopsy sheet, keeping my place.

"Have a look around," I said, getting up. "And feel free to ask questions." My standard line, usually hoping to get a conversation going with some art lover–cum–buyer, but today I hoped they would just look. Waiting until they adjusted their collars and hats and gloves and wandered to the pottery and oils, I sat again and read.

I skimmed through the parts about how the medical examiner had done the body cuts, how the vital organs looked just fine. Only one visible injury, he said. He took samples of something white under the boy's fingernails, blood samples, tissue samples, made note of lividity where he had lain for so long in the woods, pools of blood on his front side, as he had lain facedown. It was all very graphic, clinical, as if he was just a specimen, one of several that day, bodies that used to be alive but walked this earth no more. Thinking of them walking and talking and being alive was probably not a good idea for a forensic pathologist. It was easier to think of them as dead, as dead they were.

I wondered if anyone had ever finished those lab results, found out if he'd been drawing with chalk or wearing sunscreen or shooting heroin that day. Probably not, I guessed. The gunshot wound to the head had killed him. That was apparently that.

I stared at the opinion of the doctor at the end, read it carefully this time.

> Findings: Death caused by gunshot wound to the back of the head. Surface tattooing of projectile gunpowder indicates a distance of more than one but no more than three feet. .22 caliber bullet found lodged in the cerebellum at an upward angle. Lividity on the frontal portions of the body, the lack of injury to the face, and grass and dirt on the palms indicate the victim was lying prone, face down, at the time of the gunshot. Brainstem trauma caused near instantaneous death. Consistent with intentional wounding or homicide."

"Everything all right?"

I looked up to find a grandfatherly type with a soft cap in his hands looking at me with concern.

"That gasp. I thought maybe you got some bad news," he said.

"Oh." I tried to smile as my eyes ran over the words again. *Lying prone* . . . "I'm fine. Thanks for asking."

He smiled and moved off, whispering to his mate. She frowned and took another look at me. I straightened up and tried to become the professional art dealer. It was a struggle today.

Consistent with intentional wounding or homicide.

I took a deep breath. I looked at the sticky note again. "Miss Elliot says to call." I walked quickly back to my railroad desk and spun the Rolodex until I came up with Peg Elliot's number. I felt a flutter of dizziness and pushed it back. Back at the gallery desk I drummed my fingers impatiently, watching the milling customers obviously just killing time on a weekend afternoon, and went ahead and dialed the coroner's number.

"Peg. It's Alix, I got your message."

"Oh, dear. Yes. The cat has just knocked over some statuettes. Wait a moment, won't you?" Her high-pitched scolding of the cat devolved into a nice-kitty routine. I waited, but not patiently. One of the ladies in the gallery chose this moment to inquire about a large painting in the side gallery. I told her just a moment as Peg returned to the line.

"So sorry, Alix. The cat is—"

"Peg," I interrupted. "I'm in the gallery. Can I stop over later?"

"Why, of course. But why don't I stop over? I'm off for my walk in a minute."

She promised to be in within the half-hour, sooner than I could get away. The customer was interested in what I called a postmodern vision of the West, semiabstract, half pure color, a barely representational version of mountains and sky, with many artificial angles in the clouds. It was something that I wasn't particularly keen on; the artist was from Arizona, but kept in inventory for precisely this kind of customer—the kind attracted to the colors and shapes, who thought the vision quirky and neat. Usually someone whose artistic consciousness was raised in the 1950s as modernism revolutionized art.

"This reminds me so much of the pieces the art students did after the war in my hometown," the lady said. She was mid-sixties, I reckoned, with a bit of New England in her accent. She required a full biography of the artist, someone much younger and considerably hipper than she was, but I failed to mention those facts. Art is such a personal thing, and I've long ago given up looking down on taste. It is what it is. Yours ain't mine, and we can be thankful for the reverse too. That didn't mean I didn't have opinions. I was plagued by them.

Peg Elliott blew in with a small white dog in her arms, with a gust of wind and a flurry of dry leaves. She fussed and cooed at the dog while I finished up with the customer. It turned out the lady was just curious about the style, and the artist, as often happens. I said good-bye to her and her friends and picked up Peg's leaves as they went out.

"So who's this?" I asked, scratching the dog between his ears.

"My new project." Peg nuzzled the dog, her own steel gray curls a nice match to the dog's white ones. "Seymour, I call him. Like that song, 'Suddenly Seymour.' He burst into my life one day last month. My niece gave him to me, quite unexpected. Well, it was a birthday."

"Not you too. I mean birthdays." I tickled his pink nose. "Nice to meet you, Seymour. A cat *and* a dog?"

She winced. "They don't get along too well. Seymour chases Kitty, then Kitty breaks things."

I tried to smile sympathetically. "Do you want to put him down?"

Peg looked around anxiously. "The floors are too nice here. Do you have a storeroom or something?"

We sequestered Seymour on a pillow in a corner of my back office and closed the door to the gallery. He was shivering, from cold or fright, and curled into a ball and shut his eyes.

Back out in the gallery I realized the coffee pot was dry. But Peg refused to let me make more, so we sat down at the desk. I laid a hand on the autopsy report. She raised her penciled eyebrows.

"Yes, I know," she said. "I kept it against regulations. I was supposed to burn it. That's what we did back then, before we had a shredder. But I didn't, did I?"

"Why?"

"I was coroner's assistant then. The coroner was also the fire chief, a fat, self-satisfied clod who did whatever he was told. I didn't. That's all there is to it. I knew what was on there was important, and yet nobody read it but him and me."

"And the pathologist, Dr.—" I checked the report. "Turnbull?"

"He was from Casper. He came in to do autopsies when we needed him. Which wasn't that often in those days, once or twice a month at most."

"So he never knew what happened to his reports."

"Didn't care, I'd say. Did his duty and went home." Peg, a firmly plump fiftyish, was dressed in a nylon purple warm-up suit, with her trademark peach lipstick. Her pale cheeks were flushed from the wind. Her black eyes darted across the photocopy. "I knew what that meant. He knew too."

"The pathologist was pretty clear."

She stood up suddenly. "Nobody cared about that boy, what really happened. It would be too troublesome, tourists and hunters would hear negative things about our little town. They wouldn't come anymore. That's what they said."

"They told you that?"

"Larry did. He was the coroner. Larry Pfeiffer."

I watched her for a moment. "What would you have done with this, if I'd never asked? If no one had ever asked?"

She turned sharply toward me. "I have a plan. There's a few more of those. Don't worry. It would have seen light. Some day. Not now, maybe. I have a good ten years to retirement."

"So when you retire." I ran my eyes over the paper again. "What should I do with this, do you think? Who should I tell about it?"

She wrung her hands. "I thought somebody asked you."

"The mother of the boy. I'll have to tell her. But that won't be the end of it."

"I certainly hope not."

"Should I take it to the sheriff?"

Her hand flew to her throat. "No!" She paced quickly to the far wall, then turned back. "Someone outside who can put pressure on. They mustn't know it came from me. I have my job to protect."

"Don't worry. I'll think of something." My morning with Danny Bartholomew brought the press to mind. But it wasn't ready yet, it was half-baked, a crumb without a crust.

"You know, Peg, I might know who did this." I tapped the report. Her jaw dropped slightly; her eyes widened. "And when it all comes out, I hope you don't wish you'd kept it in your Purge file."

Her jaw clenched. A yelp from Seymour startled us. Another yelp made her take two steps in the direction of the back office; then she stopped and stared at me.

"I want something done. Yes, I have to be careful. But if I didn't want justice done, I'd never have kept that report. I'd never have given it to you." She walked up to the desk and put a finger on the photocopy. "Something must be done. Justice."

Fine words, I thought, rereading the autopsy report for the twentieth time between customers. Fine, yes, but how to put them into action? With very little encouragement from management, three paintings, one small watercolor and two original oils, sold themselves to a crew of itinerants from Saskatchewan, Vermont, and Florida. I kept the gallery open until five-thirty when a lengthening lull convinced me the run was over.

Upstairs in my apartment I spread the report on the kitchen counter, sucked in my breath, and called Queen. Part of me wanted her not to answer, so I wouldn't have to tell her this. The other part was still worried about her whereabouts, and the use of her shotgun. Audrey's condition crossed my cluttered mind too, as the phone rang in the mountainside cabin. Just as I was ready to hang up, Queen answered.

"Outside, chopping wood," she replied to my query. As if to demonstrate a loud crash followed, the armful of wood dropping into the box next to the stove.

"I came up last night looking for you," I said warily. "You weren't home."

"I went out."

She was cryptic again. I could grill her about where she'd been, but I doubted it would get me anywhere. Instead I stared at the autopsy report.

"I got a copy of Derek's autopsy. We should talk about it."

A long pause, then: "There was an autopsy?"

"You didn't know?"

"No one told me. Dominick did—" She stopped, her composure slipping. "What does it say?"

"Can I come up, Queen? You need to read this."

"Tell me what it says."

"Just let me—"

"Read it, Alix. Just read it to me."

"Are you sure? Okay, okay." I read the autopsy findings paragraph, slowly, without inflection. Then paused at the end without comment.

"Read it again," she demanded. I complied.

When I finished the second time, I thought I heard a little cry, or gasp, on the line. But she didn't speak, for so long I thought she might have hung up. I said her name, and waited.

"Queen, are you all right?"

"Someone knew it was him. They did it on purpose." Her voice was a monotone, full of neither grief nor hatred. I didn't know how to proceed, or respond.

Finally I said: "That's the way it looks."

"Do you know who it was?"

"Not exactly. Not for sure."

"Who?"

"I don't have any evidence, Queen. I can't be sure."

"Tell me. That's the bargain, tell me."

"The bargain was, I find you these reports. This is the one you wanted, I imagine, without even knowing it existed. This one comes the closest to telling you what happened that day. But I can't in good conscience send you off hunting Derek's killers."

"There was more than one?"

"All I know is there were two boys with him that day. We don't know who pulled the trigger, or who the boys were."

"You know, Alix. You said you knew."

"I have a hunch. I have no evidence. I have an old man's rickety memory, and somebody else who won't talk. That's all I have." *Please don't make me tell you.*

"Then you have more work to do. Find evidence."

"I don't think that's possible. Not after twenty-five years."

"It's there. You just have to find it. You've come so far, Alix, don't stop. I can't stop. I think about him, all the things he's missed, I've missed. I look out my window and I see—" She let out a sigh. Her voice dropped to a whisper. "Don't stop."

We listened to each other's breathing for a long minute. Her voice twisted my heart. I wanted to stop, to bury this forever, never to confront Derek's killers. Let the waters I'd disturbed calm. But I knew I couldn't do that. Not just for Queen, or for Peg Elliot's brand of justice, or even for my own conscience.

It was the boy. I had to do it for Derek, who should be alive right now. Derek, who should be a man now, who should have a wife and children now. Derek, who was forced to lie down in the forest and die.

"I won't stop," I said. "Queen. Where were you last night?"

"In the woods."

"You didn't go visiting?"

"What are you talking about?"

"Nothing." What was I talking about? The Vargas homestead

was quiet and dark, no gunshots there. And Morris Kale had confessed to shooting his wife. What had any of that to do with Queen? I frowned and dug my fingers into my forehead again. I felt on the edge of something I couldn't see, like the blind man and the elephant, and it made just as much sense.

"I'll call you. As soon as I have anything else. Oh, Queen, one more thing."

"What?"

"They've taken your paintings out of the auction for the moment. But, don't worry, I'm working on it, I'll get them back in."

"Who took them out?"

"One of the chairmen. He—"

"Vargas."

I sighed in answer. She said, "That son of a bitch."

"I'll get them back in. He isn't the only chair."

"He's a Nazi."

"I'll go talk to him."

"The auction is in what—three, four days?"

"I'll talk to him tonight if you want."

"Alix, I need that money. I can donate my percentage, I don't mind that at all, even though that bastard is heading this up. I put in because of you, you know. Over my feelings about him. And the cause, of course. But mostly because of you."

"I appreciate that, Queen." Christ, did it have to be so personal? I felt the bonds of responsibility wrap tighter around my skull. "We'll work it out."

"I'm counting on that income for my winter expenses. I can't barter for everything."

"I know, Queen."

"If you come up tomorrow, I'll give you the first piece I promised. It's ready. The other one is almost done."

"Sure." Now I felt like a heel for accepting the painting at all. "You should sell that one. I can put it up in the gallery."

"You've worked for it, Alix. It's yours to do whatever you want with. Come up tomorrow. I don't welsh on my promises."

A challenge, I thought later, to not welsh on mine.

10

ANOTHER dinner of the single girl's delight, peanut butter on stale toast, and I was on the road again, up to the Flying V. I had to go without thinking, stay rational. It was a lost cause from my angle anyway; it would take Morris Kale to get Queen's paintings back in the auction. I hoped to get possession of the paintings at least, since I was responsible for them. I focused on that, with the taste of coffee and peanuts in my clenched mouth as I rounded the curves to the ranch.

The door was flung open by Georgia in a red silk dressing gown. She was pulling it together hastily as if she expected the fire department.

"Sorry to interrupt, Georgia," I said seriously. "Is Terry here?"

She rearranged the slight panic in her face, sliding into contempt. "He's busy."

"This will only take a minute," I said, holding open the door. "I can wait for him to get his pants on."

"He's cooking," she said, then flung up her hands and walked away, leaving the door open wide. I stepped inside and closed it. Georgia had disappeared.

The smell of garlic, onion, and butter floated heavily, leading me and my nose right, down a tiled hallway to the kitchen. In the middle of a vast island of gold-and-orange tile, Terry Vargas stood over a stainless steel stove, stirring with a wooden spoon. The overhead lights gave his dark figures a shadowy look, despite his wearing only flannel pajama bottoms. His chest was every inch the manly man, hairy and muscular. So hairy I worried about the cooking.

"Smells good," I said.

Vargas started, then frowned at me. "What do you want?"

"Queen Johns's paintings, since you're not offering dinner."

He sprinkled some herbs or something into the pan and stirred some more. "Not here. And this isn't dinner, just something for my friends."

Oh, darn, I wasn't one of his friends.

"Morris Kale says they're here. I'll just look around." I walked through the end of the kitchen, where a door led to a darkened dining room, and searched for a light switch on the rounded log wall. Vargas was on me like a tick.

"You take one step in there, and I'll have you arrested for trespassing."

I turned toward him. "I was invited into your home by the lovely Georgia. Why don't you just shoot me? Isn't that what the western man is entitled to?"

His nostrils flared. "Keep this up, bitch, and I'll do just that."

"Threats and names, Terry. They hurt me. Just hand over the paintings, and I'm outa here."

"I'm keeping them for the auction. They don't belong to you."

"I'm her dealer. You confiscated property that doesn't belong to you. Do I have to get a court order?"

"She's a disgrace to the auction. She's a fucking lunatic. Everybody knows that."

"I don't know it. The committee voted to keep her in. Is this perhaps a personal vendetta?"

"Yeah, it's personal. She threatened me with a shotgun."

"And what did you do to her, Terry?"

He glared at me, his eyes dark with anger. "I never did anything to the woman."

Over his shoulder I saw Georgia at the hall door, a grim expression on her face. I glanced down her body to the handgun held at her side. Maybe this wasn't the best time to tell Vargas I knew he was a murderer. It could wait. I could feel his breath on me, we stood so close in the dining room doorway. His chest rose and fell in quick, tense breaths.

"Then hand over her paintings. Or I'll have to call the authorities on you. That will put the wildlife auction in a new light in the papers, won't it?" I smiled sweetly. "I don't have to make up more headlines for you, do I?"

A whoosh behind him in the kitchen made us all turn toward the stove. Three-foot flames shot out of the frying pan toward the ceiling. Lightbulbs in the overhanging fixtures burst, sending glass flying in all directions. Georgia screamed. Vargas leaped toward the stove, stepped on the glass with bare feet, cursed, and hopped. The smoke alarm pierced the air. Georgia reached over the island to turn off the stove, but the flames continued. I backed into the dark dining room. As I looked around and stepped quickly across the Navajo rug to the living room, I heard cursing, shouting, and crunching glass from the kitchen.

In the vast living room two lamps shone. I looked around quickly, saw no paintings, and made for the bedroom hallway. The smell of smoke and burning onions hadn't come this far. I switched on a light in the first room on the right. There on a bed lay two paintings wrapped in craft paper. On them was written, "Johns #42" and "Johns #55."

There wasn't time to check to see if the labels were accurate. I grabbed them, slung them under my arm, and ran to the hallway. The smoke alarms still sent out their annoying cry but I thought I heard voices, calming now, Terry telling Georgia to open the windows.

A dash through the living room and out the door into the night. The original mad dash. I ran as quietly as possible, threw open the Saab Sister, tossed in the paintings and myself, and backed her out. As I turned around, muscling the old car to perform on deep gravel, Georgia was framed in the doorway with the red silk gown hanging open, bare from neck to ankle, in a blazing white slice. I waved, spun rocks, and executed the getaway.

Damn, that was fun.

Elation had evaporated by the time I got back into Jackson, despite a light dusting of snow on the streets. New snow, especially in the evening under the glow of streetlights, cheers me
more than almost everything. A silent blessing from on high,
making all the old look new, all the mistakes gone, all perfect
and renewed. Forget spring—it has a way of pissing off everybody in Jackson with its nonappearance. Snow is hard to beat
for a lift in mood in these parts. At least in October.

But tonight all it did was make the streets slick, icing up on
corners and making the old Saab dance a skip-to-my-lou as she
turned into the alley behind the gallery. One of these days I'd have
to get snow tires. And a real car.

What to do with the paintings? In my apartment I tore off the
paper and confirmed they were the right ones. I carried the wolf
one, *Imminent Domain*, into my bedroom and propped it up on my
dresser facing my bed. It was a wonderful piece, even better now
on second viewing, with power and mystery and the colors of the
wild. I sat on the edge of the bed and felt a shiver.

Now I knew Queen's story of the wolf with the blue tongue,
the one she'd used as a model for this painting. No tongue was
showing in the picture, but a hint of a smile was there, if you
looked hard enough. Carl was right; the colors in the ruff were gorgeous and rich, violets and sapphires and midnight blues.

Did it look like my wolf, the one I saw years ago? I shut my eyes
tight and tried to picture him. But Blue Wolf was too far away for
these details, too much a silhouette in the moonlight. I squeezed
my eyes harder. Why couldn't I see the starlight in his eyes, the
sparkle on his coat? I opened my eyes and sighed. The painted wolf
was realer than the one I'd seen.

What would it be like, I wondered, to see a wolf that close?
Would my reaction be like Marc's, fear and defense, immediate
and visceral, a brush with death? Or like Queen's—laughter, ac-
ceptance, smiles? I could see it both ways, under a variety of cir-

cumstances. What would my circumstances be, a shy approach, a chance passing, a bold midnight attack? Would I ever have a chance to find out? One wolf sighting in a lifetime was probably all I would get.

I lay back on the bed. It was eleven o'clock and felt like three in the morning. The ceiling had old, ugly water spots. Who was Carl with tonight? Some forest ranger with curvy calves and sturdy hiking boots, no doubt. Did I care? Mostly I didn't want to think about it. My thoughts went back to Audrey Kale. How was she? Was Morris in jail? What the hell happened to Frankie?

I rolled over and bunched up a pillow under my cheek. I would call Morris about the paintings, try to get them back in the auction. Would he be open for that, with everything else he was dealing with? How else to get them in, though?

I woke up an hour later, cold. Kicking off my boots, slipping out of my jeans, I crawled under the covers, took a last sleepy look at the wolf in my bedroom, and fell back into my dreams.

Halfway through my first cup of coffee in the morning, I remembered the gallery was closed for the week. I'd already put an ad in both papers that I would be closed "for painting," so no one expected me, anywhere. An odd feeling, one I had every year at this time and had come to both despise and relish: a free-floating nowhereness, a sense of dislocation and disorientation. I could do anything, go anywhere, and no one would blink an eye.

A sturdy sense of responsibility brought me back to my rail-road desk for a last accounting check-up before my week of leisure. I pulled out the book from my pencil drawer and saw the photo of Paolo again. Why did I keep it there to torment me each day? Why couldn't I let him go? I rubbed a smeary fingerprint off his handsome face with my shirttail. Oh, lovely boy.

I stood up the photo against my pencil cup and tried to balance the books. At least I'd had a good day yesterday to end up the week. Still it occurred to me I shouldn't be taking the week off at all, that it was selfish and irresponsible, and that I really needed to be making some money. As the only employee for these interim months—I had Artie Wacker's word he would be back at Christmas—I paid myself whatever was necessary, for rent, food, gas, general expenses. I had a small emergency cushion that I used for health insurance but nothing else. It was beginning to look like a very lean Thanksgiving.

Paolo beamed at me from the photograph. We didn't worry about money back then. We didn't even think about health insurance or how big the electric bill would be. All we thought about was us, and fun. The world was new, unspoiled, like our hearts.

I sighed and tried to free the puddle of grief in my chest. My carefree youth, and Paolo, were gone, never to return. Whatever I had with Carl, or men after him, would be a pale reflection of what Paolo and I had. I couldn't change that. People you loved died, that was the way the world worked. It happened to everybody; it had happened to my father at a cruel age, and to all of us who loved him.

Hell. It was too early to get weepy. I slammed the book closed, slipping it and Paolo back in the drawer, and turned off the desk light. With an outward show of determination, I went back upstairs and changed into my painting clothes. I didn't feel like painting, now that it was time. But I recalled that old Jack London phrase, "You can't wait for inspiration, you have to go after it with a club." I grit my teeth, drove to the studio, built a fire.

And took a nice long nap.

Monday didn't look much better, but at least I was well rested. Not much point going straight over to the studio to mope, so I wrapped the two paintings of Queen's in craft paper again and left through the back, not looking back at the dark, forlorn gallery I was leaving unattended.

The morning was overcast and gray like my mood. The thin patches of snow weren't cheery. The roads were still slick, and the Saab took it slow and easy through light traffic out to the mesa where Morris Kale had staked his claim. A mist hung on the long drive, enshrouding the big red house in a shawl of moisture. Birds sung in the evergreens, unseen, but the house was quiet.

The gravel crunched loudly as I made my way to the front door. I'd left the paintings in the car. The look of the house made me think they might be at the hospital with Audrey, or otherwise unavailable. I shivered in my father's ancient hunting jacket, frowning at the frayed cuffs. Grabbing it was an unconscious move to the old and comfortable on a day when I felt cold and alone.

Just as I was ready to turn away, footsteps approached the door from the inside. It was opened by a stocky young man in his late twenties, with an angry scowl and dark eyes like Terry Vargas. I introduced myself and said I was looking for Morris. The scowler stepped back and gestured me inside. I waited for him to shut the door, then followed his short, jean-clad legs into the room where we'd had the meeting last week.

The atmosphere in the room was dramatically different, a cold hearth, chilled, misty windows, a solitary lamp making a spot of warmth. Morris Kale sat hunched over in an armchair, while Frankie sat opposite him with his music ears on. A young woman sat on the dark green sofa, nearly disappearing into its depths.

"Somebody to see you, Morris," my escort announced dully. Morris looked up from a contemplation of his shoe tips, a look of surprise on his face.

"Alix." He rose carefully from his seat and crossed the carpet to give me a hug. In all the years I'd known Morris, I'd never gotten a hug. I patted his back sympathetically and caught a hostile stare from the young woman. As Morris released me, I nodded to her and said hello.

She extracted her petite self from the down pillows of the sofa and stretched out a hand politely. "I'm Valerie, Audrey's daughter. And you met my husband Jason?"

I shook her hand and ventured a smile at her husband, who bore a striking resemblance to Frankie, attitude-wise. "Nice to meet you. You just flew in?"

"Yesterday, from New York. We came as soon as we could."

Valerie's face was harder than her mother's, and she was smaller, but the family resemblance was unmistakable. She wore a tailored pantsuit in charcoal gray, as if she was headed for Wall Street. In contrast her husband was casual, in denim and starched blue oxford shirt. Morris looked his own impeccable self, in pressed khakis and sweater vest.

"How is she doing?" I asked cautiously.

They all looked at Morris. He stood with one hand on the large, carved mantelpiece, staring at the cold ashes. In the pause he glanced up at me, a face creased with worry. "She's holding her own. We were just going to the hospital."

"Well, don't let me keep you," I said.

But no one moved toward the door. Valerie sat back down in the sofa and examined her nails. Jason cleared his throat. "Can't go just yet," he said with a sneer.

"It was very good of you to come out, Alix," Morris said formally. "But as you can see, we're fine here, there's nothing to do but wait for Audrey to heal. But we appreciate your thoughtfulness."

He managed a small, strained smile. I realized suddenly that Audrey's children must accuse him of shooting their mother, and here they all sat so cozily. What a burden of guilt, even with an accidental shooting. And then there was my own guilt, for I hadn't come out to console them at all.

I touched Morris's arm lightly. "Can we talk for a minute?" I whispered.

He nodded, and waited, then with my hesitant glance around the room at the younger generation, he got the hint. We walked over to the bar in the corner and took up perches on two stools.

"I'm sorry to bother you about this now, Morrie. But I don't know where else to turn."

He seemed to concentrate and focus at last, giving me his old on-the-case Morris look.

"It's Queen's paintings for the auction. I got them back from Terry last night, but not without a fight."

"He called me," Morris said. "Words were spoken."

"I bet. Queen really needs the income from the paintings, and we already have her in the brochure. It's unfair that Terry can take her out of the auction without the consent of the committee. They voted not to vote on taking her out—you were there."

"There really isn't any precedence for this. If a chairman wants to remove a painting or two, the committee has no right to supercede that decision."

I stared at him. "What?"

"It's basically a dictatorship. Most committees like this are. The chairman does what he wants, as long as they keep him as chairman."

"But you're a chairman too."

He pursed his lips. The circles under his eyes had advanced to bluish bags. He looked very, very tired. Why was I burdening him with this? But what else could I do? I felt angry, and betrayed.

"You aren't going to do anything?"

He looked away at the three silent bodies in the upholstery. His family, such as it was. He'd married late, to an older woman, perhaps hoping to make up for lost time, the lost family he never got around to having. And now they hated him, or at least accused him. And his wife lay suffering from his own hand. I bit my tongue and stood up.

"I'm really sorry about Audrey. I wouldn't—"

A loud yawn startled me. In the doorway to the bedroom wing behind me stood a man in his late fifties in a loose blue terrycloth robe, his thinning brown hair in every direction, barefoot, with his mouth open in an enormous intake of air. He burbled to the end of the yawn and rubbed his chest through the gap in the robe.

"Morning, all. Sleep well, I hope?"

Morris stood up. Valerie too. Frankie sat forward, glaring at the man. Jason looked away.

"There's coffee in the kitchen, Corky," Morris said stiffly.

"We've been waiting for you, Dad," Valerie scolded. "We want to go see Mother."

Corky ran a hand over his thinning hair. "Coffee, you say? Thanks, old boy." And he ignored the rest of us as he made his way through the furniture toward the far door. "This way, right?"

As he passed I caught a strong smell of sweat, cigarettes, and whiskey. I turned back to Morris and said my good-byes. "I'll stop in to see Audrey later."

"She'd like that, I'm sure," Morris said. A clatter in the kitchen was followed by the sound of crockery breaking and a strong curse. Valerie turned hesitantly toward the sound as if to help.

"Leave it, Val," Morris said.

She stopped midstep, looked sympathetically toward the kitchen, then back at Morris's hard jaw. "He'll cut his feet," she said.

"Just leave it."

Valerie shuddered slightly. Frankie stood up then and took off his headphones. "Let's go. If we're going, let's just fucking go," he said, heading for the door.

"Frankie!" Valerie cried. "Stop it. We have to wait for Dad."

"The fuck we do." The boy, who no longer looked much like a boy but more like a very angry young man, turned to his stepfather. "You coming or not?"

Morris Kale stared at the boy's face, then went calmly to where a leather jacket was draped over a chairback. He picked it up and turned to Valerie. "Take the Cherokee. We'll meet you there." And they were gone.

I stood frozen for a moment but as I heard the door open I mumbled good-byes and ran after them. They were driving the black pickup out before I had a chance to turn the Saab around. With a sigh I looked at the two paintings in the backseat.

Mission Not Accomplished. Driving back through town, I debated going straight up to Queen's, possibly leaving the paintings with her, or stashing them back at the gallery. In the end I stopped off at the Second Sun and locked them in the storeroom. I didn't want Terry Vargas hearing about them at Queen's and making another scene there. Anything to keep those two apart as long as possible. Queen was sure to keep pressing me about digging out evidence on the two companions of Derek on the hunting trip. And I had promised to do it, for that lost boy.

The bad feelings of the extended Kale family, combined with the day's gloomy weather, hung over me on the drive up through Kelly and along the Gros Ventre River. The forest had a dark primeval look, perfect for a wayward wolf. Queen must have been out searching for him that night, keeping him away from the traps and the wildlife rangers. Keeping him safe and free. I had a mental picture of that smiling wolf face with his blue tongue, loping through the misty woods, nose to the ground. That cheered me as I pulled into the gravelly yard by Queen's cabin, relieved to see a light on inside.

Queen met me at the door with a smile. She wore a yellow-and-green flowered muumuu today, with cowboy boots. Her cabin was cozy and warm on this damp day, bright with kerosene lamps and tea on the stove. I told her about my failure with Morris Kale as we drank cinnamon tea. She seemed philosophic about it this morning.

"Something will come up. You'll see," she said, her eyes crinkling over the teacup.

"I could try some of the other committee members. Candace Gundy was pretty vocal against Terry, she might back me up."

Queen shrugged and looked out the window.

"Or," I continued, "I could just take them to the auction myself. What's he going to do then?"

"There might be a scene," she said.

"I doubt in public. But even if there is, Terry Vargas is going to be the loser. Because he would have to initiate a scene."

"Morris Kale might, it sounds like."

"Morris Kale isn't going to do anything at the auction. He'll be lucky if he makes it there."

"They aren't going to arrest him for shooting his wife, are they?"

"You heard about that? I doubt it. He's a rich white guy, and he's got a big blowhard attorney."

"That cowboy lawyer—Penn?"

"I don't know this guy. I hear he's a player. His name is Garrett."

Queen set her cup down carefully. "I know that name." Her fingertips pressed her downturned forehead. "There was a governor named Garrett back in the fifties. Only lasted half a term, got thrown out on an election racket, stuffing the ballot boxes or something."

"It might be him. But this guy looked about sixty. In the fifties he'd have been—"

"Too young."

"Maybe a relative." I frowned at her. "This guy's first name was Sonny. The governor's son?" Did what the old sheriff told me work here? "Did you meet any lawyers that night? Somebody working for the other boys?"

Her eyes took on the glaze of memory. "I was hysterical that night."

"Maybe at the sheriff's. He would have been trying to keep the sheriff away from the boys. They never were interviewed, except at the scene."

She shook her long gray locks, pushed back the black forelock. "I think I was at the morgue, with Derek."

"Where was the morgue?"

"In the old hospital."

I looked at my watch. Was it too late to catch old Sheriff Gass before his morning nap? It was close to eleven. He'd be into his afternoon nap by the time I reached the nursing home. Sonny Garrett had to be that lawyer. But how could I use the information—sketchy and intuitive as it was—to elicit a confession out of Terry Vargas? Or, at the very least, find solid evidence that it had been Terry hunting with Derek? Who the hell was the other kid? Would Terry tell, was he the kind to rat out his friend, assuming he hadn't been the actual trigger puller? Personally I could see Vargas doing almost anything, but his macho code might extend to snitches. They'd kept a good secret for twenty-five years. Hell, maybe the pal was dead by now.

I pulled a manila envelope out of my backpack and handed it to Queen. She laid it in her lap unopened. "You know what it says. But it is pretty clinical. Autopsies are like that."

"I understand." She set it carefully on the side table and laid her palm flat on it, as if some vibration of Derek's being could still be felt in copier paper—a gentle, hopeless gesture. Then she stood up, straightening her muumuu. "I have the painting for you. Only the first one."

I followed her into the kitchen, where she lifted a large oil off the wall. It was at least four feet across, a Teton view, in the fall with aspens all golden in patches of fir and pine, with a first glazing of snow on the mountains and a hard glare to the sky. I loved the wolf more, but this was the kind of painting that sold in the gallery faster than almost any, a well-loved mountain scene for city dwellers to take home a slice of wild to their city digs.

"It's beautiful, Queen. Lovely."

She handed it to me, already framed with a tasteful black-stained wood moulding, ready to go, ready to sell. "Thank you so much for this," I said.

She shook her head. "It was an arrangement. You've done what I asked. And if you can just find out a little more, we'll be square. You know it pains me to have to do this because I hate to be beholden to people. I feel better now that you have the painting. *Silver and Gold*, I call it."

It was tricky getting the large canvas into the Saab's backseat. I respectfully refused a bowl of soup for lunch, pleading auction business. A small lie, as I felt no loyalty to the Auction for Wildlife now, with the shabby way they'd treated Queen. Yes, I would get her paintings into the auction by hook or by crook, and would buy them myself if I had to. (A brave but desperate thought.)

But after this year, I would find some other October cause. A few more days, I grimaced, wringing the steering wheel as the car twisted and turned out of the mountains and back to the pale green sagebrush flats and Jackson Hole.

11

THE Second Sun looked lonely this afternoon, with its dark eyes gazing on the deserted streets of Jackson. I stashed Queen Johns's painting in the storeroom with her others, locked it tight, and turned on the alarm system when I went out the alley door. This time of year burglary seemed unlikely, but those paintings of Queen's made me edgy.

In the interests of simplicity, purely, I made a run through the drive-through at the golden arches and emerged with giant-size fries and a chocolate milk shake. I turned back into town and was almost done with my shake by the time I pulled into the lot at St. John's Hospital. Sheriff Gass crossed my mind again, but there was no point bothering the old man again. The obnoxious lawyer with a father in state government had to be Sonny Garrett. As I washed salt and grease off my hands in the lobby ladies' room, I had another thought. Just to be sure.

"Danny, my man," I purred into the pay phone. "I need a very tiny favor."

"Or two or three." He sighed. "What is it?"

"I need a little history on a former governor named Garrett. He was in office not even a whole term, back in the fifties or sixties."

"Never heard of him. Wait, I'll ask Maymie—uh, Russ. Hang on."

In a moment he returned with the news that Wade Garrett had been elected governor in 1960 then thrown out of office on election irregularities in 1962. He and his son then practiced together in Casper until the old man croaked in 1973.

"Then what happened to the son?"

"Well, that's Sonny Garrett. He got the hell out of Casper when his pop died."

Nothing like hunch confirmation to put a jump in your step. But the gloomy faces outside Audrey Kale's room took the wind out of my sails. I slowed as I saw Frankie slumped on the floor, his head buried against his knees. Across the hall Valerie was in Jason's arms, her face against his chest. I stopped at a distance and leaned against the wall, feeling the blood rush out of my head.

Was Audrey dead? The words pounded in my head. I settled against the wall, inert: I couldn't ask the kids. I remembered the moment my mother told me my father was dead, the day the bottom fell out. I would never forget. Why was it so hard to remember that wolf in the Little Belts? Because I was still grieving for my father?

A clearing of a throat, full throttle, preceded the kids' father, Corky, around the corner. He was dressed now, in rumpled corduroys, black turtleneck, and a pile jacket that was too small. He smiled broadly at me.

"Don't I know you?" He wagged a finger at me.

I looked at Frankie and turned my back in that direction, hoping Corky would keep his voice down. He cocked his head. "Don't I?" he repeated.

"From this morning, at Morris's," I whispered, stuck my hand out. "Alix Thorssen. I was just checking on Audrey."

He shook my hand limply. "Bad business, that. When you got guns in the house—" He burped dramatically. "Somebody's gonna get shot."

"Is she all right?" A sour fragrance wafted off Corky. I glanced over my shoulder. Valerie was now staring at her father from her vantage point in Jason's embrace.

"Decidedly not. They rushed her to surgery again. Sounded to me like a big bleed."

Frankie still had his face buried. The poor kid. Poor Audrey.

"They'll fix it up, won't they?" I asked, sounding about Frankie's age.

"We'd like to think so, wouldn't we?" He patted down his pockets suddenly. "Got a match? Seem to have forgotten my lighter."

"I might." I dug through my backpack and scrounged a battered matchbook from the Snow King Hotel.

"Come outside with me, would you? Smoking alone makes it seem criminal." He laughed. "But I guess it's getting that way, right?"

I followed him back through the lobby and out the front doors. Anything to get away from that family scene. In the outdoor air I felt the clenching of my heart lessen a bit. Hospitals were not my favorite milieu.

Corky lit his cigarette inside cupped hands. I stood upwind and wondered if it was really necessary to keep this man company while he made his eyes more bloodshot, his complexion more waxy, and his fingers more stained. A big white Cadillac pulled to a stop at the curb; Sonny Garrett emerged, white-haired, gray-suited. He was all business, his mouth in a thin line, his eyes grave as he made a beeline for the hospital doors.

"Morris's lawyer," Corky said out of the side of his mouth. "Old Morrie could be getting into a heap o' hurt."

Corky's speech patterns and accent had me a little stumped. Sometimes he sounded New England, sometimes Nashville.

"You mean, if she should die?"

"Even if she doesn't. The sheriff's thinking about filing charges of reckless endangerment, or something like that."

"That's bogus. He must be listening to somebody."

"Some county prosecutor, Sonny says. Running for office."

Our Phil Burke, running for state attorney general. Just Morrie's luck. "Where're you from, Corky?"

"Connecticut."

"Let me guess. Wall Street."

A smoky laugh. "No, I run Granddad's foundation. He was loaded, and we've been doing our damnedest these last twenty-five years to give it away."

"Must be rough."

"Damn near backbreaking." He winked through the fumes.

I wanted to ask about him and Audrey and all that, but it seemed like prying. Besides, it didn't matter. So I smiled and said, "I'm working with Morris on the wildlife art auction."

He raised his eyebrows in polite disinterest. "You don't say."

"It's Wednesday night. You should come if you're still in town. Give away some of Grandpa's money. We encourage that."

He tipped his hand, dropping ash near my feet. "Love to, thank you for asking. I'll probably be gone by then. Damn well better be."

I was squinting at that comment when the doors opened behind me. Sonny Garrett, out again. He paused to look for the Cadillac, which had moved off to handicapped parking.

"Gotta go. Nice talking to you." I waved behind my back at Corky as I sprinted toward Sonny Garrett. He was on the move again, having spotted his vehicle, when I startled him by bounding up at his side."

"Mr. Garrett."

He stopped and glared at me. "I'm a busy man," he said, and kept walking.

"I know, I'm not a reporter. I'm a friend of Morris Kale's."

He stopped again. "What did you say your name was?"

I told him. "I own a gallery in town. I just need a minute."

He paused on the grassy median and folded his arms. "What is this about?"

Taking a big breath, I set down my backpack and tried to look casual. *No big deal. Just a murder twenty-five years ago.* "It's not about Audrey, or Morris, it's something else. Something that happened twenty-five years ago."

He looked at his watch and arched an eyebrow.

"Right," I said. "It's just not that easy to explain. You repre-

sented Terry Vargas twenty-five years ago when he and a friend
were involved in a hunting accident where a boy named Derek
Wylie was shot and killed. I need to know—"

"Hold it." He put a soft, pink palm toward me. "Where did you
get this information?"

"From official sources. I need to speak to Mr. Vargas about
this, and well, I figured it would be better to go through his
lawyer." *For my physical well-being.* I took a breath. "I was going to
call your office, but then I saw you here. Visiting Audrey, I assume,
like I was."

"I'm sorry, little lady, your information is incorrect. I have no
idea what you're talking about, Mr. Vargas is not my client, and I
am late for an appointment."

He turned to go.

"I know you represented those boys. I know you badgered the
sheriff until he decided to forget about even interviewing them. I
know the autopsy report was suppposed to be shredded, and their
names purged from the incident reports. I have evidence."

"What evidence?" he said quietly.

I shook my head. "I need to talk to Mr. Vargas."

"You seem to think you know everything."

"That's between him and me. There are reparations that need
to be made."

"How do I know you're not bluffing?"

"Have I told you anything wrong so far? You're familiar with
the case."

His face was expressionless. "I'm afraid I can't help you, Miss
Thorssen." He stepped away toward the car.

"You put me in an awkward position, Mr. Garrett. If I can't
talk to your client, then I'll have to talk to the authorities."

Garrett didn't turn until he got to the Cadillac. He opened the
back door. As he paused to stoop and get in, he turned his cold
eyes on me with a chill I felt down to my toes. I stood frozen for a
moment, watching the car pull around the parking lot and roar
back toward town. Had I started some kind of awful chain reaction, one I would be sorry about later? My throat felt dry, burning.

I picked up my backpack. The sun had come out, weak but

cheering. In front of the hospital, Corky stood smokeless, staring. I waved and headed to my car.

Back in town an overpowering need to share the information I'd gleaned came over me. It was fear, of course, but that didn't make it less potent. The steely eyes of Sonny Garrett had put a double-gloom whammy on my day. I tried to envision his next move. Would he call Terry Vargas and report all I'd said? Probably. What would Terry do? What *could* he do without tipping his hand to me, and everyone? I shivered. Of all the people to piss off, what—three times in one week? And this time, it was deadly serious.

The atmosphere inside the newsroom at the *Jackson Hole News* was completely different from the last time I'd been here. A buzz of activity, clacking of computer keys, phones ringing, talking, shouting, laughing: it was deadline day for the twice-weekly. I rounded the counter and headed for Danny Bartholomew's desk on the far left of the room.

He was hunched over his keyboard, glaring at the monitor. I waited a second for him to look up, but he didn't. I put my arms on his monitor and stared down at his curly black hair. "Danny? It's me."

He glanced up for a second and murmured something, then went back to his computer.

"Got a second?"

"Nope." He typed for a minute, then stopped. "What? I've gotta get this done, Alix."

"I really have to talk to you. About this hunting accident thing, the one from twenty-five years ago. I—"

"Sorry. Can't. Got a deadline in—" He looked at his watch. "Forty-five minutes."

"It won't take long, I promise. Please, Danny."

He sighed. "Look, sweetheart. I've got a planning commission story that is deadly boring. I've got a reaction piece putting together fifteen interview comments. And that doesn't include my lead story about the wolves in the park. I can't do it. Not now."

"What about the wolves? Has something happened with Marc?"

"Oh, yeah." He spun around in the chair, grabbed a printout

off a table behind him, and spun back. "If I let you read this, will you go away?"

"You sure know how to make a girl feel wanted. Okay, give."

The news story was already laid out in columns, ready to go. The headline made my heart sink.

Danny was watching me. "It's not pretty," he said.

12

Teton County Sheriff's deputies arrested Marc Fontaine on Monday, the horse wrangler who admitted shooting a wolf on private land two weeks ago. The arrest was orchestrated by U.S. Fish & Wildlife agents, working through the U.S. Attorney's office.

Fontaine was taken into custody on the Bar-T-Bar Ranch deep inside the borders of Grand Teton National Park, one of several private ranches remaining from the days before the federal government took over the parkland. He had no comment for reporters as sheriff's deputies took him to the Teton County lockup.

The official charge for Fontaine is slaughter of an endangered species. The wrangler admits shooting the wolf that he claims attacked him on the ranch owned by Bud Wooten, third-generation Teton County cattle and horse rancher.

Federal agents report that wolf #145, as the dead wolf is called, is from the Leopold Pack inside Yellowstone National Park. The pack is named for naturalist Aldo Leopold, who advocated wolf reintroduction in the park back in 1944. Official reintroduction took place there in 1995. Wolves and other predators were exterminated by park rangers in the early years of the century. The wolves now number over 100 and have been migrating outside the park for the last couple years, often coming into conflict with ranching interests.

Rancher Bud Wooten appears to be implicated in the charge, although Fish & Wildlife officials won't comment on the record. Unofficially one agent told the *News* that he believes that Wooten and Fontaine had seen wolves previously, and Wooten gave orders to shoot to kill any wolves on the ranch.

I folded the papers and tucked them into the kindling bucket next to the red enamel woodstove in my studio behind what was once Paolo's house. It was still hard to think of the cream-colored bungalow as his sister Luca's, although she'd made it her own with orchids and new paint. Paolo was my partner, my lover for a while. We came to Jackson Hole together, but he was gone now. He'd sacrificed himself, saved me from a gunman. We'd buried him here. Life went on here in paradise. Here in the wood shack of an old garage where I'd done my own radical painting on the walls, the canvases lay thick with dust. A busy summer, nose to the books and the customers—I'd made it over here only once or twice since my spring painting week in early May.

Outside on the tiny stoop I sat on a stump and looked at the sky. This was all I really wanted this week for, a bit of cloud-watching, no strings attached. But my mind raced with troubles and conflict—Audrey in the operating room, Morris under possible arrest, Terry Vargas and his lawyer planning something special for me, Queen's paintings excluded from the auction. And now Marc Fontaine in jail.

A solitary mallard quacked loudly, flying low overhead in the wrong direction. Lost in the clouds, without direction, friends, or even a winter plan, but still honking like mad and flapping away. I sighed, feeling very mallard. The clouds brightened as the sun lit them from within, jewels on the pale ocean sky. Then a very distant V of Canadian geese passed over, high and orderly. As if to remind me that there was a plan; I was just too far away to get a glimpse of it.

Back inside the studio I spent half an hour idling with the

paints and brushes, checking the condition of bristles, making note of needed colors and such. Paolo once told me there was nothing he liked better than a brand new, plump tube of gentian blue, or was it Venetian green? I couldn't remember any more. He was fading, and I hated that. I squeezed my eyes, pictured him in the photograph again, young, happy, unaware of fate.

"Hey there." The voice, and accompanying knock, were soft but startled me anyway.

"Maggie."

She stood grinning in the doorway, taking in all the colorful wildness she had helped me paint: yellow walls, orange window trim, the twisty spirals of grass green on the skinny beams, the sky blue ceiling. "Thought I'd find you here. Got something groovy going?"

"Hardly. Unless thumb twiddling counts."

Maggie's long black hair was pulled into a messy braid, and she wasn't even wearing her customary red lipstick. As she came closer, perching on the edge of the battered table that held supplies, her complexion looked washed out, her eyes dull. She caught me watching her, and I looked quickly away.

"So, your painting week begins."

"Exciting, isn't it? I'm afraid my heart isn't in it. Maybe I should have gone hiking with Carl after all."

She shrugged and looked out the window. The circles under her eyes shocked me. Maggie Barlow was a happy person, not one prone to all-night worrying. "Supposed to snow. A cold front coming in tonight." Her voice was flat yet wistful.

"Guess I better fire up the stove then." I got busy building the fire, finding the right logs from the stack outside. Maggie would talk to me in good time. But with the fire built and her seated next to the red stove, she just stared at the flames through the small gap in the stove door.

"Are you coming to the auction?" I asked.

"Um, no, I don't have tickets," she said, blinking herself back to the present.

"I've got one for you. I got ten for helping out with things. For all the trouble it's been, it should have been more. Anyway, come with me, it'll be fun. Bring James too, if you want."

She stirred, frowning. "I won't be bringing James."

"Oh. How about Lily, then?"

She shook her head. "That's over."

So that was it. "I'm sorry."

"Don't be." She straightened up and looked me in the eye. "I was completely wrong about James. I feel like such a fool."

"Oh, Maggie. How could you be that wrong?" The few times I met him, James seemed like a decent guy, a little high-strung maybe.

"Believe me, this one tops the rest. I've been wrong about guys, but—" She swallowed hard. "Smack."

I blinked. "What?"

"He is a freaking heroin addict. Or at least a frequent user—I don't know anything about heroin. How could I miss something like that? Jesus Christ, I made love to the man and never noticed needle marks. It took him stealing money out of my purse to get me to wake up."

"I never would have guessed." Now that she mentioned it, though . . . his unreliable nature, inability to cope some days and wild confidence the next. But those were traits of almost any single guy in Jackson.

"You'd have thought his lovely ex might have mentioned it."

"Maybe she didn't know. Would she have left her daughter with him? Thank God you were there, Maggie. Poor Lily."

"I hope he rots in hell," she said viciously, then opened her eyes wide and laughed. "I mean, I hope he gets some help, really, really soon."

She slumped on her chair and looked so sad. I remembered the look on her face when she'd come to the gallery with Lily, a mixture of wonder and aggravation. She would miss that sweet thing.

Maggie rubbed her face hard and expelled a big breath. "So. What's new with you?"

I paused a moment to see if she was serious. But I knew the impulse to hear someone else's woes, anything to distract from the pain. Her eyes were bright enough now, and fixed on me. So I launched into the tale of Queen Johns's son, his short life and untimely death, everything I knew, down to the dirty facts on Terry Vargas.

"I hope telling you all this doesn't get you in trouble," I said. "I tried to tell Danny, because I want him to write about it eventually. I feel a little weird, knowing the dirt on people." I felt a little grubby for all my digging. Shouldn't I have let it all lie, as it had for twenty-five years? Hadn't I recommended that to Queen? But the worms were out of the can now.

Maggie had been quiet through the story but listening attentively. She pulled her dark eyebrows together. "Is someone threatening you?"

"No. But I told Sonny Garrett that I'd go to the authorities with what I know. And I will. Trouble is, I don't really have evidence that it was Terry Vargas, just old Sheriff Gass's memory."

"Which is none too reliable. I know, I carry his insurance." Maggie sat forward. "I also carry the Flying V."

I closed the door of the stove and adjusted the dampers. It was cooking now, almost too hot for the small studio. "Nothing fishy about the ranch, is there?"

"Like forged titles, bodies buried in the drainfield?" She smiled at my hapless shrug. "What are you going to do?"

"I guess I'm waiting to see if he and Sonny Garrett take the bait. Maybe they'll make me an offer to keep quiet."

"Then you'd know for sure it was Terry. But what if he doesn't?"

"Got any ideas?"

"Sic Danny on 'em?"

"Worked once, didn't it? But not yet. It's not ready."

We tossed around some lame ideas and let the matter drop. I was glad to have my friend to discuss things with, because Maggie Barlow was far more adventurous than I was. She'd lived here all her life, except for a couple party years at the university in Laramie. She would do almost anything if I asked her, but she didn't have any ideas for this one. She asked me a few more questions about Derek Wylie, and we both felt the hollow loss of his death. We made plans to go to dinner tomorrow night, where I'd give her the auction ticket and make such important decisions as what outfit to wear.

"I'll help you with Queen's paintings," Maggie said as she was leaving. When I frowned, she said, "But you are bringing them to be sold. You have to. You can't let Terry have his way in this. There is no way he'll make a public scene."

I wasn't so sure. "I'll bring them." Maybe Terry Vargas wouldn't even notice we were carrying around large canvases. Yeah, and maybe winter wouldn't come to the high country this year.

As I watched Maggie walk back down the alley to her car, I noted more color in her cheeks and a little pep in her step. A new battle awaited; she was pumped. I hoped I had helped her forget about James, at least for a while.

I turned back to the studio, damped down the stove, turned out the lights, and locked the door. No painting today. Maybe tomorrow, maybe the next day.

Yeah, and maybe winter wouldn't come. . . .

13

AGGIE'S visit reminded me I hadn't given away my free
tickets yet. In a last-minute panic after supper, I ran
around town dropping off tickets to Danny Bartholomew,
Coroner Peg Elliot, my artist friend Martin Ditolla, and Queen
Johns. The drive out to Kelly and up into the Gros Ventres was getting automatic, the curves of the rising hillside road too familiar,
as an orange Camaro of sixties vintage screamed by me and scared
me onto the shoulder. I felt my heart thumping and was barely
breathing by the time I pulled next to Queen's cabin.

There was no sign of her, again. I knocked, called, tried the
knob. It was locked this time, both doors. The easel was still set up
in the dry grass on the edge of the clearing, but no canvas graced
it. No paints or brushes, as there would be if she'd only left for a
moment. I walked around the cabin, peering into the gloom of
forest, and left an auction ticket and note for her inside the screen
door.

The Saab paused at the stop sign at Highway 89. Left took me
home, right took me to the park, to Moose. The evening light was
fading, almost gone. A purple blush hung over the Tetons. Did I

want Carl to come to the auction? Why not, I thought, turning impulsively, gunning the Saab Sister to her max of 55 m.p.h. I had missed talking to him these last few days, I had to admit, even though things had been hectic, and I could hear what he would say about the run-ins with Vargas and Garrett.

The Park Service cabins sat in a low, homely group at the end of a dirt road behind the Visitor Center. They were neat enough, but rough and plain. Serviceable would be a kind term. The yards were treeless and barren, with native grasses shorn once in August and left to turn golden and sharp as needles. Carl's half of the cabin he shared with Kevin Stoddard was dark. No sign of his pickup truck. I knocked. As I waited, hearing nothing inside, Kevin came out the other door of the duplex and stopped, startled by my appearance.

"Oh, hi. Alix, right?"

Kevin wasn't in uniform tonight but wore jeans, hiking boots, and leather vest over a plaid shirt. He looked brushed and polished, as if he had a woman expecting him somewhere.

"How's it going?"

He nodded. "Carl's not here."

"I see that." I looked at the invitations in my hands. "I've got some extra tickets for the Auction for Wildlife on Wednesday. I was going to leave one for Carl. Would you like one? It should be fun, even if you don't buy art."

"Isn't that kind of a hoity-toity thing?"

I laughed. "Not really. I mean, there will be some money there. And possibly some Hollywood."

Kevin wrinkled his nose and looked up at the Tetons in the alpenglow. I followed his gaze, never bored with the sight, the violets and deep blues, the pinks and peachy oranges glowing on the new snowcaps like hot breath on a cool evening. Down here in the valley, it was night. Up there, where life was crystalline and transient, sunlight clung fiercely, making its magic.

"Is he out on a helicopter run? Somebody get stranded?"

"I don't know," Kevin said. "Haven't seen him today. Might be."

He looked at his shoe tips, then at the mountains again. He

knew where Carl was. I shuffled the invitations again. "So, did I talk you into it? There's a buffet with good food."

He stuck his hands in his pockets and smiled politely. "I guess not. But thanks."

"Will you give this to Carl, then? I'd stick it in his mailbox if he had one."

Kevin took the envelope. "Sure. No problem."

I turned and walked with Kevin toward his truck and my car. "I hear they arrested Marc Fontaine."

He frowned at me and nodded. "Don't see what good it's going to do, but they have to follow the law."

"It had to be self-defense," I said. "Marc wouldn't do something like that, some kind of premeditated kill."

"You know him?"

"A little. I sold my horse to them. But I wouldn't be surprised if Bud Wooten knew about the wolves."

Kevin unlocked his truck door. "Everybody knew. We had sightings reported all summer, all around here."

"You did?"

"It was just a matter of time. The fact that none of the rangers could confirm the sightings, in place, was a problem, but a short-term one. We'd have seen one, inside the park, in good time, especially after the first snowfall when we could really track them."

Carl's truck pulled up behind Kevin's. It was nearly full dark now, but the interior light illuminated him as he opened the truck's door, turned to his passenger, and laughed heartily. As he got out, the passenger called from the other side: "I thought you were going to pass out when I told you I forgot the water!"

The truck doors slammed. Kevin opened his own door and made to escape, but I grabbed the door handle. The woman came between the two trucks with a backpack slung over her shoulder and was still teasing Carl when they both saw us in the light of Kevin's interior lamp.

"Alix?" Carl stepped forward, his backpack under his arm, in cargo pants and a fleece vest. "Hey, Kevin."

"Carl." Kevin nodded. I was strangely mum. Perhaps a first even.

"Hey," Carl said again. He looked at Kevin, then back at me, then at the woman. For her part she stared at Carl, waiting pointedly. "Oh. This is Tara. This is Kevin Stoddard, he lives here, next door. And this is Alix Thorssen."

"Nice to meet you both."

Charmed, I'm sure. I straightened my shoulders. Only my name, no modifier. Interesting, Carl. "Been on a hike?" I managed to ask.

Carl opened his mouth, but Tara spoke first. "Up to Hanging Canyon. Took a picnic."

"Ah. The weather was nice?"

Tara was petite but muscular, sunglasses resting in her short black hair. She wore khaki hiking shorts and a T-shirt and didn't seem to mind the evening chill. "It rained a little. But it didn't bother us, did it, Carl?"

Carl seemed to have a tongue problem. His head dipped sideways as if he was trying to decipher whether rain bothered him. It wasn't unpleasant to watch. But I was getting cold, and I'd seen enough.

"I brought you a ticket to the wildlife auction," I said. "Kevin's got it."

Kevin, inching into the truck, pulled it from a pocket, thrusting it at Carl.

"I've got another. Do you want two?" I said, looking at my watch as if I had a big meeting soon. I did, with my pillow.

There was a longish pause, and I looked up in time to hear Tara say, "What do you think, Carl? Take me to the auction?"

Carl blushed, and even in the low light we all saw it. Kevin cleared his throat loudly and announced he had to go.

"Well, look, Tara. Here." I passed her an invitation. "If you don't plan to use it, just slip it in my mail slot at the Second Sun Gallery."

Her eyes widened. "Oh, that's you. Alix Thorssen."

"The one and only. See you, Carl."

As I walked to the Saab, Kevin's truck tires raked up gravel in a mad attempt to flee. He was almost as embarrassed as Carl. I smiled, thinking how sweet it was to see Carl blush. I'd done all right; I hadn't gotten too tongue-tied, hadn't made an ass of myself. But hell, the night was young.

As I strapped on my seat belt, Carl tapped his knuckles on the window. I rolled it down.

"Need another ticket?"

"Alix. Listen." He leaned down into the window space. "We just went on a hike, that's all. She's a mountain ranger, I take her up in the chopper to look for climbers."

"Good person to go hiking with. I bet she has strong legs." I turned on the engine, gave the choke a tweak.

Carl ran his hand through his hair, which was too short to muss. "So, about the auction. Can we go together? I can pick you up."

"I'm going with Maggie. Why don't you bring Tara? She seems eager. Maybe she's an art lover."

Carl leaned in close, the tendons in his neck tight. I smelled beer on his breath. "Why are you being like this?" he hissed.

I turned to him slowly and lit up a big smile. "Like what?"

Lying in bed later, staring at the same damn water stains on the same damn ceiling again, I thought how temporary the delight in maturity was. I had been so calm, so collected, and now I felt I might explode with anger. With betrayal, with stupidity and naïveté. And yet I'd pushed him away; there was nothing I could do. I had made my bed, and here I lay, alone.

Why couldn't I have just slapped him? That sounded excellent in hindsight. The fact that I'd never actually slapped anyone, ever, was a minor stumbling block. I'd faced down a couple of guns in my time, some miscreants and thieves and whackos, surely I could slap my boyfriend. Only he wasn't my boyfriend, and had never really been my boyfriend, if I was honest about it.

I rolled over and punched up the pillow. I didn't want to be honest. Or mature. Or calm or collected. I wanted pain, not just my own but somebody else's. I rolled back over and sighed. That was stupid. I thought about Queen, and James, and Audrey Kale. Derek Wylie. Marc Fontaine. There was plenty of pain in my little world; I didn't need to add to it.

I put the pillow on my stomach and frowned at the ceiling again. I was just too damn mature for my own good.

The telephone rang the next morning and woke me from my nest of twisted bedcovers. I untangled myself and stumbled into the kitchen. It was nine o'clock, and I had nowhere to be. Why wasn't that liberating?

I straightened at the sound of Sonny Garrett's voice. "We have some business to talk about," he said in a low voice. I imagined him looking furtively out at his secretary and cupping the mouthpiece.

"Do we?"

He ignored that. "Meet me at the Jenny Lake Lodge, one o'clock."

"Isn't it closed for the season?"

"On the porch. We'll talk."

"Just you and me?"

"That's right."

"Why out there? I can come to your office. Or let's just go up to the Flying V."

"One o'clock." He hung up.

My hand shook as I made coffee. Garrett scared me, with his icy stares and slick lawyer ways. What would happen out there? He wasn't going to have me whacked—that was too mafioso for this neck of the woods. He could threaten to whack me, a popular tactic though illegal.

Was this appointment validation of my so-called theory about Terry Vargas? Did I even need to hear what Sonny Garrett had to say? I was curious, yes, but was it necessary that I go? I drank my second cup of coffee and mulled it over.

In the end my curiosity about the way the whole thing would turn out overcame my better judgment. But I did call Peg Elliot and tell her what was going on. The coroner had a vested interest, and she was a public official; she should know. There was a long moment of silence when I mentioned Sonny Garrett.

"You aren't going alone, Alix." It was more a question than a command.

"Why? What do you know about Sonny Garrett?"

"Let's just say our paths have crossed. He's not a pleasant man, all business, all for the client."

"Do you remember him from the, um, the incident?"

"Back in 'seventy-five? No."

I had pushed down my own fear and couldn't let myself register Peg's. I had to go, I had to see what they offered, what they felt, what Terry Vargas felt about shooting his friend in the back of the head. Did he feel remorse, did he care? How did he live with himself?

"I'm going, Peg. I'll be careful. I just wanted you to know what was happening." So fearless, Alix, when the only reason for calling her was in case you didn't come back.

"What about that boyfriend of yours, the policeman? Can't you take him with you?"

"No. I can't."

I decided the best way to pretend this was just another business meeting was to carry on. To that end I put Dutch Abbott's clipping in my backpack and headed west to the old man's cabin on the edge of Teton Pass. I forgot chocolate, but intended to keep it brief.

The old man was outside chopping wood in the noontime sun. He squinted up at me and smiled. "The Hershey girl returns."

"Hi, Dutch." I set my backpack down on a log. "How are you today?"

"Not bad, a little rheumatism." He cocked his head. The dirty cowboy hat he wore slid sideways as if his head had shrunk with age. "You feel like splitting wood?"

Laying my jacket on the ground, I took the awl from him and

swung it hard on four or five pieces of wood. Winded, I paused. I didn't have time for this, I had to meet a lawyer.

"Don't stop on my account," Dutch said, returning from personal business in the woods. So I hacked away at a couple more logs, then set down the awl to stack the wood.

"Dutch? Tell me what you know about the Vargases. Terry and his father."

"Vargas? What you want with them?"

"Just curious. Have they lived here a long time?"

He took off the filthy hat and slapped his crusty Carharts on the knee, causing a cloud of dust to rise. He sat down on a rock. "Jeepers, it's warm today. Must be headed into a long, hard winter."

I looked at the old man a moment, his beard still at the four-day growth stage, still white. His blue eyes sparkled as he looked up at the sky. I picked up an armload of wood and carried it to his porch, arranging it carefully by the door. When I returned, I sat silently on the stump and waited.

Finally he cleared his throat and gave me a sidelong grin. "Okay. Percy Vargas. He came here after the war. He was some army buddy of Bud Wooten's, I guess. They used to have Saturday-night rodeo up at their spreads. Mostly at Wooten's, it was bigger. Bud sold Percy the Flying V, to keep it private, you know. That was when they was doing the last round of buying up for the park, and Bud musta heard about the rules for keeping your ranch private. What I heard was, he sold part of his spread to Percy's boy, even though he was just a kid." Dutch squinted at me. "The ranch stays private as long as the owner is alive. Same with leases."

"Bud Wooten owned both ranches? He must have had a lot of land."

"Oh, he did. Too much, some said. Him and his old man wouldn't sell to the Rockefellers or the government, wanted to keep it all free. Bud tried to organize all the ranchers not to sell. But the tourists started coming and that was that. He helped start the elk hunts inside the park. You know about that?"

"Yeah. Is Grand Teton the only national park that allows hunting?"

"Could be. Percy loved to hunt, took down animals from here to Alaska and back. Great shot," Dutch said, admiration in his voice.

"Terry, too?"

"Not bad. His old man taught him well."

How good a shot did a man have to be to shoot a kid in the back? The bile rose, thinking of Terry Vargas and Derek Wylie, in the woods. "Mostly gave him that chip on his shoulder though."

"Terry?"

"A pain-in-the-ass kid. His mother died giving birth to him, and the old man spoiled him rotten. He grew up thinking he owned the goddamn world."

Everything I'd heard about Terry Vargas confirmed my own opinion. This meet with Garrett made me jumpy. I stood up, looked at my watch, and pulled the clipping of Dutch's column carefully from my backpack.

"Thanks for letting me borrow this, Dutch. And for all the information." I slung the strap of the pack over my shoulder. "Danny was right, you are a steel trap of Jackson history. Have you ever thought about writing a book about it?"

The old man chuckled as he pushed himself up off the rock. "I know too much. Somebody'd come gunning for me, for sure."

The words pounded in my head as I tried and failed to steer around potholes on the way down the hill from Dutch Abbott's cabin. Sonny Garrett was a respectable citizen. Surely a lawyer of his stature had too much to lose in harming a mere slip of a girl such as myself. I smiled and tried to collect myself. Then flexed my biceps. I was no slip of a girl, nosiree. I suddenly wished I hadn't gotten rid of the gun my mother had given me years before.

So it can get you in trouble again? Christ. Focus, girl. I was better off using my wits. But by the time I crawled through town and out the other side, my confidence had leaked away, leaving me grasping for images of Blue Wolf to distract myself. But today, in the midday sun, the wolf lay somewhere in a shadow, out of sight.

✦

I was late.

Twenty minutes late, to be exact. The Tetons stretched hard and glossy like an artificial set of teeth against the mouth of the sky. I tried not to look at them, thinking I should have taken the Moose-Wilson Road despite the havoc it would have wreaked on the Saab's shocks. My personal shocks felt shot as I pulled off the park road into the clearing that held the log house and outbuildings of Jenny Lake Lodge. The big white Cadillac sat in the shade of a tall spruce at one end of the parking lot. I pulled in next to it and got out.

A chill wind blew down off the mountain and across the lake. I stood still for a moment, smelling the piny scent, the promise of winter. The air felt good, fresh. I blinked, my face washing in the breeze. Then, with a gulp of it, I walked to the lodge.

"Miss Thorssen."

The voice came out of the shadows of the small porch. Sonny Garrett sat in a rocking chair, elegant legs crossed, Italian loafers poised. He looked relaxed, even friendly. Before I wondered about that and had misgivings, I felt relieved. Then the tension set in again. He wasn't worried. What did he have planned? Was he alone?

I looked back at the Cadillac but couldn't see anyone inside. The parking lot was empty. The lodge itself was closed, a sign delineating its short season: June 1–September 1. The shutters were closed.

"An odd place for a business meeting, Mr. Garrett," I said and crossed my arms defensively.

"Have a seat, won't you?"

He looked blow-dried and spiffy in his pearl gray suit. White shirt, sapphire tie with small somethings—ducks?—in an allover pattern. Maybe they were small dollar signs, that would be more appropriate.

I hesitated then sat. The old split-log rockers were weather-worn and scratchy. I took a tentative rock back and forth. No big deal, just me and ol' Sonny doing the rocking chair thing. My hands gripped the armrests, and I kept quiet.

The sound of a car passing beyond the trees, the wind high in the limbs, the creak of the chairs. Those were our companions for a good long minute. Then Garrett said, "You mentioned reparations."

I stopped rocking. "Reparations—uh, yes."

"What did you have in mind?" he said. He stopped rocking too, and looked at me with a hard snakelike stare meant to stop hearts cold in the courtroom.

I stared back, then up at the mountains. Kicking off my clogs, I had a sudden urge to tuck up my feet and cuddle into the chair, so I did. Sonny Garrett watched with a thin smile.

"How's Audrey today, have you heard?" I asked.

"No, I haven't heard." He squirmed. "What sort of reparations did you have in mind, Miss Thorssen?"

"What sort? Oh." I played with my toes. "Justice, Mr. Garrett. That sort."

He gave a low, cynical chuckle. "Justice. How very quaint."

"Seems to have gone out of style."

Quiet descended again for a long pause. Then Garrett put both loafered feet on the wood porch floor with a slap of leather. "Look here. My client feels badly about this, although why I don't know. He wants to know what can be done. I advised him against it. Justice after twenty-five years is a very creaky concept, entirely too tangled."

"You said Terry Vargas wasn't your client."

Snake eyes again. "Look—"

"Is he or isn't he?"

"I can't tell you that."

"That's good enough," I said, smiling.

Garrett was glaring, silver eyebrows scrunched against his broad forehead. "Keep an open mind. It's a big wide world out there." He sat back, drummed his fingers on the armrests. "What are we going to do about this?"

"I don't know." I put my feet back in my clogs, no longer comfortable here. Garrett didn't scare me anymore, but something did. "The usual won't work here, Sonny. Money won't cure it."

He scratched the back of his hand. "Money goes a long way toward a cure. Maybe you want to discuss this with your client. Think about retirement, old age."

"Nothing to discuss. Money never came up. It was never an issue."

"You could be making a terrible mistake, dragging all this out again. It's been buried a long time, and that means a lot is at stake to keep it buried."

"It wasn't something I asked for. But whether or not I have anything to do with it, the truth will come out." I stood up and pulled my jacket straight. "You made a big mistake when you didn't let the shooting get investigated. That put a bad light on it, and it's shining still, even over the distance in time. Only now it's even started to stink, and it's a real bad stink."

The lawyer listened to my little speech politely, his face a study of grim blankness. I grimaced inwardly at the mess of bad metaphors but clenched my jaw. He stood up and faced me, smoothing his suit trousers and rebuttoning his jacket.

"I told my client I'd speak to you, and I have. I'm sorry we can't do business. I just hope, Miss Thorssen, that none of that stink stays on you. I won't be the only sorry one. You can bet on that."

I lay in bed that night, after surprising Maggie with a rare culinary impulse that played out as seared tuna steaks and rice, and tried to sleep. It wouldn't come. Despite my best efforts at normalcy the rest of the day, everything was off-kilter. An afternoon of serious painting (finally!), then domestication and friendship and dress-swapping, all for naught.

In the dark I smelled turpentine faintly on my forearms, a fishy smell on my fingers. My stomach felt satisfied and warm, my head buzzing with wine, the apartment full of Maggie's recovered good humor. Outside the village lay still and silent, the stars hidden under a blanket of clouds.

I put on my robe, a new one from my brother Erik, and padded downstairs in my wool socks. The gallery was dim, only the security light near the door shining. I flipped the switch in my office and unlocked the padlock on the storeroom. Queen's paintings were still there, the three of them. I picked up the wolf, *Imminent Domain*, propped it on my desk chair, and stepped back.

What was it about this wolf, Queen's wolf? Had he been caught? Was that what I was feeling tonight, his pain and fear? Was it Derek Wylie coming back to tell me that he needed justice, that his mother needed release?

I know that. I understand. I tried to breathe deeply, to relax, but my breaths came in gulps. I rubbed my arms, hearing Garrett's words again. *Hope none of that stink stays on you.* I sank to the floor and grabbed my knees.

Someone was afraid tonight. Someone hurt.

14

THE violet in Paolo's hair was turning out perfect. Too bad about his nose.

I stared at the small photograph, the one I'd been fingering in my pencil drawer for months, tacked now to the wall of the studio. Difficult to process out the emotion, to see an object or person as just a series of lights and darks, streaks and shades, to compartmentalize a human spirit into lines and squares and dabs and dribbles. I'd been struggling with it since early morning and was proud of myself, leaving the apartment at the crack of dawn despite a restless night. This was what my painting week was for, me and my painting. Not Queen's paintings, not Queen's pain. Not the wildlife auction, not Carl Mendez's hikes. Just me and tubes of oils. No bullshit, no requests, no problems.

My stomach growled; I ignored it. I gulped down the rest of the thermos cup of coffee and poured out more. What time was it? I hadn't worn my watch on purpose. I stared at the dusty portable radio and shook my head. No, stay on task. The phone was off the hook. The sun was high in the sky. I was painting.

I shook out my cramping shoulder, unaccustomed to long painting sessions. Paolo needed work, he was calling me. But I had to stop, go outside. The day was cool and invigorating, or should have been. I messed around in Luca's garden for a minute, watering some dead flowers, splashed icy water on my face and neck. Then I went back inside and painted for another hour.

Outside again, I sat in the sun on the stoop and leaned against the door. By the angle of the sun I knew it was getting into mid-afternoon. I would have to quit soon. Maggie was coming by the apartment to pick me up for the auction, and help with Queen's paintings. We'd hatched a plan last night to slip them into the auction lineup, but we had to prepare.

I closed my eyes. The warm sun and fatigue washed over me simultaneously. The next thing I remember, Maggie was shaking me, her face close and frowning.

"Alix, are you all right?"

I lurched forward. "What time is it?"

She looked at her watch. "Three-thirty. Are you okay?"

I stood up, and she followed. "I just fell asleep. I thought maybe it was time for the auction already. I've been painting all day, come see Paolo. He's almost done."

I opened the door and stepped into the studio. Maggie hesitated, a queer look on her face, then came in too. She eyed me like I was sick, then turned to the easel.

We stared at the Argentine's face, laughing, stirring beans in his undershirt. He looked so happy. I'd painted him in vibrant colors—orange, purple, sunshine yellow. He was alive in those colors. I still didn't like his nose, and had opened my mouth to say so when Maggie gasped.

"Oh, my God," she whispered then burst into tears.

We'd cried plenty over Paolo, but not in a long time. I put my hand on her arm. She said, "It's just like Morris."

I let out an astonished laugh. "Mags, I'm not that bad, am I? It's Paolo."

She wiped her eyes and turned to me. "You didn't hear about Morris Kale?"

I stepped back from the easel and stared at her, speechless. Last night's vibe of pain and fear and confusion slapped me. It hadn't been just my imagination.

"He—" She stopped, gulping air to calm herself. "Alix. He shot himself last night."

I sat down. "What happened?"

"He left a note, I heard. Everybody's been calling me. My mother had to come over and lie on my couch in the office. She hates suicides." Maggie rolled her eyes. "We all do."

"Suicide?" I shook my head. It wasn't possible. Of course he was in trouble about Audrey's shooting, but that would be cleared up. She wouldn't testify against him. She hadn't died, had she? I felt sick, my heartbeat loud in my chest. I thought about her greasy ex, Corky. Maybe his being around had made Morrie—no. Ridiculous.

"Poor Frankie. That mixed-up kid," Maggie said. "Good thing his sister's still here."

"Yes. She's very nice."

Maggie looked at me closely. "You sound terrible. I thought you'd already have heard. I'm sorry." She leaned down and held me for a moment. I felt weak, hands limp at my sides, unable to hug back.

She straightened up and looked around the studio, suddenly businesslike. "Okay, let's pack it in here. Lids on tubes, brushes wiped down. You put 'em in turpentine or something? Okay, let's do it."

She set me to tasks, and I performed them mechanically, numb. I kept getting a picture of Morris in my head. When he came to the door of his daughter's room as Audrey was showing me around the house. We'd been admiring that small painting, and he stared at it with something strange in his eyes. He'd turned to me and barked about Terry starting the vote, and I'd run back behind him, his footsteps silent against the thick carpeting.

As Maggie handed me my jacket and picked up my thermos, she peered into an empty wastebasket. "No food. You eat today?"

I shook my head. "Just coffee."

A few minutes later, as she handed me the bag of Big Macs

and fries in the McDonald's drive-through, I looked into the warm, steamy grease and said, "Morris wouldn't kill himself."

Maggie turned her Jeep back toward the town square. "It's hard to take. It always is."

"No, really." I popped six fries in my mouth. "He must have been murdered."

She frowned. "Hand me a Big Mac."

"Or it was an accident. He was cleaning his gun, or Frankie was using it and Morrie was taking it away from him. Something like that."

We stopped at the light. "He left a note, Alix. I already talked to Charlie Frye, he told me. There's no doubt."

"Somebody could have made him write it."

"Alix." Maggie pulled into a parking place right in front of the Second Sun and turned off the car. "Take a bite of that sandwich, that's an order." She waited while I unwrapped the hamburger and took a huge bite. "Now, look at me. We have to go to the auction tonight. I don't want you bringing up murder theories to Morris's friends. Most of his close ones probably won't even be there, but we have to go. We—"

"I'm not going."

Maggie gave me a sympathetic look. "We don't have to. I thought they'd probably call it off, but Candace came over to pick up her check and told me they'd polled the committee, and they all felt like Morris would have wanted them to go on with it."

"They didn't poll me."

"You had your phone off the hook." Maggie laid her hand on my arm. "What about Queen? You told her you'd get those paintings in."

"Fuck a duck." I threw the hamburger back in the bag. "Everything that has to do with this auction has turned to shit. Every goddamn thing."

Maggie was smiling, her black eyes cleared from crying now. I glared at her. "What? What is so goddamn funny?"

"Nothing." She grinned wider. "You just sound like yourself again."

✦

Walking up the wide stairs into the vast marble lobby of the Jackson Lake Lodge never failed to move me, and despite anger, denial, sorrow, too much coffee, animal fat, and bad hair, to-night was no exception. The mountains were framed by the majestic windows. In the marshland below, a moose waded through the reeds. Hawks and ospreys soared in the evening sky.

Maggie and I each carried a framed, wrapped painting. The lobby was deserted tonight. Only those headed early to the Auction for Wildlife meandered in the direction of the large meeting hall off to the right. I nodded to several members of the com-mittee—Candace Gundy, the banker, the artist—but no one seemed eager to chat.

I couldn't get my mind off Morris Kale. It seemed so senseless, so impossible to accept. I decided just to go with that feeling, not try to explain it, and see if I could get through the evening. I tried not to think about Audrey or their kids, but that was hard. Maggie had been chatty and distracting, and I loved her for it.

We had concocted a simple plan to leave only a number on the wrapper of the two Queen Johns paintings and put them behind the auctioneer as if just waiting. The rest of the pieces were sitting against the walls, on tabletops, around the room. Art lovers and potential buyers could view them as they drank and ate, before the auction started. One obstacle remained, how to get the auctioneer to change what Terry Vargas had no doubt told him: that the Queen Johns paintings had been pulled.

"I say we just hogtie Jake Laughlin in the little boys room. I can be stand-in auctioneer," Maggie said, puffing out her small chest. "I can do it, sure." She looked very nice in my green cash-mere sweater and her black velvet jeans, but she wasn't an auc-tioneer. She tossed back her black hair and began to mumble into her fist as if auctioning cattle.

"It's a thought," I said. "Is there anyone else, though?"

The room was still nearly empty, the banquet folks putting out food on the buffet tables and setting up napkins on tables. Someone that Terry Vargas wouldn't expect to be auctioneer, someone unconnected with me. Candace Gundy was in a tight clinch with the Vargas girl, Georgia, at the other end of the room. I wondered what that was about, and figured it was Morris. A wave of loss washed over me, and I sat on the edge of the auctioneer's platform with Maggie.

"Who's coming?" she asked. I shrugged. No one I'd given tickets to had given me a definite. All of the committee members would be Vargas-shy. All but Candace maybe, and she was too flighty to depend on for this delicate task.

Maggie and I sat, contemplating, on the edge of the platform. The room began to fill; people began to load plates with food. Maggie dragged me through the buffet line, keeping up a torrent of chatter about people she knew as they came in. I had no interest in food but ate some vegetables to make her happy. We sat at an empty table and munched and tried to think of a creative way to get Laughlin to auction the paintings.

"This sucks," she said. "We are a couple of no-minds tonight."

"We'll think of something. Go get us some wine."

"Of course. The essential ingredient."

While she was at the bar across the room, Danny Bartholomew and his wife Geri caught my eye. They looked out of place, and a little nervous, in the room filling with diamonds and leather and Gucci and Rolexes. I waved them over to the table. Danny wore his usual jeans and shirt with a nice plaid vest, but Geri had dressed up in a flattering short blue dress.

"Sit down. You guys look great. I mean you, Geri."

They pulled out chairs and sat down. "Thanks, Alix," Geri said. She was shorter than Danny, with cropped blond hair and an infectious laugh. But now she frowned at me, then at Danny. In the silence I crunched hard on a carrot.

"We heard about Morris," Danny said finally.

"Didn't we all."

He looked at me as if trying to figure out if I was losing it. I smiled. "A hell of a way to go," I said. "Not my choice."

Danny and Geri nodded solemnly. What was there to say about a suicide? We were all sorry as hell. But what we felt meant nothing. We were just left to pick up our lives and go on.

"You hear about the note?" I asked Danny.

Geri stood up suddenly. "I'll get you a sandwich," she told her husband and moved off toward the buffet table. Danny watched her go, his face tight with anger.

"Her brother committed suicide when he was nineteen. This brought it all back," he said.

I watched her small hands at the tableware, her careful motions. "Fuck."

"You can say that again." Danny sat back and sighed. "What note?"

"Morris left one. That's why it was so cut-and-dried."

He eyed me, his keen black eyes intense, then rubbed his beard. "There was no note. But I talked to several of the deputies who went out—they were pretty sure. They have to do the usual forensics, powder tests and all, but it was suicide."

"Without a note? How can you be sure?"

"Only a small fraction leave notes. You've been watching too many old movies. The deputies say it happened late at night, two or three in the morning, everybody was in bed. The stepdaughter heard it and found him and called it in immediately."

"Not Frankie?"

"No, the girl."

"That's something, I guess." It seemed like Morris really cared about Frankie, really tried with him. But what did I know? I could have made all kinds of educated guesses about that family before today, and they'd all be wrong. "They tell Audrey?"

Danny shook his head. "They're going to wait till she's stronger. That's what the doctor recommended."

"But she's better?"

"Looks like she'll pull through." Danny gazed off at the ceiling, frowned, then raised his eyebrows.

"What?"

"Just wondering if it was the same gun. Not that it matters now."

A tap on my shoulder made me turn to find Peg Elliot carrying full plates of food in both hands. We snagged an extra chair and pulled her into our circle. Danny went to help Geri at the buffet table as Peg carefully buttered a roll.

"Tell me what happened," she said, her iron curls hard with hair spray tonight. She looked older, as if remembering what she should have done years ago when Derek Wylie died had aged her overnight. "With Sonny Garrett," she whispered.

"He's not here, is he?" I scanned the room and didn't see him, then took a sip of wine. "He wouldn't say for sure it was Terry Vargas."

"Just being cagey, I suppose."

"Maybe. Whoever his client is, he wanted to pay me off."

"Rich, then."

"Somebody with enough clout to stop the investigation."

The room was full of rich people, like the banker on the auction committee whose grandfather had started the bank, or the gaggle of film people like Maggie's ex-boyfriend James. Those boys could be any one of dozens of rich middle-aged men who lived in Jackson Hole twenty-five years ago. Why should it be Terry Vargas, just because a very old man seemed to remember the name? But it was my only clue, and the man seemed to ask for it with his arrogance.

"Terrible about Mr. Kale," Peg said, shaking her head. "The autopsy's set for the morning."

"Everybody says suicide."

"Can't be sure until we do the tests," she said. "You concerned?"

I shrugged. Should I be? Morris Kale had so few enemies. My chest ached thinking about Frankie and Audrey and their grief.

Peg patted my arm. "I'll let you know. Soon as we're done."

Maggie came back with wine at the same time Geri and Danny returned with plates of food. By silent consent we stopped talking about the suicide and returned to plotting the sale of Queen's paintings. Maggie and Geri both agreed to start the bidding on either painting if no one else did, and I told them if by chance they actually bought one, I would buy it from them. That made us all feel conspiratorial and brilliant, and the wine helped too.

When Jake Laughlin waddled through the crowd on his way to

the podium and the teenagers from the Jackson Hole High School art club pulled on their white gloves to carry the artworks forward in an orderly stream for auction, we were still stumped about how to interrupt Jake. But we no longer cared. Someone from the back of the room sent us up two bottles of wine, one red, one white, and we managed to drink them merrily.

We had located the spots in the lineup for Queen's two paintings in the elaborate brochure. The printing was slick and colorful, but I looked in vain for some attribution to yours truly for her awesome descriptions and general good deeds. Terry Vargas strikes again, whose name could be found almost everywhere, even above Morris Kale's on the opening page. I hadn't seen Vargas yet, but with Georgia here, I was sure he'd show up sooner or later to get his standing ovation.

I had been sipping carefully on my wine, since it sometimes had a tendency to make me weepy. I didn't need to get that going tonight, I needed balls, and a small amount of wine gave just the right fortitude. I was prepared to spring up from the audience when the time came and charge Jake Laughlin like a cow elk in heat. Maggie gave me a toast with her wine across the table, and drained her glass.

Jake began in his loud and toneless way to auction off the pieces. Paintings and sculptures sold, some for thousands more than anticipated, some for thousands less. Not all the artists would be happy; some would even buy them back. Usually I kept track of prices for future reference, but tonight I was too distracted. The two craft-paper-wrapped squares behind the platform had all my attention.

The first Queen Johns was next to last before the end of the half. I tensed as the sculpture before it, a sweet little bronze of two playful river otters, sold for an ungodly sum. I could see it now on a doctor's reception counter, his latest tax deduction. May he live long and prosper. And buy more art next year.

There was a pause, a rifling of paper through the room as pages were turned. Jake looked down at his notes through tiny John Lennon glasses sitting precariously on his bulbous nose. He began to announce the next piece.

"And now the last piece before—"

I stood up. I was sucking in a big breath when the shout came from the back of the room. Jake stopped his speech. Heads turned to the purple muumuu and streaming white hair, black cowboy boots under the dress striding up the aisle. Across the room Candace Gundy threw her napkin on the tabletop, her hard blue eyes flashing. I caught her eye and nodded toward the podium, where Queen was headed.

"As a special treat, mister auctioneer, sir," Queen was saying as she walked toward him, "I would like to carry my own painting, to show it to these good people."

In the back of the room, Georgia slipped out the doors to the lobby. Candace and I converged on the platform, where Jake Laughlin stood at the podium, his mouth sagging. He swallowed hard and looked down at his notes. He seemed to collect himself as Queen stepped up on the platform and crowded in beside him.

"Madam, please. I am the auctioneer, this is not the way we do it here, if you will please take your seat."

"I see nothing wrong with holding my own painting for the folks," Queen said. She was as tall as Jake but seemed larger, more vivid, especially in the purple muumuu and that amazing hair. Her silver bracelets jangled as she stretched out her arms beatifically to the crowd. "You see anything wrong with that?" She smiled, they smiled back. They'd never seen nothing like Queen Johns.

Behind the platform I tore the paper from the first painting I reached. Jake was mumbling into Queen's ear. She was ignoring him, still eating up the crowd with her grin.

"What a magnificent group of art lovers you have gathered here," Queen said loudly. "And wildlife lovers. People who care about the mountains, the sage plains, the elk, the griz, the moose, the eagle. Even the wolf." A stirring in the back of the room made me peer over the painting. "Isn't that right, Bud Wooten? Even the wily wolf. We love them all."

The rancher was sitting at a large table near the back. Not surprising he would be here; he was one of the founders of the Land Trust. Several other cowboy types sat with him. Even Marc Fontaine. My God, Marc Fontaine was here. He was out of jail and at a flashy society event with his boss. What torture.

Wooten stood suddenly, his face red with anger, and turned to Terry Vargas, who stood with Georgia at the back. Vargas frowned and crossed his arms. Wooten walked up to him, spoke into his face. Vargas listened, gave him a small push back, and stepped around him.

"I'm sorry, everyone," Vargas said loudly. "Queen Johns removed her pieces from the auction. We'll move on—" Vargas walked to the nearest table and pointed to an open brochure held by a woman. "To the last piece, a fabric design titled *Flathead Lake*, by the Montana artist Dana Broussard. Number 46, Mr. Laughlin, please."

Candace Gundy had been standing, arms crossed and face a terror, on the other side of Jake Laughlin. She couldn't contain herself any longer, and pushed the auctioneer sideways. Queen Johns caught his arm, righting him, and held his bicep protectively against her bosom.

Candace's voice boomed through the loudspeakers. "Ladies and gentlemen. Queen Johns did not remove her paintings. That was done as part of a personal vendetta by the chairman of this auction. But now," she said, becoming more articulate and less full of spit as she calmed, "let us remember a man we all miss tonight, whose warm friendship and quiet generosity made this auction the success it is, our colleague, our friend Morris Kale. In his memory I suggest we put aside differences and get on with the auction to raise funds to help this valley's wildlife. That's why we're here, right?!"

"Damn straight," somebody hollered.

"Would you, Alix?" Candace turned to me. I glanced back at Terry Vargas. He stood against the wall again, an odd expression of compliance on his face. Maybe he missed Morris too.

Candace took the pass-off of Jake Laughlin from Queen, as Queen took the painting from me. It was her winter landscape. I stepped to the microphone and began to describe it. In a few minutes it had sold for $3,600, and we all were beaming. We placed Jake back in position behind the podium and stepped back, arms linked in feminine solidarity. Somehow Jake auctioned off the last piece in his limp fashion and stepped away in a daze. I announced the fifteen-minute break, and the room exploded in chatter. Before she could step down, I grabbed Candace's arm and gave it a squeeze.

"Thanks," I whispered. She winked.

A strong urge to hide out in the ladies' rest room came over me. I plowed through the milling crowd toward the doors to the lobby. The ladies' room was downstairs, a short hike away, and I would probably pass Terry Vargas on the way. I kept my head down and buffaloed through. I should talk to Marc Fontaine but didn't really want to here, with newspaper people and his boss around. I should be looking after Queen too. Where had she disappeared to? I just felt like hiding for a minute after my fifteen seconds in the spotlight. But in the lobby overheated voices made me slow my pace.

Georgia and Candace were nose-to-nose near the shuttered coffee shop on the far side of the lobby. The willowy Georgia was shaking her finger in the shorter woman's face. Candace exploded back at her, expletives included. A small crowd was forming, as if fisticuffs were next. Nobody wanted to miss a catfight.

I frowned at the gawkers and pushed through. When I reached Candace, she was telling Georgia in no uncertain terms what a spoiled bimbo and misogynist bitch she was. You had to give Georgia credit; she didn't even flinch.

"Come on, Candace," I said, pulling her away. She yanked her arm out of my grasp.

"I'm not done with her yet." Candace was huffing like she might explode.

"Yes, you are. She's not the enemy," I said.

Georgia crossed her arms and gave a slick smile. "That's right. The enemy is the white male chauvinist NRA fundamentalist anti-abortion racist pigs."

Candace leveled her gaze at Georgia. "And the women who suck their cocks."

Georgia's smile drooped. A smattering of applause rose from

the crowd. I grabbed Candace again, dragged her away to the rest room. While she was splashing water on her face, Maggie burst in, laughing.

"God, Candace, that was great!"

"Don't encourage her. We still have another of Queen's paintings to auction off." I startled. "Is somebody watching it?"

"Don't worry. I gave it to Danny and Geri to guard." Maggie checked her lipstick in the mirror, watching Candace run wet fingers through her spiky hair. "I see the wolf killer is here."

Candace tensed. "What? The cowboy?"

"Sitting with the big boss, Bud Wooten. That's what Queen was talking about, loving the wolf. Didn't you—"

"Get out of my way." Candace pushed me aside roughly as she ran for the exit. I could hear her footsteps on the steps back up to the lobby.

I rolled my eyes at Maggie. "Good going. Now she's off to pick another fight."

"Oh. She's the one Marc thought was throwing blood on his gate, wasn't she?"

"And on me, remember?" Maggie and I washed our hands. I rolled my eyes at her in the mirror. "Do you think we'll make it out of here alive?"

Somehow we did. The bidding on Queen Johns's wolf painting went sky-high. She insisted on holding it like the other one, roving around the tables, showing it to the admiring crowd. I didn't have to auction it this time, Jake Laughlin knew he was beat. He got close to six thousand for it, so I was happy, Queen was happy, the committee was happy.

Was everybody happy? Not quite. Georgia and Terry left as Jake began to auction *Imminent Domain*, their disapproval thick on their faces. It must have killed Vargas to not get his way in front of all these people. And with sweet Georgia defending him too.

Bud Wooten gave Candace the evil eye every time she passed by the Bar-T-Bar table. Her arms were fisted and stiff at her sides as she glared at the cowboys, then went on to pick up a napkin or an olive at the buffet table. I was surprised Wooten could intimidate her, but grateful for the lack of further violence.

The auction kept going, and my interest waned. The room was warm with too many people. Danny and Geri said they had to relieve the baby-sitter and went home. Peg Elliot left at halftime, and Maggie was chatting up an old high school beau. I had to get some air.

Outside on the terrace the moon was shining, half full but bright in the dark autumn sky. The air was cold, with a west wind blowing up from the marshes, smelling of fish and bird nests and wet moose. I leaned on the railing and took gulps of air before I heard the match striking in the shadows behind me and saw Marc Fontaine light up a hand-rolled cigarette.

He walked up to the railing and stood next to me without a word, taking a deep drag on the cigarette and blowing it out. Finally I said, "Surprised to see you here, Marc."

His eyes flicked at me, then back at the black water, the mountains beyond. "Command performance. Boss wants us showing no shame, no fear."

"Ah." What was it like to work for a man like Bud Wooten? He sounded like a tyrant. "You weren't in long, were you? He bailed you out?"

Marc nodded quickly. "Just overnight."

"I'm sorry. I never thought it would come to this."

"You and me neither, Alix." He let out his breath long and mournfully.

We talked for a minute about Farley and Hal and Valkyrie, then he stubbed out his cigarette on the stone terrace under his boot, gave me a sad smile, and went back inside. I felt hollow, like something bad was going to happen to Marc and nobody could do a damn thing about it. It made me angry. It was ten o'clock, and I should have been tired after my long painting day, the tragic news, the auction, but I felt a weird buzz. Things still undone, things that mattered. I turned back into the lobby of the lodge, wondering what the vibe meant.

I stuck my head inside the doors to the auction. Jake Laughlin looked worse for wear, a high sheen on his balding head and sweat rings on his shirt. Marc sat with Bud Wooten again, very still, hands in his lap. Maggie was nowhere to be seen, nor Queen. Just before I closed the door, Candace Gundy rose from her chair and charged toward me.

I held the door as she stalked through. Her heavy boots thudded on the stone. She had dressed up a little for the occasion, in khakis and a blue batik blouse. She paused in the darkened lobby. Small glass candleholders on cocktail tables and dimmed wall sconces made the cavernous room shadowy. The moon reflected off the dark marble floor through the windows. Candace squinted at its glow, then at me.

"Almost over," I said, tilting my head at the closed doors. "Thank God."

Candace walked to the nearest Navajo-print chair and sat down.

And began to cry.

I watched, stunned for a moment, then sat down in the chair next to her. She sobbed silently for a minute, then seemed to remember where she was. Her tears turned off as quickly as they'd turned on, and she wiped her face with the heel of her hand.

"It's that damn Morris," she said angrily. "How could he do this?"

I'd been trying to not think about Morris all evening. I bit my lip.

Candace went on, spitting her words. "It's like he hated this auction, hated all of us, to do it right before. Like everything we did was in vain, useless. I can't help it, I take that really personally, you know? I have dedicated my whole fucking life to wildlife, and here we're raising money for the animals, for feeding the elk, for paying off ranchers, for keeping species alive. Alive!! I mean, isn't that what we're about? Life? And what does he do? He goes and blasts his motherfucking brains out right before the auction. I could kill him for that." She threw herself back in the chair and stretched out her boots, slamming her heels on the rug.

"Why, Alix? Why?" She glared at me with those icy blue eyes. "Can you fucking explain it to me?"

I shook my head slowly. I didn't want to explain anything, I couldn't.

"Why don't you go home, Candace? This is over for us."

Her face reddened. "Over? I'll say. Do you believe that asshole Vargas? And now he's saying he feels so bad because he and Morris have been friends for fucking years—like we even believe that Vargas has a heart? That he cares about anyone but himself and his guns and that—that cunt—"

I stood up to cut her off. "Go home, Candace. Do you need a ride? I'm going as soon as I round up Maggie. Can I give you a lift?"

Rubbing her face, Candace walked down the lobby stairs to the doors. She said she had driven her own truck, pointing out a suspiciously familiar navy Ford pickup. I walked her out to make sure she was only angry, not drunk and angry. She surprised me by giving me a quick hug before she drove away.

Her tirade left me rattled as I walked back through the doors and found Maggie and Queen coming out of the ladies' rest room together. They were laughing and talking, in high spirits.

"There she is," Maggie said, grabbing my wrist. "Do you mind if I ride back with Sid, Alix? Will you be all right? Queen needs a ride, and I told her you were going that way, more or less. Okay?"

Maggie gave me her keys and went back up the stairs to find her old boyfriend. Queen and I walked through the moonlight to Maggie's Jeep. I would have preferred not to drive tonight, the way I was feeling, but maybe having to focus on the white glare of headlights against pavement was just what I needed. Regardless, I got it, down through Moran Junction, across Antelope Flats, turning off to the Gros Ventre, and up the long hill to Queen's cabin. She was quiet, and I felt wrung dry. I looked over at her as we drove, her serene face in the blue glare of the moon, her eyes scanning the hillsides as we climbed.

I pulled the Jeep up to her cabin and left the engine running. "I'm glad you came, Queen, and that the paintings sold so well."

"Wowed 'em, didn't we?" She was smiling.

"The wolf was hot. I knew he would be."

She made no move to leave the Jeep but gazed across the moon-silvered grass. "He hasn't come back," she said softly.

"He will. When things quiet down."

"No. I saw him in the woods, far up on the mountain. His head was down, and he was on his way." She turned to me, and I saw tears in her eyes. My heart thumped hard in my chest. "He's not coming back here. He told me. Derek isn't coming back."

I held my breath. Her gray eyes pleaded with me. "It's Derek, don't you see? The wolf came back here, he smiled at me. I took care of him. It's Derek come back. To see me." Her voice trailed off in a wisp. "And now he's gone."

We stared out the windshield for a long moment. Then her strong hand gripped my arm. "They can't catch him, they'll hurt him. I have to find him, I have to!! He's my son, my only son." A sob choked her throat. "Oh, Derek."

"Take it easy." I smoothed her hair like she was a child. "It's all right."

"No, it's not!" she shouted, batting my hand away. "Derek was here, and I scared him away. You said it yourself, the blasts of the gun scared him. Derek was always afraid of loud noises. He hated hunting. Why did he go hunting? Why did he go that day?" She began to sob again. I had no answers, and in the vacuum of my knowledge, she had concocted her own reality.

"I don't know, Queen. I wish I did, I'm sorry."

"Everyone is so sorry." Her voice was crazy and bitter. It cut through me like a knife. "Derek is dead and everyone is so so-ooo sorry. They don't know what happened and they don't care. Because Derek is dead and you're not. You're not, I'm not. Just Derek. Derek is dead."

She gulped air for a second. "But he came back. He can roam the forests now. He's strong and brave, until someone scares him with guns and traps. I scared him, my own son! I'm sorry, Derek. I'm sorry."

She hung her head against her chest and covered her face with her hands. I put a gentle hand against her hair again. For a moment we sat like that, quiet. Then she jumped from the car without another word. I jumped out too, but she was opening her cabin door by the time I hit the dirt.

"Queen, please, are you—"

She slammed the door shut behind her.

15

THE apartment was dark, only the red blinking light on the answering machine, like a heartbeat in the blackness. I sat on the edge of the sofa, trying to reconcile the two Queens I'd seen tonight, the proud, charismatic artist, unafraid and regal, and the broken woman, the mother who had lost her only son and her grip on reality. I shut my eyes and tried to meld the two halves in my mind, then shook my head and stood up.

All the way home I'd thought about my own wolf experience. I didn't think of him as "my" wolf, as Queen did. Yet there was something I was missing, something I couldn't quite touch over the passage of years. The wolf had seared my heart, made me want to live again. Something like that had happened to Queen too, but she and I were different. Our two wolves had touched us in a way humans never could. Was that what bound me to her, our mutual alienation?

The lamp clicked loudly, but the light was warm and welcome. I felt alone after Queen's outburst, after Candace's passion, after Maggie's laughter had faded. Carl hadn't come to the auction at all, with or without the mountain ranger with excellent legs. I

rubbed my eyes and wondered if it was over. I didn't have it in me
to dig deep about it tonight.

Working out kinks in my shoulders, I walked to the answering
machine on the kitchen counter. Three messages, it reported. I hit
the button. The first was Maggie, looking for me this afternoon,
before I knew about Morris Kale. The second was from Sonny
Garrett.

"Miss Thorssen." His voice was solemn and low, without any
bluster. "Please call me. I have something in my possession
that—" He paused, sighed. "Call me, and we'll deal with it." He
left his number and hung up.

Was this about Terry Vargas? Then I saw Garrett striding con-
fidently out of the hospital after visiting Audrey Kale. He would be
Morris's family lawyer, he would have to deal with the suicide, the
estate. Morris's will? Before I got past that, the next message
began, a low, smoky woman's voice.

"Alix. You maybe remember me. It's Wanda Leachman, from
up in the Little Belts herding sheep. Myron, your uncle, was in
Missoula yesterday on business, and he called me, said you'd
called a while back and asked about me. You always were such a
sweet thing. He gave me your number, and I thought we might
talk, but you're out."

There was an awkward pause, and I leaned in, thinking she
might have hung up. But her voice came back, dreamy with memories.

"I guess I just wanted to check up on ya. You talked a bunch
that summer about your dad, do you remember that? You had this
picture of him you kept with you all the time, from when he was
young, and I said he looked like James Dean in those old movies,
with that cockeyed smile. I know you've grown up, your uncle told
me about you. I've grown up too." She barked a laugh. "I was nineteen that summer, and I guess I should apologize for some of the
things I did. I sure enjoyed having you around, made it go quick,
our talks about men and fathers and the big sky and the way hearts
get broken."

She took a breath. My chest burned, remembering.

"Your uncle said you were asking about when you thought you

saw that wolf out there, and nobody believed you. I remember that. I didn't believe you either. No wolves been seen around there in years. But the next summer I was up by the Hi-line at another spread watching sheep again, and guess what. I saw a wolf myself. Weird, but it kinda changed my life. I got over that son of a bitch boyfriend of mine and went back to college. I don't know if it was the wolf who changed me, but who knows? Coulda been." She laughed, a contented sound. "So I'll say good-bye, and I'm thinking about ya, kiddo."

I knew I wouldn't sleep. My head was awash with old and new, past and present, pain and renewal, forgiveness and tragedy. I pawed through my trunk for the old photo of my father, Rollie, the one I'd had copied off an old portrait that hung at my sister's, and the black-and-white journal of that summer. I stuck the photo inside the journal, grabbed my keys, and drove the Saab Sister to the studio.

The moon was almost down, disappearing into the treetops and mountains. The studio felt chilled to the bone. I made a fire in the woodstove and stood in front of it. The flames licked the wood, crackling. Why was I here? I couldn't accomplish anything tonight. I wasn't going to fix Queen's problems. Morris Kale was beyond help, and his family needed more than I could give. Paolo, smiling from the easel, was little comfort. He had left me, like all the other men in my life.

I flopped down on the ratty sofa and tried to feel sorry for myself. Thinking about Rollie made it easy for a while—Rollie, who had left us so young. But it got boring after a minute. I rummaged through the small cupboard, found the mice had gotten to the Saltines. But there was three-quarters of a jug of red table wine, the cheap variety I kept on hand to serve people who I'd rather hadn't come at all. I found a clean jelly jar and poured it.

I was three glasses in when I started with the paint. It was idle, like finger painting, squeezing blue onto the palette, mixing green in with my fingers, a little white, some yellow. It got ugly. I added more blue, started again. My hands were covered with paint. I slipped off the flannel shirt and pulled over a dusty canvas I'd painted a bunch of yellow somethings on last spring. I blew off the dust.

A wolf. A blue wolf. I would paint a blue wolf. The stove was cooking; it smelled of enamel and iron. The studio was getting warm, too warm. I took off my T-shirt, smearing it with paint. My camisole was thin, and black. I'd put on my old paint jeans before driving over, but they were confining. I took them off and sat in my underpants on the short stool and smeared great blue smears on the canvas with my hands. Art therapy, for the damaged heart. For the confused mind. It felt pure, unstudied, a relapse into kindergarten where nothing you painted was wrong, when there were no bad choices or miscalculated relationships. When there was always time to fix your mistakes. I took another gulp of wine.

The canvas started to swirl and twist, its shape oblong now, kidney now. I was drunk, but happily so. I didn't care, it was too hard to care. I felt cut loose, wild. I squeezed out huge lumps of blue, white, black, dabs of this and that. I colored my arms blue, with white tattoos. I laughed and massaged sky blue into my chest and neck and face. I stood up, feeling free, and smeared paint directly out of the tubes onto my legs like that old drugstore artificial tan goo. A freaking blue tan! A world where the sun turned you blue! Where you matched the sky: how right, how true blue.

My underpants looked too white, too virginal, for a blue world. They caved to blueness. I pushed back my hair and blued my ears, my forehead. I stared at myself in the reflection in the window-glass, poured more wine and turned out the light. The flicker of the fire was eerie and right, a primitive glow for the uncomplicated blue world.

The night called to me. In the middle of Luca's lawn I raised my jelly jar high. Praise to the night, I whispered. Then I shouted it. "Praise to the night!" I twirled around like a forest nymph and giggled.

The night was friendly but chilly. I grabbed a blanket from the studio and spread it on the grass, lay down, and stared at the sky. It was covered with low, pinkish clouds. There were no stars tonight, no shooting streaks, no northern lights, no moon, no planets, no blue.

And no wolf.

I shivered violently and rolled inside the blanket. My body smelled, a heavy, sweet, oily odor. I felt suddenly like crying. But I closed my eyes and felt my stomach lurch and my body pitch. I stuck a foot out on the grass to anchor myself and felt the wet, earthy chill against my toes.

You could paint yourself blue, invent a blue existence. The whole blooming world could be gentian, azure, lavender blue billy billy, lapis to the max-is. Sky blue from tip to toe, from the cocky cornflower to the peacock's plume, from midnight to marine. From prussian to sapphire to the egg of robin, it could all be blue, blue, blue.

But you still couldn't have the wolf.

I lay on the grass in the blanket for a long time, an hour maybe. Not asleep, not awake. Somewhere in between. Finally I rolled over on my back and looked at the sky again. I felt clearheaded, sober, and dry-eyed.

The clouds were more defined now, clumps of gray and white, churning in a far-aloft wind. An unseen hand stirred them, and they thumped and humped and bumped into each other, like an angry crowd. I pulled out my hands, smeared with color. How did one decide that this living was too hard? What came over you at that moment, what made you get the gun, what made you pull the trigger? I clenched my fists and shook them at the sky. Living was hard, but it was something. It was hope, it was tomorrow.

Silence floated down on me, a calming silence. I was alone, and what I made with my body, my mind, my soul, whether I painted it blue and rolled in the grass or went to church on Sunday, was my own business. Success or failure, jolts of happiness or pitches of sorrow—they were all I had.

Was the wolf inside me? Did he make me wake up? What was he telling me? I strained to listen, I stretched my neck off the damp blanket, propped my elbows up, felt the wind in my ears, in my hair. What was he saying?

Talk to me, lobo. Tell me the secret.

16

"WHAT'S this?"

Maggie set down her coffee mug and swiped at my earlobe, coming off with a smear of blue paint on her fingertip. I pulled my head away slowly, feeling the slush in my sinuses shift. Nothing like a red wine hangover to make you quit the grape.

Before she'd arrived with muffins from the Bunnery, I'd managed to chug a gallon of water and scrub my skin relentlessly in the shower with turpentine and soap and water. I hadn't expected to get it all; it was a mathematical impossibility. No matter how hard you try, compulsively searching every inch of skin and scalp and hair, paint remains. My fingernails had a quaint lavender cast that no doubt matched my stomach lining. Still, I didn't feel terrible about last night. In some unknowing way, such mayhem was necessary. The world felt more balanced today, even if my head didn't.

"I was painting yesterday, remember?"

She eyed me. "After the auction?"

I shrugged. "It came over me. A frenzy of painting. Sort of."

"So, what today? More painting?" She looked at her watch.

Some people had to work. They had regular jobs, paychecks even.

"What's the weather like?" I peered out the north window and saw distant sunshine and blue skies.

"Nice, not too warm."

"Maybe I'll go on a hike."

Maggie smiled. "No sign of Carl last night."

"Maybe there was an emergency, up on the mountain."

She let that one lie. We munched chocolate cream cheese muffins, my favorite, in silence. I was frowning at the oil slick on top of my coffee. Maggie asked me why.

"Queen got strange last night. Told me she thought the wolf that's been hanging around her house is her son, the one that died twenty-five years ago."

"Like, reincarnated? Wow." Maggie picked up crumbs and set them on her napkin. "Are you still trying to find out how he was killed?"

I told her where things stood, which wasn't much but hunches. She hadn't any warm feelings for Terry Vargas but found it hard to believe he would shoot somebody like that.

"Why? I mean, what would he have to gain? Derek Wylie was just a kid. Why would Terry shoot him? Do you think he's so evil he'd do it just to . . . do it?"

I shook my head. "It's so long ago, we'll probably never know. Maybe Derek died with some secret about Terry, something Terry'd done."

"Isn't there some kind of statute of limitations?"

"Not on murder."

Maggie found another smudge of blue on the back of my neck before she left. I went back into the bathroom and searched and scrubbed and washed for another half-hour, until I felt faint with fatigue. I was headed back to bed when the telephone cried out in agony.

The coroner, Peg Elliot, was slightly breathless, as if she'd been running. "Alix, I found you. I tried your studio. Is your phone off the hook? I was just over there."

"Sorry." I rubbed my eyes. "I unplugged it. What's going on?"

"The autopsy. You wanted to know?" She was a little huffy,

which was difficult for me this morning. Or afternoon.

"Yes, of course. Morris Kale."

"Morris Kale." She sighed. "Definitely suicide. Powder on his gun hand, everything's consistent. I'm sorry."

"No, don't—" I took a deep breath. "I'm just glad to know, for sure. There was no note?"

She paused. "I don't know about that," she said finally, as if she really did know. "I just deal with the postmortem."

"Right. Well, thanks."

"And thank you for the ticket to the auction last night. It was very nice."

"I'm glad you enjoyed yourself, Peg."

"Did they let that woman sell her other painting?"

"Yes, it sold very well."

"She looked so familiar."

"Queen Johns. She grew up here." I woke up a little, my head clearing. "You know that Queen Johns was Derek Wylie's mother?"

A quick intake of air. "Oh."

I needed to take another aspirin. "I'll talk to you later, Peg. Thanks for the information," I said and hung up the phone. I lay down on my bed after gulping the pills, and by the time I woke up, it was dark again. I felt better, my headache gone. I closed my eyes and conjured up my father, but he was a faded black-and-white picture, a relic, a frozen memory. I couldn't hear him laugh anymore, or remember the way he smelled. I felt his loss, but it was muted, almost as if he was still here, telling me not to cry anymore. I'd stopped crying a long time ago, but he wanted me to stop it on the inside too. He wanted me to laugh now, the way he'd laughed, hearty and lusty and loud, not caring who heard it. Trying to hear it made me smile.

I made myself macaroni and cheese and ate it all. The phone didn't ring again, and I went back to bed and slept the sleep of the righteous.

When the telephone did ring, I was washed, dressed, and coffeed. It was early, the late October dawn just breaking. I had my hand on the doorknob, planning to open the gallery today, to move on, and almost didn't answer.

"Sonny Garrett on the line for you. Will you hold?" a pert voice asked.

"Yes." Although one of my pet peeves was holding for somebody who wanted to talk to you.

He didn't make me suffer long.

"Ms. Thorssen. I have something here for you. Something Morris Kale left you."

I blinked, frowning. "What is it?"

"An envelope. He left me some instructions, and one of them was to see that you get this envelope."

"So he did leave a note?"

"To you, yes. And to me."

"Not to his family?"

"I can't really discuss that."

What would Morris have to say to me? A thank-you for giving Frankie some time over the summer? I drew a circle on the kitchen counter with my fingertip, as a lightbulb blew up in my head.

"Morris was—he was the client you were talking about at Jenny Lake."

Garrett didn't speak.

"He was the one who wanted me to quit investigating Derek Wylie's death," I continued.

He didn't deny it. "Come over and read the letter. It will be on my desk if I'm not in. My secretary will give it to you."

"Have you read it?"

"It's sealed."

"But you know what it says."

He sighed. "More or less."

I hung up and cursed aloud several times. It wasn't possible. Morris Kale didn't live in Jackson then, no, Terry Vargas did. But, wait, what had Candace said?—that Morris and Terry were old friends. Was it possible they knew each other in '75? I squeezed my eyes shut. I didn't want to think about it. He seemed so level-headed, so kind. Yet is suicide a levelheaded act? I covered my mouth with my hand, smelled the turpentine, the lemon soap. Felt my eyes fill.

Oh, Morris.

Forty-five minutes later I held the envelope in my lap in the Saab, parked in an overlook in the park. Through the windshield the mountains looked immovable and solid, just what I needed at this moment.

Garrett hadn't been in, on purpose, I supposed. The young secretary had handed over the envelope as if it was good news—Inheritance! Insurance settlement! Her smile told me she didn't know.

I ripped open the flap, took out the single sheet of stationery with Morris Kale's name embossed across the top. He had been Morris W. Kale III, a regal name, one worth handing down. The note was handwritten in blue ink from a fountain pen.

> To Alix Thorssen, Jackson, Wyo
> October 28, 2000
>
> I have mailed today a letter to Ms. Queen Johns, relating to her the exact nature of my role in the events that led to the death of her son Derek Wylie. It is my hope that by this confession, a task long overdue, I can lay the matter to rest at last. I take full responsibility for the death, which was due to my own faulty judgment. No one else need feel guilt or responsibility. I will forever be guilty, and I can only hope that the Lord forgives me in the next life. I have no hope for forgiveness here on Earth.

He signed his name. There was no more on the back.

I looked up at the mountains and felt the frustration grow inside me. I wanted details, the why, the how, the when. Morris had punished himself, wracked with guilt. He must have convinced himself it would never come to light after all these years, and when it did, all the guilt overwhelmed him.

I stared at the fine ivory bond but got no more. No answers, no motives, no reasons. Had he told Queen more? *The exact nature,* he wrote.

I folded the letter and put it back in the envelope. A stony brick of guilt hardened in my chest, making breathing difficult, and I laid my forehead against the steering wheel. If I hadn't pressed the issue, if I had convinced Queen to let it go, Morris would be alive. He wouldn't have felt cornered, reliving his misdeed until the burden was too much. I didn't know it was Morris. I didn't think it could be someone I liked, I admired. I didn't realize the heart could be so cruel, so unyielding. Oh, Morris. The years of pain, and now, the terrible release. Was it my fault?

I started the car and pointed it north. But he killed him, he killed Derek. Would there have been an end to it if Morris hadn't killed himself? And what end would it have been—family disgrace, imprisonment? At the highway I skirted over to Kelly, gassed up at the store, and drove up the Gros Ventre again. The morning sun hurt my eyes, and I'd forgotten my Ray-Bans. I squinted and drove on.

Queen's cabin looked forlorn and cold, no smoke from the stack. I knocked hard on the door and called for her. I walked around to the back door and gave the knob a jiggle: locked. I called again, into the woods, again and again. *Queen, where are you?* I felt sick.

Back at the front door, I tried to jam it open with my shoulder. But she must have had a deadbolt, because the thick wooden door didn't budge. I peered through the window, cupping my eyes to see in the darkness. But the room was empty and still. She was gone.

On the radio as I drove down the mountain, the news came on. A reporter was telling about a rancher near Dubois who claimed that sixty-two calves turned into summer pasture never came home. Lost to wolves, he claimed. Then the newsman mentioned Marc Fontaine.

"Fontaine's case, the alleged shooting of an endangered wolf on a private ranch inside Grand Teton National Park, has taken on a new twist. U.S. Fish and Wildlife agents say political pressure is being placed on them to drop the case, and they resent it. When asked who was applying this pressure, the agents wouldn't name names. But a call to the field office of U. S. senator Willard Ferguson revealed a high level of interest in the case. What does this mean for Marc Fontaine? He enters yet another round as a political football."

Marc's troubles made me think of Valkyrie. I didn't want to go back to the cold, silent gallery, and painting had lost its allure. I turned off the highway and drove through the morning sun to the Bar-T-Bar Ranch, hoping Big Bud Wooten had gone back to Denver where he belonged. I found Farley forking hay from a round bale into a pickup truck in a pasture behind the barns. The old cowboy squinted at me for a minute, and I introduced myself.

"That's right," he said, jumping down to the ground like a man half his age. "Couldn't see you in this blasted light." He squinted at me from under his beat-up hat. "You look different. You been having some trouble?"

"Not bad," I said, taking off my slouch hat and letting the wind ruffle my hair. It was a cold wind, and smelled like snow. "How about you?"

"Just the usual." He nodded toward the main house. "Boss is back."

"I heard. Any sign of that old horse of mine?"

"Come to ride, did you?" Farley looked off to the west. "I think Marc's on her today. He'll be back soon. He's taken quite a liking to that mare."

We chatted and walked back toward the bunkhouse. Farley offered me a drink of water, and I accepted. It seemed the neighborly thing to do. We sat on the porch steps.

"Am I keeping you from your chores, Farley?"

He shook his head. "Boss went in to some meeting. I'll make busy when he gets back." He looked sideways at me. "Not every day a pretty girl comes to call."

I smiled at him and drank my water. I felt restless and wondered why I'd even come.

"You find out anymore about Derek?" he asked quietly.

"I guess I can't talk about it. Not yet."

"I understand." Farley took out a pocketknife and began to chip away on the edge of the steps, digging the tip of the blade deep into the old pine planks. "That reporter came out here, the one who talked to Marc. A friend of yours?"

"Danny Bartholomew?"

"He was asking me all sorts of questions about that wolf what was captured and brought into town, back in '75." He paused and glanced at me. "I guess because of Marc and all."

"Did you work on that, when you were a deputy?"

"Yup. Sad thing, some punks coming in and shooting the animal."

"Wasn't he going to be killed anyway?"

"Oh, yeah. But it was bad anyways. I had to help clean it up. Shot all to hell, like for target practice."

"They ever catch who did it?" I asked.

"No, but I always felt like some people knew but kept their mouths shut. Guess it don't matter, not anymore."

"I guess not." I frowned. "Could it have been Derek Wylie?"

"Don't know. He didn't take much to hunting."

So many questions unanswered. I wondered if Morris Kale's role in the shooting would now come out. Would Queen tell everyone?

"How is Queen?" Farley asked quietly. Carefully.

"Okay, I guess." What did you say about somebody who thought their son was reincarnated as a blue-tongued carnivore? Who was probably somewhere tearing out her hair, mourning and grieving all over again? "You should give her a call sometime. She could use a friend."

Farley cocked his head. "Yeah?"

Marc and Hal rode up, finished with riding fence for the morning. I led Valkyrie off to the barn, helped Marc put away the saddle and blanket, and brushed her for a while, feeling her strong, warm muscles. She was calm, happy, and hungry. I poured her out some grain and walked back outside. Marc was working on some tack.

"I heard that thing on the radio about the senator wanting your case dropped."

He didn't look up, but the anger radiated off him. "It won't happen."

"Why not?"

"There are people who want to press the issue, want the wolf declassified. They won't let the issue die."

"Like environmentalists?"

He glared at me. "Ranchers. So they can shoot wolves. Now you can't shoot one unless you catch it in the act. And that's hard."

"So they'd let you go to trial?"

"They want it to go to trial. There is nothing they'd like more than to have it out with the government in a court of law."

"You sound pissed off, Marc."

He threw down the latigo. "I am nothing but a pawn in this. What I want doesn't matter. It means squat. It's the big picture, that's what they keep telling me. The big picture."

"Meanwhile your small picture is going up river."

His mouth was set and hard.

I climbed up on the fence and sat on the top rail. "Marc, what really happened that night?"

"I shot the damn wolf—"

"You just said you were a pawn. You didn't do it, but you're taking the fall for it." I stared at him until he looked up at me. I could see the pleading in his eyes. "I'm right, aren't I?"

He didn't say anything for a long time. I thought he might stalk off. It wouldn't have surprised me.

Then he said, "What difference does it make who shot the wolf?"

"A hell of a lot to the guy who takes the fall."

He put down the harness. His voice was very low. "I never thought it would come to this." He turned to me. "What would you do? If I told you."

"I don't know. It depends."

"On who it is?"

"Maybe. Who is it?"

"Would you promise to not do anything I didn't want you to? Not go to the papers?"

"If you don't want anybody to know, don't tell me. Don't tell anybody. You tell me, and it means you want the truth to come out." I stared at him. "Marc. Look at me." He had a helpless, defeated look in his rugged face. "Don't protect some big-shot rancher. Even if it's your boss. You have to tell the truth. This is way too complicated for you to protect somebody. You have to protect yourself. And let the chips fall."

He scuffed his boot toe in the dirt. "I better not."

"You're right, Marc. You shouldn't. But if you don't, what will happen to you?"

He stared at me for a long second, then twisted away. He blinked at the mountains several times. He swallowed hard, then told the story.

17

SNOW began to fall as I left the Bar-T-Bar Ranch and headed back into Jackson. My windshield wipers did a less than perfect job, keeping time to an old Neil Young song on the radio. The sky was gray and cottony with winter, and I shivered. It was here again, winter.

The snow thickened as I dropped into the basin by the Elk Refuge. Already the animals had gathered there, ready to be fed. They stood like dark smudges in the white-gray canvas of pasture. Hard to believe they once almost died out, their forage eaten, no hay left in the valley to feed them. Hard to believe that once three-quarters of the calves didn't make it through their first winter. They looked fat and happy now. No wonder the wolves were hanging around in the hills whitened with the first heavy snow, frosted cupcakes with sprinkles of pines.

In my apartment I shook the snow out of my hair and called Danny B.

Danny had to talk about Morris Kale for a minute, and I mumbled along. There was a candlelight prayer service tonight at eleven, he said. Not the memorial service but just a place for people to go, to grieve together. I didn't know if I'd make it, I told him.

"I've been talking to Marc Fontaine," I said. "He told me everything."

"Ah," said Danny. "He tell you they were out hunting for wolf before?"

"He told me the real story, Danny."

I filled him in, trying to use Marc's words. I told him it was Terry Vargas who had shot the wolf, angry because Marc had done nothing to prevent livestock losses. That Bud Wooten had discussed it with Terry on the phone, then set up Marc to take the fall. I told him about my worries about Marc and Hal losing their jobs, and wondered aloud what to do to end the mess.

"We could get all the culprits in the room, like in a story, then the detective points out the one who did it," he said. "Now that might get the juices flowing."

"What culprits are there, besides Terry Vargas and Bud Wooten?"

"You'd want all the cops, the Fish and Wildlife agents, the feds who brought the prosecution."

"If I was Marc, I'd want my lawyer."

"Sonny Garrett. Okay, I'm making a list."

"Would be Sonny. You really want fireworks? We could ask Candace."

"Hmmm. She's in the maybe column. Definitely if we need some drama."

I had a feeling we'd have enough drama. We tossed around a few more names, and Danny said good-bye. He wanted to get it in the Monday paper—he had a headline in his mind already—so he had to get going. It was Friday night; he wanted to arrange the meeting for tomorrow, at the latest Sunday.

I got Morris's letter out of my backpack and set it gingerly on the kitchen counter. I hadn't told Danny about the confession; I doubted I'd tell anyone. The family had suffered enough. The rest of the questions about Derek Wylie nagged at me, unanswered, but my head wasn't there right now. Marc needed out of the hole he'd had so enthusiastically dug for him.

My refrigerator was a sad case. A hard hunk of Gouda, half a jar of olives, some flat Pepsi in a plastic liter bottle. But it was snowing outside, not the optimum time to search for wherever they moved the grocery store to this time, or to renew my annual pledge to get snow tires. So I dug deeper, found a slightly stale piece of flatbread, dumped some olives on it, and called it good.

With my mouth full, I dialed Queen's number. It rang and rang, and I set the receiver down on the counter and chewed. But she never answered, and I hung up. Where was she? I looked up Terry Vargas's number, dialed it, then pinched my nose and disguised my accent when Georgia came on the line.

"Eees Monsieur Vargas at home please?"

Too much Inspector Clouseau. Georgia gave a half-laugh and called him. When he got on the line and said hello, I hung up. Voices were not my spec-i-alité. Besides, Terry Vargas was scum. I just wanted to make sure Queen hadn't blasted him yet, so I could sleep tonight. But where in blazes was she?

At ten-thirty the snow was still falling, thick, fat flakes floating languidly to Earth. The church was three blocks away, short enough for a walk and long enough to enjoy the snow. I pulled on my slouch hat, my down jacket, and a pair of wool mittens. Not ready for boots yet, I slid down the alley in my clogs. The snowflakes kissed my cheeks, and I wondered how in hell Morris could throw this away. The world was new tonight, and he didn't know it.

The good winter smells—wet wool, chilled skin, puddles—gave way to melted wax and smoke as the shadowed church filled with mourners. I took my white candle with its cardboard dripshield, already lit and ready, from a sweet young girl who had no business at funerals at her age, and filed down the aisle. Not a large church—none in Jackson were, unless you were Mormon—it was already half full. The lights were dim, the candles bright, the faces solemn.

Men filed forward to give witness to the man, a few women too. I watched the flame on my candle, and the ceiling, and hoped that Morris was at peace. Church was only ritual to me now, but I hoped for Morris's sake there was someplace for him, someplace where he could spend eternity without suffering anymore. A flicker of anger passed over me again, like the candle's flame, and went out. Why did we have to suffer so much in this life?

As we stood to leave, blowing out our candles in unison—an act so touched with gravity that I began to cry—I saw Valerie and her husband in the front of the church. Behind Valerie was Frankie, slumped and shuffling, his face ruined by tragedy. Why had they forced him to come? My eyes cleared as I thought poorly of Valerie, then tried to let it go. Maybe he had wanted to come, to say good-bye. But he sure didn't look it.

Terry Vargas and Georgia sat across the church and filed now down the side aisle, his hand on her elbow. At least he had enough feeling to come. I had such plans for Vargas, plans to make him be the villain in the Derek Wylie story. Plans Morris Kale had thwarted. Yes, he would get his due in shooting the wolf and framing Marc, if I had anything to say about it, but it didn't matter. Not against the loss of Morris.

In the vestibule Danny and Geri paused to button their coats before plunging back out into the night. Danny caught my eye, but Geri's face was blotchy with crying, and they escaped out the door. I shuffled behind some strangers and felt the cold on my cheeks willingly.

The snow had stopped. The mourners left trails through the wet snow on the sidewalk. I stepped aside and let the quiet groups pass, pulling on my mittens at last. I twirled my scarf around my neck and looked up at the wooden church, modern and plain like good, solid Americans, not gaudy or famous or even particularly holy. Just a plain wooden box, good enough for any man, any woman, to seek the answers to life's questions or provide a moment's solace.

The deep breath I took felt both clean and painful, the cold hurting my lungs. Hapless blundering, one mother's suffering relieved, one man's suffering multiplied: was that the trade-off? If it was, the price was too high.

I looked around suddenly for Queen. But she hadn't come—no flowing white hair, no inappropriate colors. She didn't know

Morris, why should she come? The boardwalks were slick and icy as I headed toward home. Up in the hills somewhere Queen searched for the boy she lost. It would be a futile search.

The search for my car keys was almost as futile. I found them finally in the kitchen drawer and stepped back outside. I didn't know where I was going, but I knew I should be going there. It was a reckless feeling, that I couldn't stay alone with my thoughts, that what I did tonight didn't matter, that *I* didn't matter. They scared me, these thoughts, and yet I couldn't stop them. A rage of guilt, and the only way to get to the end of it was to ride it out.

The skating-rink streets sobered me quickly. I made a turn up toward Snow King Mountain, where a crowd was crawling out of the ice arena parking lot after a hockey game. As soon as I could, I turned off onto a side street and fishtailed all the way to the corner, then stopped to catch my breath. This was insanity. But I had a stop to make, if I could just figure out what it was. Sometimes a girl just had to drive.

Until, of course, she slides into a ditch. It happened so fast I didn't see it coming. One minute tooling along at five miles per hour, next minute one front tire low in a shoulder's pothole and no way out. I spun the back tires for a few hundred revolutions, then gave up. I turned the car off and looked down the street. Where was I? It couldn't be far to walk home.

Out on the street the temperature was dropping. Ice formed quickly in the slushy tracks of passing automobiles. Heavy snow weighed down the limbs of old pines and overgrown lilac bushes. Crackling of cold wood as the limbs broke punctuated the silence. A pickup passed, going in the other direction, spraying me with cold slush. I cursed, pulled up my collar, and began to walk toward the square. My clogs were hopeless, and my socks soon soaked through.

A siren ahead, then the ambulance attached to it. It came slowly toward me, as if it was going to pick me up. Twenty feet away it turned carefully into a driveway, the red light bouncing off the snow.

Adjacent the driveway I looked where it had gone and realized I was in front of the hospital. The snow had camouflaged everything, but now I saw the St. John's sign. I blinked and tucked my chin deeper into my coat. My feet were cold and wet. Was this where I was supposed to go tonight? I walked in the tracks made by the ambulance, then cut off to the side entrance. Even this late, it was open. Yes, this was where I was meant to go.

Trying not to think, my feet found the way to Audrey Kale's room. At the end of the corridor they faltered. What would I say to her? Did she know? If she didn't, I couldn't tell her. I made my legs work, made myself walk down the corridor, past a deserted nursing station, toward her door.

At the door I froze again. I stared at it, checked the tag on the side. Her name was printed there, same as before. I just watched the door as if it would give me a sign. Then, as I stared, it opened.

Corky stepped out and eased the door shut. He looked pale and drawn, as if he hadn't slept, but I remembered that this was his habitual look. His hair was messy, his tweedy jacket catching dandruff. He sighed deeply, rubbed his face.

I cleared my throat. Corky looked up, startled, and squinted. "Corky. Alix Thorssen. How are you?"

He relaxed, stuffing his hands in his pockets. "Been better. What brings you out?"

"I went to the prayer service. And somehow I . . . " My words trailed off. He seemed to understand. "Does she know?"

He nodded. "Val told her this afternoon."

"Is she okay?"

"Not really. I told Val to wait, but she couldn't." He pursed his lips. This was a Corky I hadn't seen, a caring, concerned friend. He wasn't smoking and didn't smell like booze. He looked at me, his gray eyes seeing me as if for the first time. "You want to talk to her?"

I tried not to grimace. I was here, wasn't I? I must have come to see her. "If she's awake."

"They tried to give her a pill, and she wouldn't take it. Guess she wants to suffer."

He opened the door. I knew how Audrey felt. I didn't want to sleep tonight either. I stepped into the darkened room with a chill that spread from the back of my arms up my neck. The room was warm and medicinal. A single lamp set up on a small table shone a circle of yellow light near the bed.

Audrey Kale lay still, her hands on the covers, her head turned to the window. Her hair was clean and curled, but the blond highlights were flat and dull. Her vibrant tan looked artificial and gray, her skin slack on her bones. A thin gold chain draped against her collarbone above the light green hospital gown. Corky stepped in behind me and whispered her name.

"Somebody to see you, dearie," he said quietly. She didn't turn her head. I looked at Corky questioningly, and he urged me on. He left the room, left me alone with Audrey and her grief and sorrow. Every instinct in my body told me to run, flee.

In the silence Grandma Olava, she of infinite cleanliness, came to me. If you can't say anything, touch them, she said. The human touch speaks loud and clear.

I obeyed Olava's voice, laid my hand softly on Audrey's, and spoke her name. "It's Alix Thorssen." No response. "I'm so sorry. I don't know what to say. Just that I'm sorry."

Audrey took a deep breath and exhaled it. Her eyes were open but still looking at the blank window. "Is it snowing?" she said.

"Um. No, it stopped." I took my hand away from her cool skin. Olava would have given her a fierce hug, but I couldn't do that. I hoped someone could, someone who loved her.

"The service was nice. Lots of people talked about Morrie and—" My voice broke then, my throat close and hot. I hadn't talked about Morris, and couldn't now.

"He would have liked that, I guess," she said. Her voice was light, otherworldly. "Or maybe not."

Audrey turned to me suddenly, an angry light in her eyes. "Five years, that's all I knew him. Just five years."

"That's a long time," I said.

She shook her head. "Not long enough for someone like him."

"I guess we never really know another person, all of them."

"My children, I know them," she said, accusing me of something.

"Yes. Of course."

She covered her eyes with her left hand, and I was afraid she was going to cry. Instead she spit out: "No. I don't even know them. Frankie, he's so—he's almost gone from me. I know nobody. And no one knows me. I am all alone. All alone."

"You have your children, and Corky. You have friends."

She put her arm down, and I could see she favored her other shoulder as she raised herself a little off the pillow. "We're all alone. We share little things, ideas or moments or even a little affection, but in the end we go alone. You do, I do, he did."

Not that tonight we needed to remember that. Tonight life seemed so fragile, a narrow thread ready to snap. "That's why we should try to live life to the fullest, don't you think?"

She fell back on the pillows, her eyes still dry. "And go out with a bang?"

After a long pause, I said, "Did he try to do it before?" I motioned to her shoulder.

"This?" An odd chuckle. "He wasn't even there. But he was the martyr, wasn't he? He'd suffer for anybody, take on all their burdens, but he wouldn't do it for himself."

"He didn't shoot you?"

"It was an accident. Frankie—he didn't mean it." She looked at me and sighed. "We had a fight, he ran out of the house with a gun. When he finally came back, well—I tried to take it away from him. Morris wouldn't let the sheriff know it was Frankie. He said a boy shouldn't have that on his conscience. As if the sheriff had some lock and key on a boy's conscience."

Frankie shot her? "I'm confused. I thought—" I stopped, my thoughts jumbled.

"We all want explanations, don't we? Well, there's a letter. It's there, on the table. You're welcome to read it. Not that it makes any sense."

"I couldn't." The suggestion was appalling, and tantalizing. "He left me a short note."

Her mouth twisted cynically. "Oh, really."

"He said—he said he was responsible for the death of a boy twenty-five years ago. Did he tell you that?"

She gave an exasperated sigh. She was in an odd state of fury.

"The letter's not personal, I can assure you of that. What he did was so selfish, so irrational, that whatever feeling I had for him is dead now too. I just wish to God I knew who he was."

I looked at her tortured face, the pain in her eyes, wanting to read the letter but ashamed of my curiosity. Had he wanted to hurt her, I wondered? Was that what suicide was about?

She rolled toward the window, hiding her face from me. I looked at my hands. *I should leave.*

"He never let me close to him. Not in any way." Her voice was small. "Our marriage was a sham. I suppose he thought he was doing me a favor."

She turned back suddenly. Her eyes were full but still fiery. "Read it. Maybe you can figure out what sort of a tortured man he was. Then somebody will know." She pursed her lips. "I won't think less of you for it. We hardly know each other, do we?"

I cleared my throat. The room was very quiet. "I had such a good time with Frankie over the summer, I'm sorry we didn't get to know each other better. I'd like to make up for that, if we could."

She wiped her tears. Her eyes glowed hot and dark. Her anger surprised me, and in some way, reassured me. She had life in her, she would not fold.

"Just read the damn letter," she said.

Audrey, Valerie, and Frankie:

I first started this letter My Dearest Audrey, Valerie, and Frankie, but after you read this you won't appreciate being dear to me. I feel very calm right now, this is a good time to write to you. I haven't felt this calm for a long, long time. For years now my head has been swimming. I have tried to hide what I really am. I got very good at hiding it.

—I find I am losing courage now. Not to do what must be done, but to tell you why. But you deserve to know, you deserve so much more. I fear—no, I know you won't understand. But I must tell you. A long time ago, another gun, another man. He wasn't a man though, only a boy, and I did something terrible to him, something for which I can never forgive myself, and I do not hope that you would forgive me.

I have been living on borrowed time, *his* time, and I can't do that anymore. I thought when I found all of you I could begin again, be someone else, a family man, respected and loved. Coming back to Jackson was wrong, very wrong, and all that happened in my head since we moved back ends now. You didn't even know. I was here when I was in college. I came with a friend to go hunting. And it turned so badly, so horribly bad. Yes, I was young, but not so young I didn't know what I did was wrong. That I let myself be persuaded is no excuse, in fact it makes it worse. I am a coward. You deserve a man, Audrey, not this poor excuse.

One thing I can tell you now, because you will find out with the will. There was no dry-cleaning franchise. There was no Morris W. Kale. I am sorry for everything, for deceiving you. For hurting you. If you had known the sort of life I led before, you wouldn't have wanted me. I wanted something I thought you could give me, but it was out of your power. I accept now what I am. How I wish I could have told you everything, but you were so happy. I could not spoil that.

18

I woke to snoring. It was nine according to the kitchen clock, but could have been any hour according to my internal ticker. The television set jumped happily with cartoons, the sound a whisper. The snoring stopped when I woke up on the couch. The telephone was ringing. I lay, sleep-frozen, and listened to the answering machine.

It was Danny. I threw myself off the sofa and lurched to the phone.

"Nice growl," he said. "Tie one on?"

"No, for your information." I rubbed a tender spot between my eyes. I did have a glass of wine somewhere along the line. Three A.M.?

"Well, can you make yourself presentable in two hours? Because we're having a powwow with all the chiefs."

He filled me in on the meeting he'd set up. Sonny Garrett had agreed to have it in his conference room.

"Vargas agreed to come?"

"Yup. He thinks it's something else. I had to fib a little."

"What'd you tell him?"

"Ranchers getting together to discuss the wolf problem. Which isn't too far off."

"One question. Does Garrett make good coffee?"

The minuscule possibility that I could wait two hours to find out gave Danny a chuckle. I hung up and made a pot, sat like a zombie in front of the set until the caffeine began its magic, and got another cup. Now I knew how those Norwegians I'd visited last spring in Oslo made it through the long, dark winter. Either coffee or a well-timed hibernation.

I found a half-empty box of Cheerios and ate them by hand. I really had to do something about the state of my self. Tomorrow, I promised Grandma Olava, I would clean the apartment and the gallery, and buy groceries. Today, however, I was content to slump in front of the tube and chew cereal dry.

At ten I got in the shower. Despite the warm water I felt a chill, remembering last night. The eerie candlight service, the snow, Audrey, the letter. I'd mused all night about Morris's assertion that someone else had persuaded him to kill Derek Wylie. What to do with Terry Vargas? Was he Morris's "friend"? Morris's strange wording of the letter to Audrey and the kids made me confused. Why was he being so obtuse? What did he still feel necessary to hide about himself? And then Vargas. How could I make him pay? Was revenge this cold even purposeful? Was I in over my head, obsessing from my own sense of vanity, of pride? Should I drop the whole thing?

I rubbed myself briskly with a towel to get the blood flowing and to stop the barrage of questions. Queen echoed in my head. I'd called her several times late last night. I wrapped the towel around myself, went into the kitchen, and dialed her number again. Six, seven, eight rings. I hung up. Should I call someone? A neighbor, the sheriff? I looked at the time, smacked myself in the forehead, and ran for the bedroom.

Sonny Garrett stood in the corner of his large, plain conference room, talking to Marc Fontaine. Brother Hal stood to one side, examining an oil painting of mallards rising off a lake. The

Fontaine brothers wore what they always wore: denims and western shirts, boots and bandannas. Sonny's attire was more reflective of the weekend, for him: navy cashmere sweater and gray flannel slacks. He was half a head taller than Marc, with his silver hair and perfect tan. When Marc turned to see me at the door, he looked nervous.

We said quick hellos. This didn't seem like the time to rehash things, when Vargas could walk in. Garrett had us sit at the table, the brothers together but me at the far end. "Just sitting around shooting the breeze," Sonny explained, trying to ease the tension.

Danny bustled in next, full of energy. He looked around quickly, then said, "I left Watson outside, to get a good shot as he's coming out." His eyes twinkled. "Nothing like the photo of them coming out of the lawyer's office."

"Or the jail," Hal said sourly, squinting at Danny.

Danny's grin faded as we remembered his paper's shot of Marc in handcuffs. "Sorry, Marc."

Marc's lips were tight. He gave a short nod.

"Is Bud Wooten coming?" I asked.

"He left for Denver this morning," Hal said.

Danny shrugged. "We tried. But we couldn't force him." He sat down across from Marc and Hal, midway down the long table. "So we'll let Sonny start, okay?"

"What's he going to say?" Hal was getting on my nerves.

"Hal," I said, trying to be soothing, "maybe it would be better if Sonny and Marc spoke for themselves. If someone asks—"

"You want me to shut up?" Hal stood up, his face reddening. "Well, I won't, not anymore. This whole thing sucks. I won't keep quiet anymore."

Marc put his hand on his brother's arm. "You don't have to, Hal. That's why we're here. We aren't lying anymore. Just keep your mouth shut and be patient." He pulled Hal down into the chair, where he slumped back, scowling. Marc turned to me and Danny. "He just wants to help. And to get this over with."

"We all do, Hal," I said.

Sonny outlined how he would present the hypothetical story of a rancher who is having trouble with wolf kills, then present it to the group for solutions. If necessary, Marc would then chime in with specific details. We would try not to make accusations, to put Vargas on guard, but to let him know we knew what really happened.

Vargas might get the message, but would he crack? Would it push him over the top? A confession was our only hope, not unlike my other inquiry. I sighed and tried to relax. Where were the cops and wildlife agents? It was after eleven.

As if on cue the outer door opened and five officials filed in—two uniforms, one of the county sheriff and one the Fish and Wildlife Service, two in suits, and one in jeans and leather vest, holding a fat file under his arm. This last one was the federal prosecutor, a black man named Ivan Fields, who introduced himself around. He sat down next to a female attorney from the Wyoming Farm Bureau and an FBI agent. The attorney, Amanda Little, hailed from Cheyenne. She had a hefty briefcase with her and seemed to know the FBI agent, Bill Simmons. They were chatting merrily, sitting down facing the door, as Vargas and Georgia appeared in the doorway.

Vargas's black eyes made a quick survey of the room, and his jaw tightened. Then Marc stood up and smiled at him, extending his hand. "Bud couldn't make it today, so he sent us," Marc said. As if he was Wooten's representative. Brilliant.

Relaxing a little, Vargas ushered Georgia into the last chair next to Danny and circled the table so he sat at my right hand. I smiled at him, which he returned, then frowned and gave me a second side glance. He'd be wondering what I was doing here. Maybe my attendance was a mistake. I swallowed hard.

"I thought this was a rancher's meeting," Vargas said loudly, glaring at Danny down the table. "Where are the rest of them?"

Danny sighed and looked at his watch. "They should be here soon. Shall we wait a few more minutes?"

Ivan Fields cleared his throat, patting his overflowing file folder. "I think we should get going. I have less than an hour." He looked bored. I wondered how much Danny had told him. The reporter finished setting up his tape recorder and gave the lawyer the sign to begin.

As Sonny Garrett began to tell his story, the hypothetical rancher under fire from all sides, from falling beef prices to weed control, inheritance taxes to conservation easements, encroachments on private property rights to predator losses, Georgia caught my eye. She was wearing a steel blue silk shirt and black suede pants, her hair swept up off her slender neck. But her eye was cold. I tried to smile and look nonthreatening, but she held the glare until I jerked away.

I squirmed in my chair, crossed my legs, and listened to Sonny.

"What is the rancher to do? He has worked from dawn till dusk and then some, all his life on this land. He loves it like his mother. It feeds him, clothes him, shelters him. But now an animal who has no respect for that, for that toil and blood and tears—especially tears, we'll come to that—this animal trots right up to the herd of sheep, or horses perhaps, and simply snatches away a life. Not just a life, a business property, a piece of capital, of enterprise, of what makes this nation great. What this nation, my friends, is founded on. And if this rancher cannot protect what is his, what kind of an American is he? Tell me, what kind?"

"The piss-poor kind," Vargas said in a shallow whisper.

"What's that, Terry? The poor kind? That's right," Garrett continued.

"What's the point of this?" the Fish and Wildlife agent complained. "We've heard all this before."

"The point is," Ms. Little said, "that you never got the point."

"I got the point," the agent returned. "I just see two sides to the question. Unlike the Farm Bureau."

"Tell me this," Garrett said to the agent. "If you are threatened by a burglar, if someone climbs in the window of your house, would you shoot him?"

"Maybe," the agent conceded.

"You would be justified, wouldn't you? And the law says you are justified."

"But the law also says if you are attacked by a wolf, you can shoot the wolf. You just have to prove you were attacked," the agent said, staring at Marc. The cowboy looked up with a scared face at the wildlife agent.

"All right," Garrett said, putting up his hand. "Back to that burglar throwing a leg over your windowsill. What if you shot first, and found out later he was unarmed?" He looked at the sheriff's deputy.

The deputy shrugged his shoulders. "Accidental?"

The attorneys around the table murmured. Ivan Fields said in his baritone, "Accidental with intent."

Garrett smiled. "If only there were such a category of motivation. You mean protection, but you maim or kill. The point is that your first motivation is to protect yourself and your property. Correct?"

"And if you knew there happened to be an armed killer, or armed robber, in the neighborhood? Wouldn't that be justifiable homicide?" Terry Vargas piped in.

Garrett raised his eyebrows. "Interesting. Justifiable if you knew a robber—any robber—was armed?"

Fields sighed. "Just because he's armed isn't due cause to shoot a man. You have to prove you were threatened, seriously in fear for your life. Otherwise people would just go around shooting anybody they suspected of packing a firearm. It would be chaos."

"Okay," said the wildlife agent, obviously annoyed by this tangent. He had a slight Minnesota accent and reminded me of a Boy Scout. "So the animals aren't armed, but they can kill. They have that capability. But it doesn't mean you can shoot them. That's the law. These wolves are an endangered species. We brought them back."

"Experimentally," the Farm Bureau lawyer added.

"It's an experiment that will be permanent, you know that. There's no going back."

The lawyer opened her mouth to rebutt that, but Garrett cut her off. "Let's ask the rancher. Terry, what would you do if a wolf was threatening your herd of cattle?"

Vargas sat back and frowned. "Bring them in from summer pastures, set up night patrols, fire into the air periodically. Try to scare 'em off."

"And if that didn't work? If you had actual losses?"

"Well"—he stuck out his lower lip and folded his arms across his chest—"I guess I'd be more vigilant. Try to catch one."

"You mean set traps?" Garrett asked.

"Maybe."

"What else?"

A tense silence, broken only by the FBI agent clicking his ballpoint pen. Marc stared at the pen until the agent stopped.

Hal turned toward me, his mouth twisting. I caught his eye and gave him a tiny head shake. *Not yet.* The boy reddened, closed his mouth, stared at his calluses. Terry Vargas unfolded his arms and sat a little taller. He glanced at Georgia, but she was looking out the window, her swanlike neck twisted away from him. He cleared his throat.

"I guess I—" He stopped, licked his lips.

"Would you shoot a wolf?" Sonny asked. "Would that bother you?"

"Bother me?" Vargas gave a breathy laugh. "It wouldn't keep me awake at night."

"Because they deserve it?"

"Well, sure. They're killers. Everybody knows that. Bringing them back was just something our fat-ass feds would do. Don't think about the long-term consequences, just placate the eco-whackos who have absolutely no stake in the future of this state. They want little cuddly playthings, and the feds bring them killing machines. It's laughable, but oh so predictable."

The Fish and Wildlife agent had a ticked-off look on his face. He folded his arms, though, and stayed silent. Amanda Little gave Terry a smile of encouragement and a clenched fist that said, *Nice going, soldier.*

"So how would you deal with the wolf problem, Mr. Vargas?" Ivan Fields prodded.

"Kill 'em. It was an unsuccessful experiment. We killed 'em off once, didn't we? What's to stop us doing it again?"

"Well, the law, for instance," the wildlife agent said.

"Laws serve men, not the other way around," Vargas said. "Change the law. Set it right."

"If you don't believe in a law," Fields asked calmly, "would you have any compunction about breaking it? If you're not hurting another human being?"

"Shame, you mean? Remorse? I went to college, Mr. Prosecutor. No. No *compunction*, as you say." Vargas sneered at the prosecutor. "Laws are made by men, they should serve. If they don't—"

"Blow 'em off?"

"Blow 'em away," Vargas said, smiling roundly. "With my semiautomatic."

"Even if these laws serve the common good?" the FBI agent, Bill Simmons, said, speaking at last.

"And what, pray tell, is that?"

"The betterment of society, the fulfillment of goals that serve the public will, the stability and civilized nature of society."

Vargas stared at Simmons. "You got the Constitution crammed up your ass?"

Simmons's facial muscles twitched, but he simply stared back. "I respect the Constitution, Mr. Vargas."

A tense moment stretched long as I waited for fighting words or actual fists to come into play. But the moment passed. Garrett straightened in his chair. Danny took the break to flip his tape over then scurried back into his seat with his notebook. We all looked to Sonny Garrett. He stared at his notes.

Marc cleared his throat. He said nothing, just fidgeted then fell still. Another moment passed. Then, finally, his soft voice: "Not many people know this but once I killed a mountain lion. I was seventeen, still living at home. The ranch over by Pinedale. Back when we had a ranch." He glared pointedly at the Farm Bureau attorney who blinked rapidly then shrugged to the FBI agent.

"It was a pretty little spread, not big enough to live on, not for more than one or two generations and by the time my dad came along he was fourth. It was a struggle, even with us boys helping, and every calf meant meals on the table. There had been some cat sign about, we knew something was up, but spotting a big cat is always tough. I was scared, I admit it, and I took to carrying my rifle with me that summer. Wherever I went, the rifle went with me. But still I was scared. I loved those woods, the smell of them after a rain, the light filtering down. I had hideaways from when I was little that I remember even now, hollowed out logs I shared with bugs, and tree stumps that seemed magical."

He cleared his throat again. "Then one day I saw the cougar. I had a feeling all morning that somebody was close, some being, probably the cat. Then, as I got off my horse to eat lunch, there she was. She wasn't watching me, but had her eye on a calf. I'd been trailing them up into high country, and she'd been trailing us. I stood up, and cocked my rifle.

"She turned to me at the sound. She could have run, I gave her time. I wanted her to run. But she turned back to the calf, and kept creeping toward it. I took a step toward them, hollered. Still, she paid no mind. So I shot her, clean through the chest like I been taught.

"Did I feel good about it? No. I tried to for the sake of my dad. He was happy it was over. But I kept seeing her lying there, bloody and dead. And doing what she was taught too. I did lose some sleep, Mr. Vargas. I did lose some sleep over that one."

Eyes shifted to Terry Vargas. He had folded his arms again, and set his jaw. With the question his eyebrows jumped. "And not the wolf, Marc?"

"No, Mr. Vargas, not the wolf."

"No? And why is that? Got over that childishness?" He smiled indulgently.

"The cat was a beautiful creature, made by God to serve a purpose on this earth. Same as the wolf. The reason I didn't feel that way about the wolf I think you know."

A long pause while all eyes stared at Vargas. Then Georgia sprang to her feet, indignant. "What is the meaning of this? Is this some kind of legal hearing? Because if it is—"

"Sit down, Georgia," Vargas bellowed.

She stared at him, nostrils flaring, and flounced into her chair.

"This is all strictly informal, is it not?" Vargas smiled around to all concerned who smiled, in a pinched sort of way, back. "Information gathering, hypothetical situations?"

Marc sat forward and looked for the first time straight down the table to Terry Vargas. "Why don't you tell them why I don't feel remorse about shooting the wolf?"

Vargas colored and slapped the table. "All right, you little pissant. I'll tell them. Because you have a yellow streak up your backside a mile wide. Because you can't stand the sight of blood, your girlish heart might faint away. Because even though you are ranch manager, you couldn't manage your way out of a wet paper bag. Because I had to kill the wolf for you, because you were a lily-livered son of a bitch."

Hal closed his eyes. Marc looked at the ceiling as if invoking prayer. Georgia put a hand over her eyes. I let out a breath. Ivan Fields leaned in. "You killed the wolf?"

Vargas stood up. "Not that you can prove it."

A new voice came from the doorway. "Wouldn't bet on it."

Candace Gundy leaned against the doorframe, waving a piece of paper. "I had a suspicion, you see, that there was more to this wolf shooting than met the eye. So I talked to the forensic people out in Oregon, told them to check for toxins. They do a routine screen, but not a full one. I even had to pay for it out of my organization's funds." She smiled at Terry Vargas. "Best four hundred dollars I ever spent."

"Here is the report." She slapped the fax down on the table in front of the federal prosecutor. "Says here this wolf was drugged. A combination of Nembutal and meperidine—that's Demerol to you and me. Enough to make her so groggy that somebody could get close and shoot her. Make it look like self-defense, or like she was attacking the livestock. You have anything to do with that, Mr. Fontaine?"

Marc stared at her, eyes wide. "No, ma'am."

"I didn't think so. That's why I had a narcotic trace done on all sales of the Nembutal and Demerol in the state in the last six months—did you know the feds are kinda picky about narcotics? One Terrence Vargas was on that list. He bought several large supplies of both drugs through a pharmacist named Georgia Tensrud, who was last registered with the state at a Laramie Shopko. Georgia Tensrud—that name ring a bell?"

Sonny Garrett turned to Georgia, sitting next to him. In his glare she crumpled, pulling herself inward, covering her face with her hands. Then Garrett turned to Terry Vargas, still standing at the other end of the table. But Ivan Fields beat him to the punch.

"Well, Vargas, do you deny buying this substance?"

"Why should I? It's legal."

"And how do you explain its presence in the carcass of the dead wolf?"

"I don't have to. That isn't my ranch. I had nothing to do with it."

"You deny discussing disposing of the wolf threat with Bud Wooten?"

Vargas snapped his head. "He never said that."

"Didn't he?"

"Even if you can link me to the drug, you can't prove I killed the wolf. The bullet killed her."

Ivan Fields stood up, an equal height to Vargas. "Actually, my man, we have two witnesses who say you shot the wolf."

"Who—them?" Vargas gestured at Marc and Hal. "That's a joke. He's charged with it, so he's suspect, and that's his goddamn brother. They're in it together."

"We could talk to Bud Wooten." Ivan Fields looked at his watch. "Agents are meeting his plane just about now."

Vargas began to move. He walked briskly around the table. "Come on, Georgia." She rose and moved to his side. But Candace Gundy blocked the door.

"Sorry. The meeting's not over yet," she said, smiling menacingly. She was a head shorter than both of them, but the glint in her eye would shatter glass.

"Move aside." Vargas put out a hand but stopped short of touching her. "Get out of my way."

"Hold up, Mr. Vargas," the deputy said behind him. "We have some more questions."

With that, dear, sweet Georgia landed an uppercut on Candace Gundy's chin that would have knocked most men flat. They skipped over her prone body, hand in hand, like fugitive lovers in a bad movie. I hoped Watson was still out there for a snap.

The deputy sprang into action, hurdling Candace and catching up with Terry Vargas on the front steps. Georgia burst into tears. Vargas swore. Watson took pictures.

19

ATE that night I sat in a corner of the Six Point with Maggie, nursing a glass of wine. The saloon, in all its stuffed head and barnwood glory, was deserted. Rusty stood behind the bar, slowly wiping glasses he'd no doubt wiped three times already. The smell of cigarette smoke clung, stale and lonely.

Neither of us had said anything for a long time. I'd told her the story about catching Terry Vargas, and taking Candace to the emergency room to have her jaw and skull looked at (she was fine, or as fine as one can be after being walloped). I'd told her about the drugs found in the wolf, and Marc and Hal telling the story a new way. We'd congratulated ourselves. We'd clinked glasses. And then the feeling passed.

I had brought up Queen Johns, and we'd discussed driving out to her cabin. We used Rusty's phone to call her. I didn't know how Maggie felt about it, but I was feeling pretty hopeless about the whole situation. On my third glass of wine I told Maggie about Morris's involvement in the killing of Derek Wylie, and she was appropriately shocked. And saddened all over again.

When it looked like we both might cry, I made Rusty drive

Maggie home. I walked the three blocks, feeling the cold air in my ears like they belonged to another person. I felt very strange. It wasn't the wine, it was the crusty patches of snow left from the morning's melt. It was the way the wind smelled clean and ancient at the same time. It was the way the mountains never answered me when I asked them hard questions.

I lay in bed, alone and lonely but not feeling the cold. Ice was forming on the inside of the old panes of glass, but it was beautiful, magical. I closed my eyes.

When I woke up, it was dawn. Something woke me, a buzzing behind my eyes, a nagging. Loose ends, niggling at me.

With a steaming cup of coffee I curled up at the table in my robe and wool socks. The apartment was frigid, but I was counting on the java to warm me for now. I opened the Casper newspaper and skimmed the headlines. Nothing interesting. I read the funnies, refolded the paper, and pushed it aside. On the way to refill my coffee cup, as I emerged from my sleep cloud, I saw the pile of documents under a rock—Queen's documents, the ones she'd wanted me to find for her. I slipped off the rock, tucked them under my arm, and marched back to the table with a second cup of coffee.

I spread them out before me, chagrined again about their small number. One police report, two newspaper articles, one autopsy report. And one suicide note—cryptic.

A big gulp of hot coffee helped focus my eyes. I held the first report flat, reading and rereading each line, looking for something, anything. I tried the old trick of reading it upside down but got a headache and switched it back. Took another gulp of coffee and a last penetrating look, then shoved the police report aside. Maybe another talk with Farley Platt would yield something.

I pulled the first newspaper article around. It was pitiful in its smallness.

LOCAL BOY DEAD IN HUNTING ACCIDENT
The sheriff's office reported yesterday that a local boy was shot while hunting near Fish Creek late Saturday night. Sheriff Gass said the incident was unfortunate and tragic, and could have been prevented with better hunting safety

measures. He reminded local hunters that wearing a bright orange ("hunter's orange") cap or vest is required by law.

According to department documents, the boy was Derek D. Wylie, age 16. His parents were Dominick V. Wylie and Queen Johns Wylie of Jackson.

The reporter seemed to think informing people of the hunter's orange law was more important than Derek's death. A sort of "too bad, and let's not do that again" attitude. As if boys were dispensable.

The second article just made me sad. The details of Derek's short life, so meager, so sketchy, as if because he wasn't a "somebody"—a high school quarterback, star of the drama club play, a top scholar—he hadn't really lived. Well, maybe he hadn't, but he hadn't gotten the chance to grow into somebody. These summations of a life always make me think about my own obituary. The really swell people, who have lots of college degrees and honors and grandchildren and gave money away and loved God and served their fellow man six ways from Sunday—those are hard to read. But the really short ones are hard too. They both make me think about how sniggling my write-up will be if I don't hurry up and do something important with my life. Like discover the next Matisse of the Rockies. Or paint like the female Picasso. Or at least have children. And preferably get married first.

Cripes. Another cup of coffee was required.

The next document was the autopsy report. I felt fortified enough to read it again. With the coffee cup holding down a corner, I went through it line by line, squinting to read the words, to make them speak to me in a language I understood. I went through it twice, sat back, and sighed. I pulled the phone over to the table, called directory assistance, and dialed Peg Elliot's home number.

She was asleep, but in true public servant style, she woke up and came to attention.

"The autopsy report? Of Derek Wylie?" She was stammering.

"Yes, Peg. The secret one you gave me."

"What about it?"

"There's a part here I don't get. Can I read it to you?"

"Just a sec." Yapping and scolding, then a door slammed. "All right, go ahead."

"It's here when the pathologist is describing all the sampling. He does fingernail scrapes and finds a white powder. It says: 'Fingernail scrapings contain mostly a fine white powdery substance.' What could that be?"

"Well, any number of things, dirt, powder. Drugs, maybe."

"Were the tests ever run on the samples?"

"I doubt it. Everything was hush-hushed, like I said."

"You don't remember for sure?"

"I would remember, dear. It was very sensitive, and just keeping that copy could have gotten me fired."

"Okay, Peg. Thanks. Sorry for waking you."

I hung up the phone and held my chin in my hands. What else was there on this report? What else was strange and unexplained? Was Derek taking drugs? It was possible, even in the seventies, even here in Backwater USA. But if he was, what did that prove? That he was killed over a drug deal that went sour? That Terry Vargas and Morris Kale were somehow involved in drugs?

I sighed loudly and pushed it all back. This was getting nowhere. I didn't need to read Morris's note again. It said so much about so little, or was it so little about so much? Either way, it wasn't going to help. If someone had convinced Morris, persuaded him, to shoot Derek Wylie, he had taken the secret to his grave.

I stretched out on the sofa under the comforter. The Sunday-morning light was thin and weak, struggling to rise over the peaks to the east, hitting the clouds with pathetic rays. Pulling the soft covers up to my chin, I shut my eyes and tried to will sleep. This never worked. My eyeballs began to buzz again. I opened my eyes and stared at the dull gold stars under the ceiling, very much in need of a wipe-down. Grandma Olava would approve of one big apartment/life wipe-down, even if it was Sunday. That was what I really should do with this energy.

I burrowed deeper into the covers instead. All the characters in this tragic farce swam in my head, Sheriff Gass, Marc Fontaine, Dutch Abbott, Farley Platt, Terry Vargas, Georgia the pharmacist, Queen Johns, Candace Gundy, Morris Kale, wife Audrey, son

Frankie—who else? There were so many fingers in this messy pie. Oh, Sonny Garrett too. He had hushed up the whole thing twenty-five years ago. But getting more information out of him would be as easy as plucking feathers from a pit bull.

Who was I missing? What was I missing? I closed my eyes again and let the faces float in front of me, the old, wrinkled faces, the unhappy faces, the grieving faces. I sighed deeply and relaxed into the sofa. Maybe I would sleep after all.

The late-afternoon sun lit the windows of the high school, turning them into flashing orange rectangles. I drummed my fingers on the steering wheel. No snow remained on the asphalt parking lot, but in the shadow of the brick building traces streaked the still-green grass. I held onto those streaks in my mind. If they melted, the fragment of blooming order in my chaotic mind might melt too.

I'd been driving around for two hours, trying to get things in place. My morning nap had been troubled, and sent me out the door with no particular destination. I'd been up to Queen's, out to the Flying V and the Bar-T-Bar, I'd watched the elk inside the tall fence of the refuge. I'd been through the drive-through at McDonald's, up the mesa to the quiet manse of the so-called Kale family, by the plain suburban ranch house of Leroy Leonard. I'd used half a tank of gas.

And I ended up here. I had to talk to Leroy again, and he wasn't at home. The high school building looked deserted. In twenty minutes no one had come and gone through the heavy double doors on the end of the north wing. There were other entrances, but from here I should see a car, any car. And so far, nothing.

Not that I expected anyone. I hoped to find Leroy but had no great hopes. He could be anywhere. My timetable had more to do with an impulsive brain than the workweek. It was still Sunday, after all. Who goes to school on Sunday?

I got out of the car. The air was cold and dry, the kind that seizes nose hairs. I shook myself and snapped up the down coat. It was time to do something, anything.

The windows on the west side were at eye level, offering little in the way of spying even if the reflection of the sun hadn't been blinding. I walked down the row, peering, cupping my hands against the glass, then turning to scan the lot, the entrances, the street. All was quiet. I kept moving until I found the room I thought was right. Six, seven, eight doors from the end, west side.

I went back around the building, head down, on the soggy ground, stomping my hiking boots on the cement walk at the building's main entrance. A blue sedan pulled up and parked, an old one with rust spots. A young woman got out, possibly a student but dressed a little better. She looked at me brightly as she swung keys around her finger, walking quickly toward the doors.

"I bet you need something out of your locker," she offered. "Forgot your math book or something?"

"Yeah," I said, trying to smirk like I was younger than she was. Student teacher maybe. We walked together to the entrance. Whoever she was, in her nice black slacks, I liked her.

As she unlocked the door, she smiled at me again. She was pretty, with blond hair and pink lipstick. "I'm new this year. Mrs. Anderson, English. Mostly freshmen. You're a senior?"

I nodded as we went into the darkened hallway. She flipped on the lights. I hoped she didn't ask for my name, or where my locker was. We walked together past the auditorium as I got my bearings. She paused at an intersecting hallway.

"I'm this way. I'll be at least half an hour, and I'll have to lock up then. You'll just be a minute, right?"

"Right. Thanks." I let my hair fall over my face and hunched into my coat, lurching away down the hall. I hoped to hell there were lockers this way.

Around the corner I stopped to listen for her footsteps. The hallways echoed with every tiny noise. It must be a cacophony full of chattering students. Down the hall a row of lockers hung on the wall. I rattled a couple, and they were all locked. Stopping to listen again, I crept back to the corner. Silence now. She was in her room. Was it near my destination? We would find out.

Slow progress, tiptoeing in hiking boots. At least the rubber bottoms were fairly silent. I went in Mrs. Anderson's wake down the side hall, looking for a light in a room ahead to signal her presence. I saw none and crept on.

The voices arrived before the footsteps, bouncing off the linoleum floors. An old man's voice, creaky but loud. I looked wildly for somewhere to hide in a barren hallway. Lockers on both sides, locked rooms. I yanked the boys' bathroom door— locked. I jogged to the girls'—ditto. But it was too late to move on. The voices rounded the corner. I shrank into the doorway of the girls' room.

Two men. That was all I could tell from the sounds. I dared not stick my head out to look. Then they walked right by me. I froze in the shadows. The old man I didn't recognize. But the other one was Leroy Leonard.

The old man was hunched but still taller than Leroy, with tufts of white hair and an old brown suit. His gait was hampered by a limp and a cane but strong, even in cowboy boots. Leroy had his hands in his pockets, head down, as if the old man had been berating him.

They were silent now except for the old man's wheezing. Leroy got his keys out and unlocked his room, turning on the lights. The sun had gone down. The fluorescents flickered on. The old man's words were slurred from this distance: "There are things . . . years . . ." A clatter—a cane against the floor? I slipped out of the doorway and along the hallway.

There was a small space at the end of the row of lockers, right behind Leroy's open door. The glass in the door was frosted, but I could hear what they were saying. Leroy's voice, small and frightened, began.

"I want to clear this up, George."

"Bullshit. Stir it up, you mean."

"I want this over."

"It is over. Christ, these chairs are uncomfortable."

"For the boy—"

"Shush. Let him rest in peace."

"I wish I could. I want this for him."

There was a long silence, then one of them blew their nose loudly.

The old man spoke, harshly. "So you diddled with him, didja?"

After an over-long pause Leroy spoke quietly. "No."

The old man snorted. "Bet you thought I didn't know. All these years. Bet you thought nobody knew."

"There's nothing to know, Uncle George."

"Right. That's why you're married, got all those invisible children."

"Not everybody gets married."

"Okay, sure, play it your way. He was your student."

"Yes. I cared about him. I still do."

"Sounds like diddlin' to me."

With relatives like this, who needed enemies? Leroy was silent for a long minute. When he spoke again, he was farther away. "I want to make it right."

"He's been gone for twenty-five years. Nothing you can say or do can change that. Let it rest. What the hell we doing here anyway?"

"I want to show you something." Footsteps. Metal doors. Clanking. Footsteps.

Long pause, then, "What the hell is it?"

"We made it. That day."

"What? A deer track?"

"That's right."

Shuffling. Grunting. "All right, I saw it. Let's go get some pie."

I shrank into the corner as the old man's boots clomped out the door into the hall. My heart thumped hard in my ears. What now? How could I get away before Leroy locked his door?

I snuck a peek at the old man, Uncle George. George Leonard, the county attorney twenty-five years ago. The man who orchestrated the cover-up, with the help of Sonny Garrett. He was old now, but hardly powerless. One look at the glare he gave the dark hallway told me that.

Metal doors clanged again in the classroom. It was now or never. I pushed back the door and stepped into the hallway, giving Uncle George's startled face a mean stare, then rounding the door. Leroy was locking a cabinet in the back of the room, fiddling with keys.

"Leroy." I stepped into the classroom. George was on my

heels, sputtering. Before he could make any proclamations, I said loudly: "I'd like to help make it right."

The teacher spun on his heel. His color rose, turning him crimson. George was pounding the floor with his cane.

"What's the meaning of this? Were you eavesdropping? Who are you? I could have you arrested for trespassing, for being a Peeping Tom, for—"

I turned to the old man calmly and smiled. He ran out of gas, or misdemeanors, which seemed only to infuriate him more. "Leroy, who is this?" he shouted.

But Leroy couldn't speak yet. His mouth worked, but no sounds came out. I turned back to George. "Someone who could have you arrested for obstruction of justice, for malfeasance, for suppressing evidence."

The old man's hand shook on his cane. He took a seatback with his other hand to steady himself.

"Leroy," I said. "Where are the wolf prints?"

"W-what?"

"Didn't you find some wolf tracks to cast the other day at Queen Johns's?"

"Oh. Yes." He walked quickly to the windowsill. "Here." He held out a round circle of plaster of paris. "Is this what you want?"

I stepped up to him and took it in my hands, a bigger circle than most on the windowsill, nearly eight inches across. The wolf's print was large, its nails digging deep into the earth, its footpad wide. I remembered Blue Wolf's big, pigeon-toed feet, and smiled.

"Now the other one," I said, handing the plaster round back to Leroy.

He frowned, glancing back at Uncle George. Then his eyebrows popped up. "Oh, here. The reverse."

I took the round, the original that had been poured over the earth. The first one had been a casting from the original poured over the track, with raised surfaces, the nails tiny hills, the footpad a plateau. A reddish-brown powder like cinnamon was sprinkled on the surface.

"No, Leroy." I put it on the windowsill, then turned to the men. George still stood defiantly, blocking the door. "Not that one.

The old one. The one you really came here to see."

"Who are you?" George thundered again.

I smiled at him again and debated answering him. "Just a friend of a boy. A long-dead boy."

"How did you get in here? I can get you arrested for breaking and entering!"

"A teacher let me in." I smiled at Leroy. The chaos in my mind had settled, and I felt a strange calm that scared me. It was too good to last.

"Get out of here right this minute. Leroy, get her out of here."

Leroy looked at his uncle. "It's too late."

"The hell." George walked toward me and put out his hand to grab my arm. I let him get a grip on it, then crossed my arms across my chest.

"Can you carry me, Mr. Leonard?"

I pulled my arm out of his grasp. He teetered back, catching himself on a desk. Leroy tried to catch him, but the old man cursed at him.

George was gasping. "This will ruin the family, Leroy. Stop this right now."

Leroy just looked at him, as if he too was feeling a strange calm.

"You never were one of us," George spat. "I never should have let my brother send you out here. He just wanted to get rid of you, didn't he, Leroy? Get the queers out of town, was that it? Send him to George, he won't care, was that it? Well, Bert never had a lick of sense—"

"Don't speak ill of the dead, George." Leroy's voice was strong, almost menacing, and the old man looked at him long and hard.

"The faggot gets a backbone," he muttered. "Will wonders never cease."

Leroy's eyes narrowed. "Whether or not I am a faggot is none of yours or anybody else's business. I just care about my students. I'm a teacher. He was my student. Not even a good student, but a good kid." Leroy turned to me. "He wasn't great in class, but he knew the land, he loved nature. We both liked to hike, and we went for long hikes with the plaster, looking for tracks."

He turned to the rows of plaster tracks, round like small plates dotting the windowsill. His fingertips caressed their peaks and valleys. "You've heard that phrase, Take only pictures, leave only footprints? Well, I wanted more than a picture, something to make the kids realize there are living beings out there who must survive, if we are to survive. So I started taking footprints too. Track castings. I started in Boy Scouts. I earned a merit badge."

George snorted. "Boy Scouts. You never grew up."

"I suppose you're right. I stayed in school. I didn't get hardened and cynical and bitter. I still hike like I did back in Boy Scouts. I still love nature, and animals, and trees, and mountains. If that makes me a kid, then I'm glad to be a kid still, in here." He pounded a fist on his chest, so like Queen expressing the fullness of her heart for the wolf that I had a moment where strange feelings converged. The sentiment in Leroy was so similar. They both loved Derek.

Leroy's eyes were misty. I looked away, hoping his uncle didn't notice.

"The other wolf, Leroy," I whispered. "What happened to the other wolf?"

He turned to the windows, now dark. Our reflection wavered there, but he seemed to see beyond it, to the mountains, to something I couldn't see. He stared for a long time, then went back to the locked metal cabinet, took out his keys, unlocked it. From the back of it he pulled out a small cardboard box.

He set the box on the windowsill next to me and eased off the dusty lid. Inside were more plaster rounds. Two sets, original and the track duplicate of two different tracks. They looked like the newer one, with a big footpad and deeply cut nail marks. Leroy set them in a row along the edge of the sill.

"These are tracks we made in the pen. It was hard; we had to do it through the fence because the wolf was close. The pen was awful, small and cramped, with an old crate for the den. Kids poked at the wolf with sticks, threw rocks at him. He paced and snarled, which only made things worse with the people watching." Leroy shut his eyes. "It made me sick."

George was sitting on a desk now, both hands resting on his

cane. He had a look of disgusted resignation on his ancient face. I wanted Leroy to continue but bit my tongue and waited him out.

"We were still killing wolves then. They weren't protected," he said. "People thought of them as bloodthirsty and evil, like in fairy tales. They never cared to really understand them, they just hated. Wolves ruined the hunting, wolves killed the cattle and the sheep. They were blamed for everything. Only they hadn't been around for a while, so people were curious. But their hate came back, a deep memory, even though most of them aren't ranchers any more."

"Still plenty of hunters though," George added.

Leroy nodded. "Oh, yes. And what a great assortment of human beings they were."

"Every man in your family is a hunter," George declared. "Except bleeding-heart you."

"Small favors," Leroy said coldly. "Derek and I got these tracks after trying for four or five nights. It would have been easier if we could have gone during the daytime because wolves are nocturnal. But we both had school. I was happy to get these, they are really one-of-a-kind."

He turned back to the track castings and touched them tenderly. "Derek distracted the wolf while I got them. You have to wait, let the plaster harden. It takes fifteen, twenty minutes, at least. I thought we were done, I was happy. But Derek wanted to go back again. There was a football game that night, and all the teachers were expected to go. So Derek went by himself to get the casting."

Leroy swallowed hard. "Only he couldn't get any that night. He didn't tell me why. But on Monday morning the paper said the wolf had been shot." He turned to me. "There had been controversy about when to kill it, why it had been trapped at all. Some people didn't like it caged in town, like me but for different reasons. They wanted it dead, now. And so they were happy, the wolf was dead."

"They were going to kill it anyway," George said.

"So what did it matter? Absolutely."

I stared at the tracks of the long-gone wolf. Where had it come from? Had it roamed south from Canada? Was it a pet wolf someone had released, or had it escaped on its own? Could the wolf I saw five years later have been from the same pack?

Leroy sighed. "Later that week I had a visitor. He told me to go looking for tracks along Fish Creek on Saturday, that there were some excellent deer tracks there, and to bring Derek. He said if I didn't, he'd tell the school board I'd—been intimate with the boy. I'd lose my job. It was my second year, I didn't want to leave."

He closed his eyes. "And so I brought Derek to Fish Creek." He took a ragged breath. Was he done? I felt no sense of winning, no victory. Then he opened his eyes and looked at me. "I had him killed."

The old man said testily, "Oh, don't make it into something it wasn't. It was an accident, and you know it. You didn't do anything to that boy."

Leroy stared at him. "I had him killed. I brought him there."

"It wasn't an accident," I spoke to the old man. To Leroy, I said, "But you didn't know. You didn't pull the trigger."

The teacher shook his head slowly. "Might as well have. I was scared."

"You weren't even carrying guns that day, were you? Derek Wylie didn't even have a gun, and people thought he was hunting." I looked at the old man. "You must have been some persuasive county attorney. A boy who hated hunting and wasn't carrying a gun, killed in a hunting accident."

"You don't have to be a hunter to be killed in a hunting accident," he croaked, smiling.

"Painfully true," Leroy said quietly.

I turned back to the teacher, who stood stock-still, staring at the blank windows.

"He saw them," I said. "He saw them kill the wolf." Leroy hung his head. "Who were they, Leroy?"

"All right. Stop right there, boy." George Leonard drew himself up to full height and tapped the cane on the floor. "It's one thing to get something off your own chest, it's another thing to start blaming other people. If they got consciences, let 'em use 'em."

"I didn't see it," Leroy said. "I can't tell you what happened. He was ahead of me. I should have stayed with him, but I stopped to examine some tracks, and he went on. I tried to tell myself it was real, that the tracks were the reason I was there. I convinced myself. Then I heard the shot. Just one. And I ran down the trail, and I found him."

"That's enough. We're late for supper. Your aunt will skin me." George rapped the floor again.

"Did you see them?"

"Leroy!" George hooked his cane around his nephew's arm. "Now."

"It's too late, Uncle George. Morris killed himself, he's gone. He couldn't take the guilt anymore." Leroy pulled the cane off his arm and dropped it.

"Well, you're not going to off yourself, are you?" George was softening a little. "What about your aunt's peach pie? Drive me home, boy."

"You saw Morris?" I asked.

He shook his head. "He came by my house, just before he left town. He never said anything directly, but I knew he was there. Wanted to apologize, I guess. He was just a college kid, he went back to Yale or somewhere."

"Who came to see you, Leroy? Who killed the wolf? Who planned Derek Wylie's murder?" I grabbed his arm, shook it, my desperation seeping out.

Leroy looked into my eyes, sad, resigned, bitter. "You know, Alix."

My stomach clenched. "Him," I whispered.

20

FROM high above, the mountains took on a peaceful tranquillity, their snowfields making patterns of the wild, transient randomness of nature. Blue and violet shadows danced down the gulleys and crevasses, trees stood straight but minuscule against the granite boulders carved by eons of ice. The chopper's blades beat a rhythm inside my chest and skull that the headphones could barely diminish. The swooping from heights to inspect tracks had caused loop-de-loops in my stomach, but I was hanging in.

Twenty-four hours had passed since I got the confirmation of my—fears, hopes, guesses?—about Terry Vargas. I still had told no one. I went to Queen Johns's last night again, beat on her door again, and finally spoke to her nearest neighbor and found he had a key. Together we went into Queen's cabin and found (to my relief, for I had begun to fear she was dead) everything neat and tidy and closed up for winter. Had she simply gone away? The neighbor and I didn't think so, but we didn't have any other theories either. I searched surreptitiously for the letter from Morris, but didn't find it.

Beside me, in the chopper's pilot's seat, Carl Mendez looked very professional, his eyes sweeping the ground, his hands strong on the controls. He was distant on the phone this morning, but when I explained that I thought Queen was missing in the mountains, he warmed to the task. It was my only theory all night long—and it was a long night—that Queen had gone in search of the wolf Blue, the smiling wolf with the blue tongue. Who was her son.

"We'll just go up this drainage and around the back of that peak," Carl hollered into the microphone. "There's a bunch of trails back there, along—" He consulted a map book. "Along Carmichael Fork, here."

I looked where he pointed on the map. It wasn't far from Queen's place, as the crow flies. But the backcountry was vast and varied, and the ease with which one person could get lost and never found, unfathomably huge. I felt the drag of hopelessness and glanced at Carl. We'd been at this an hour already. He smiled at me and gave me a thumbs-up. I smiled back. And went back to worrying about my other problem.

"Use the binoculars," Carl said a minute later, snapping me out of my funk. I put the binoculars up to my eyes and leaned forward, sweeping the lenses down the tiny thread of blue creek, along ridgetops and trails, in clearings and rocky scree. An occasional line of tracks, but small, close together, a small mammal like a hare or a fox or a marmot.

Danny's news flash—or splash—played over in my mind's eye. The photo of Vargas and Georgia bursting out of the law office, with the deputy close behind. The headline that said it all: "Rancher Revealed as Wolf Shooter." The choice quotes caught by Danny as Vargas was handcuffed and put in the car, the agonies cried by Georgia as she too was arrested. A head shot of Georgia with her mascara running down her face. Too cruel.

By the time I read the article this morning, what satisfaction had come from clearing Marc Fontaine has dried to a trickle. Now I knew more about Vargas. I knew he was capable of much more than shooting a wolf and blackmailing somebody else to take the fall. He'd done worse twenty-five years ago, and gotten away scot-free. He'd taken a life—two, actually, when you consider what it did to Morris—and the unfairness of it grated on my soul.

We flew on, up the drainage, around a peak where the creek split into two. Carl chose the bigger fork, and we kept going, up, up, toward the Continental Divide not far away to the east. I scanned the ridges again. There, there was something.

"Look," I shouted to Carl. "Over there."

He slammed the controls, shifting us in a severe right and downward maneuver. I held onto the seat, feeling us plunge toward the earth, then slow and hover over the ridge. I handed him the binoculars. He looked at the tracks for a long minute, then took the lenses from his eyes.

"Looks like wolf all right. Good eye."

He turned the helicopter downhill. We had discussed this heatedly before we left. Do we track the wolf, find it, or find tracks and backtrack to where a person might be following? I had won. I wanted to find Queen, I didn't care if the wolf kept going to Boston.

As we moved slowly along the ridgeline, keeping the tracks in sight, I wondered if this was the right wolf. There was no way of knowing.

Within minutes we had lost the trail in a large forested hillside. We searched for another forty-five minutes, trying to find where the wolf had entered the trees, where he had come from. But there were no tracks going in, only going out. Was this a female, denning in the forest? Had she been in the forest since before the snow? There were too many questions, and we were out of gas, both literally and figuratively. Not even time to go back up to where we'd found the tracks. We were done.

Carl set the chopper down with a bump. The yellowed grass was damp and flattened by the melted snow around the helicopter landing site, just a large painted circle in a clearing near the Visitor's Center in Moose. We took off our headsets and sat for a minute, watching the rotors slow and droop.

"I'm sorry we couldn't find her," Carl said quietly.

"It was a long shot."

Another awkward silence. The rotor made a last turn and stopped.

"How did the auction go?" he asked.

"Fine. Made some money." I looked up at him. He was staring ahead. "Missed seeing you there."

"It was your night."

I shook my head slowly. "Not really." It seemed so long ago now. "You heard about my friend Morris Kale?"

"Yeah. That was bad." He looked over quickly. "He was your friend?"

"Sort of." Christ, what was I saying? "Yes. He was my friend."

There was more—too much—to say. I opened the door quickly and hopped out of the helicopter, leaving the headset on the seat. I slammed the door shut, felt the warmth of the afternoon sun on my arms and face, and headed to my car. I didn't want to talk anymore.

But Carl called to me as I unlocked the Saab. I watched him jogging over, his lean body healthy and strong, his teeth flashing in a smile. My heart felt a stab, then sank back to its tired-but-holding-the-line-on-depression zone.

"Hey," he said, putting his forearms on the roof of the car and grinning over it. "Do you want to go to dinner?"

"I don't feel up to it, not tonight."

His dark eyes caught mine. "Then tomorrow."

I fiddled with my keys. A burble of happiness pulled at my mouth. "Okay, tomorrow."

Olava's cleaning spirit hit me hard that night. I did the bathroom, the kitchen, and changed my sheets before going downstairs to mop the gallery floor. At eight o'clock I stopped long enough to feel hunger pains and call out for a pizza. On the phone to Domino's, I suddenly gave my studio address. In minutes I was out the door, moving at warp speed. I had a suspicion the quiet, colorful studio would slow me down, and the food would help. But instead I felt trapped there, staring at Paolo's half-finished face, him staring back at me as I gulped down a sausage pizza. If I could finish Paolo's face, would I never have to remember again? Why couldn't I let him go? I was too tired to answer tonight. I locked up again and stood in the night air.

The stars were out, but not too bright, dimmed by the city lights. The smell of winter was strong. I looked at the constellations and tried to figure out what to do with Leroy's confession.

"Whatever you want me to do," he'd said. "I'll do it, whatever you think is right."

How I hated being the arbiter of justice. I wanted it done, it had to be done. But how did you decide when the deed was so long past? How did time passing affect the evil done? And what evil had Terry Vargas done, exactly? His intentions were malicious. But just talking people into things, threatening them to do your bidding—? What was that? Accomplice to murder? Conspiracy to murder?

I rubbed the bump on my nose and let a long sigh drift vapor trails into the cold night air. A shiver went up my neck. Maybe I would sleep tonight.

The autumn sun shone bright on the treetops in the town square the next morning. The front steps were swept of leaves, the floor sparkling and clean. The plate glass had submitted to a bottle of Windex before the postman handed me the mail, brochures and junk mail and bills. Then a large, square package that looked like a painting. I took it all inside, the tinkle of the door's bell echoing in the empty gallery.

An envelope was taped to the cardboard package, with no return address. The postmark said Friday. I tore it off the box.

Dear Alix, it read. I flipped over the single sheet. At the end: *With love, Queen.*

> It's over now, dear. I've had a letter from that man, Mr. Kale. He told me everything, how he shot Derrie and how his conscience was so bad he was going to kill himself. Of course, by the time I got it, I heard about him. But I'm glad he wrote, and now that he's dead too, I can forgive him. At least I hope I can. He says his life was a fraud, that his grandfather was head of a crime family and he didn't have the stomach for it but he had something to prove to his father because his father under-

stood him all too well. Nonsense to me, but it must have made sense to him. I feel a sort of pity for him, it's strange.

Here is the painting I promised you. I hope you like it and can make some money on it. You earned it. And I thank you for everything. You won't see me for a long time. I have some lost time to make up. I will always remember you and all you did for me and Derrie. Between you and the wolf, my heart is new. Happy trails.

Late that afternoon I stood outside in the sunshine on the boardwalk. The slanted rays didn't do much warming, but they helped my mood, which had been troubled and sad all day. The slow business hadn't helped, giving me extra time to mope. I looked back through the plate glass at Queen Johns's painting where I'd hung it on the side wall. I was staring at it, arms folded, leaning against the porch rail, when I heard the voices.

"Stop following me, you freaking pest!"

On the corner Terry Vargas and a man in a navy pinstriped suit walked briskly ahead of Danny Bartholomew. Danny chased them, bombarding them with questions.

"Did Bud Wooten give you express instructions to shoot the wolf? Was that over the telephone or in person?" Danny bounced on his toes, trying to keep up with the long strides of the taller men. I tried to stifle a grin, watching him in action.

"No comment," the suit said over his shoulder.

"Is it true Bud Wooten is like a father to you?" Danny asked as they approached me. Terry Vargas stopped abruptly, causing Danny to crash into him. The lawyer pulled him away.

"Look, you vermin, whoever you are. I know you orchestrated this whole thing. You were at that meeting. And I am going to personally sue everybody who was there for harrassment, conspiracy, and slander. I will see to it you never work in this town again." Vargas was red in the face, poking Danny in the chest with a single finger. "If you print that, I will sue you for libel too." He turned, took two steps toward me, and stopped again.

"And the same goes for you." He pointed at me now. I straightened up, put my arms at my sides. I would have liked nothing better than for him to take a swing at me.

"Easy, Terry," the lawyer said calmly. "Let's just go back to my office."

"How can I take it easy with these vultures around me constantly?!" Vargas yelled, turning back to Danny. The smaller man took a step back, keeping his notebook in front of him as a shield. He wrote furiously now, a slim smile on his lips.

"What the hell do you people want from me?"

"How about the truth, Terry?" I said.

He spun on his heel. His beard had been trimmed but looked as if he'd been twisting it. His eyes blazed. "Truth? And you'd have some pipeline on that, Little Miss Knowitall?"

"Not really. I just recognize it."

"You calling me a liar?" He stepped forward. I smiled, finally enjoying myself. His lawyer pulled on his arm frantically.

"If the shoe fits," I said.

Vargas sputtered, tightening his fists at his sides. His neck was taut, his jaw thrust out. But I stepped even closer to him. When I spoke, it was a whisper.

"You won't hit me, will you, Terry? You're a coward. You shot that wolf, a poor, drugged animal who couldn't run away. You get other people to do your dirty work. Like Georgia—she's probably regretting ever meeting you now, isn't she?"

"What do you know about Georgia?"

"Nothing." I shrugged. "But I do know about something else. It happened twenty-five years ago. When you had somebody else—somebody who was *your friend*—do your dirty work."

Vargas was motionless, his eyes boring into me. I stared back, willing him to break away first. His breath was fetid and sour. He smelled of sweat, and fear. Finally his eyes flickered, and he said, "I don't know what you're talking about."

"You do, Terry. You know, and I know. Others too. We know the truth. And somehow, some day, the truth will come out."

"Get out of my way." He pushed me aside then and stalked down the boardwalk, his lawyer hopping along behind him. Danny stepped next to me.

"What happened twenty-five years ago? What's this about?" he asked.

Vargas and his lawyer stepped down the wooden steps into the street. As they reached the opposite corner, Terry did what I was hoping for, a sign of sorts. He looked back at me. I smiled.

"Wait a minute. Is this about the wolves in the pen? That was twenty-five years ago. Was Vargas involved in that?"

"You'll have to ask him, Danny."

"But you said you knew the truth. Don't hold out on me now."

I looked at Danny, his pen poised over his notebook, ready for the next big story. Down the street Terry Vargas and his lawyer paused as a pickup truck stopped next to them. A cowboy stuck his head out the window and howled like a wolf. Then he laughed, and the truck sped away. It was Hal Fontaine. I gave him a wave, but he was too busy laughing. Vargas and the lawyer stepped quickly away, into one of the doorways. Off to plot strategy, and worry, I hoped. And fret and get ulcers. I would call Leroy Leonard tonight, and tell him to give his story to the sheriff and see what happened. I couldn't control that.

I put my arm around Danny's shoulders and felt a burst of something—joy? I laughed. A strange yet familiar sound—my father's laugh. A shiver went up my spine, and I heard the low, guttural chuckle again in my head. The picture too of the wolf in the Little Belt Mountains, Blue Wolf—had he been my father's spirit come to teach me to live again, to laugh? Was that what happened that night, the searing of my heart? Was it my father's doing? I didn't know. I only knew that laughing, and remembering, felt good. Tomorrow I would finish Paolo's painting, I vowed. But I would never forget him.

Inside the gallery Queen's new painting drew my eye again, a wolf climbing through snowy rocks, searching for something he knows is there, that he trusts will feed him tomorrow. Purple shadows, blue wolf, green pines, white snow. Queen would be searching in the mountains tonight. I hoped she found whatever it was she was looking for—a companion, a peace, a full heart, a future.

In the painting the wolf looked back over his shoulder, scanning the hillside for enemies, for pack mates, for prey. The wolf was restless, knowing, fierce, watchful. I would be too. Maybe I didn't have to find justice for everybody. Maybe it wasn't up to me to balance the world. Maybe it was true about what goes around, comes around. In the case of Terry Vargas, I hoped so.

"I've got a story for you, Danny boy. About a man who told everybody he was a dry-cleaning millionaire."

"But he wasn't?"

"Do you think they release records of people in the Witness Protection Program after they're dead?"

"I can find out."

"He might have been from New Jersey like he said."

Danny was scribbling again, and it made me happy. "So . . . mafia informant?"

"Possibly."

He stopped writing and looked down the street where the men had gone. "What about Vargas?"

What about Vargas? I wanted him punished so bad I could taste it. I wanted him to suffer like Derek had suffered, to spend years at it like Queen had. Yet—a frustrating, humbling, freeing revelation—I could only do what I could do.

I laughed again. The sun was on our backs and the sky was blue.

"Oh, Mr. B," I said. "Don't you just love to make people sweat?"